Antique Virgin
Russ Crossley

Published by 53rd Street Publishing

Acknowledgments

Thanks for this book must go to Kristine Katherine Rusch and Dean Wesley Smith two experienced professional writers and educators who encouraged this humble writer to follow his dreams.

Thanks must also go to Sapphire Blue Publishing who took a chance on a new writer and first published this book.

Lastly, many thanks to my first reader, Rita Schulz, who read the manuscript and made many helpful suggestions and who laughed at the jokes in the book.

Antique Virgin

Russ Crossley

53rd Street Publishing Offices in Gibsons, B.C. Canada
and Lincoln City Oregon, U.S.A.

Dedication

For Rita, my everything.

CHAPTER ONE

"SAXONY!"

At the sound of her name Saxony Edwards looked up from the sales ledger that lay open on the glass display case overflowing with junk. A bright red neon sign, which read Antique Virgin in reverse from inside the store, sat in the dirty window facing Highway 101 where cars and motor homes streamed by.

Antique Virgin was the name of the family owned antique shop, and Sax's view of her own non-existent love life.

Yup, that's me all right, an antique virgin. In her twenty four years Sax had never had a serious boyfriend and she was sure she never would. As far as Sax was concerned her life sucked.

She yearned for someone to love who would love her back. She studied the figures in the ledger. But there had been Marty Spiers. He had come closest to saying those magic I-love-you words. He might have been the one. After his leg healed. And his brother's front teeth were fixed.

It just wasn't in the cards. Not with her problem.

"Yes, Mom?"

Her mother was in the back room where the delivery van had dropped off two large cardboard boxes. No doubt the boxes contained new pieces for the shop. New pieces they didn't need. New pieces they couldn't pay for.

According to the figures on the page in the ledger they'd sold exactly three antiques in the past month.

1

Antique Virgin

A silver souvenir spoon with GLAD BEACH stenciled into the nickel plate by a factory in China, a garish scarf with the smiling cartoon image of a California grey whale (real whales don't smile) printed on cheap nylon fabric, and a plastic piggy bank with the words GLAD BEACH WELCOMES YOU stenciled on the side.

All very touristy. All very bad.

Saxony often wondered how they called themselves an antique store when all they sold was stuff to tourists. It was false advertising wasn't it? She'd seen pictures of the exhibits at the British Museum and their antiques look nothing like what her mom and dad sold in the store.

She shook her head. What is wrong with me? Why do I stay here?

But she couldn't just abandon her parents. Her mom needed her to look after her father. She couldn't look after him on her own. She picked up a pencil and made a tick mark on the page next to a line for Queen Elizabeth key chains. She'd counted them earlier and there were still forty-seven in stock. Same as last month.

"Dear, can you come here and help me?" called her mother from the stock room.

Saxony, or Sax as she preferred to be called, set the pencil on the counter then closed the ledger with a thump.

She walked toward the stock room at the back of the store. She held the beaded curtain aside with her hand and saw her gray-haired mother bent over a waist-high cardboard box. Sax smiled to herself. Mom looked ridiculous. Her mother was struggling to remove something from inside the box. I better help her before she falls in.

She released the beads then walked into the store room. They snapped behind her. As she approached, her mother straightened and withdrew her head from the within the box. Her hair was covered in dust. With a laugh her mother shook her head to create a cloud of dust. The dusty air made Sax rub a finger across her upper lip and wiggle her nose.

Allergy season was early this year. She hated having the sniffles. She covered her mouth in time to catch a sneeze.

2

Sax stopped on the side opposite her mother and peered into the box. She sniffed. She studied the object, her curiosity piqued. A wheel? Why would she buy a wheel? "What's that?"

Her mother looked up from the strange object. "A spinning wheel, dear. Just like Queen Victoria's."

Her mother and father being the "all-things-English lovers" only bought things for the shop that were connected, no matter how tenuously, to England.

What's wrong with Greece or France? They're perfectly good countries too. Some around town called them obsessed; she preferred to think they were eccentric. Her three brothers just called them nuts, but then they didn't live with their parents any more, did they? Why was it her sole responsibility to look after them, obsessions and all? She sighed. It wasn't fair. But what's a girl to do when her brothers are out in the world living their lives and I'm here?

"Great." More money wasted on crap. She wondered if they would ever listen to her. "How much did we spend on that thing?"

Her mother frowned and her sky blue eyes narrowed. "Now don't start that again. Your father knows what's going on in the market. He has his finger on the pulse of the antique business."

If that's true then our business was about to have a heart attack. They were going to be eating cat food soon if they didn't start listening to her. She paused to watch her mother once again bend over the side of the box, grunting, trying to lift the obviously heavy spinning wheel over the side. Not that she didn't love them, but they were so impossible.

Sax snorted in frustration. Her mother glared at her. "For heaven's sake, girl, don't shuffle your feet, and don't snort. Act like a lady. That's what the Queen does."

Yeah, right, Queen Liz probably snorts in private.

Rolling up the sleeves of her heavy wool sweater, Sax reached in and grasped one end of the faux antique spinning wheel. Her mother grasped the other end. It was surprisingly heavy. For a piece of copycat crap.

On the count of three Sax and her mother managed to lift the wheel out of the box.

3

Her mother gazed at the made-in-China wheel as if it were a rare treasure. Oh, brother. Sax swiveled her hips to flex her back muscles. She'd need a hot bath tonight to work out the kinks, for sure.

Sax looked at the cheap imitation of Brit-junkana covered in smelly lacquer. Yeah, a real treasure, Mom. She stopped moving when she felt a sharp pinch in her lower back. After she set it down she groaned. Man, that thing is heavy. She hoped she didn't have to carry it any further.

Sax crossed her arms over her chest and shook her head in disgust.

She wondered if a millionaire would drop by looking for a cheap copy of an antique spinning wheel. How 'bout that, I made a funny. She covered her mouth with her hand as she snorted. Her mother glared at her.

"Hello? Is anybody there?" Sax started and her heart beat faster at the sound of a man's voice from the other side of the bead curtain.

A customer? Maybe it was the handsome millionaire coming in on his white steed to take her away from all this. Her heart rate slowed and she smiled to herself. In my dreams.

"Coming!" Sax called as she locked eyes with her mother. "I'll take care of the customer. Okay, Mom?"

Her mother stepped back, and like one of the models on The Price is Right motioned toward the spinning wheel. As if I'm going to be able to sell this thing. Sax rolled her eyes and headed back through the bead curtain.

She wondered if her father would ever fix the bell over the shop door. It's only been what, a year?

Sometimes she wondered if he realized how scary it could be if she was in the back and some scary serial killer came into the shop. I could be killed, buried in a shallow grave, and no one would ever know.

Her breath caught in her throat when she walked through the bead curtain to find a man with soft brown wavy hair framing a lean, tanned face complete with a square jaw. Oh, my. He was too handsome. If that was even possible.

4

Her heart beat hard in her ears and the moisture in her mouth evaporated. He stood in front of the fingerprint-covered display case smiling at her. He was beautiful.

The blue-eyed man's build fit his tight blue jeans perfectly. And his jean shirt had the top two buttons undone, revealing a bed of wispy brown curls. This was way too weird. I think about a handsome guy and poof, one appears. Guys who looked like him never came in here. The men that came in were usually bald with beer paunches with their blue-hair wives nagging at them.

It'd be wayyy weirder if he was rich. Which she seriously doubted.

Maybe I should ask him? Her face grew warm and she averted her gaze from his when she realized he was looking at her with his friendly blue eyes.

Oops. He was looking at her. She looked down at her dust covered t-shirt and wrinkled jeans. She was dressed like Cinderella. More cinder than rella, actually. She scolded herself. Girl, you are such a dumb-ass for even imagining he's your dream man.

Out of the corner of one eye she spotted a man and woman, both blond, studying the collection of Coca-Cola tiffany lamps, and the Chinese dragon porcelain statues lined against the back wall.

Sax teased her mother about the statues, calling the dragons the breakable Great Wall of China, and her mother really hated it when she called them that. Unfortunately, there was limited interest in large porcelain dragons on the Oregon coast, so she spent more time dusting them than selling any. They were just dust collectors that annoyed her and were a symbol of a string of bad ideas.

She tried to swallow then cleared her throat. "Uhhh...yes... can I help you?" Oh, brother I must sound like a moron.

"Yes, my name's Bryce Kelly. I just bought a house out at Emerald Lake and I'm looking for some unique items to decorate it."

"Uhhh, certainly, Mr. Kelly. Was there anything in particular you were looking for? We—"

"Hello!" Sax's mother called from the back room, interrupting her.

At the sound of her mother's voice Sax turned to see her mother coming through the bead curtain.

5

No, no, she thought, her heart stopping for a beat. Her mother was going to make a fool out of her as usual.

"I'm Bertie Edwards," indicating Sax with a nod she added, "and this is my daughter Saxony."

She had a feeling her mother would take one look at this man and immediately go into matchmaker mode. It was as good a time as any for her higher power to save her from utter embarrassment.

A smile registered on Bryce Kelly's handsome features and one corner of his mouth curled slightly. "Saxony? My, what a lovely name. English?"

One eyebrow rose on Sax's forehead and she wondered if he was laughing at her name, but before could respond her mother spoke, "Why, yes, Mr. Kelly. How did you know?" Her mother stepped up and wrapped one hand around Sax's shoulder. With her other hand she poked Sax in the ribs.

Sax glared at her mother. "Mother, please don't," she said between gritted teeth. She hated being poked. Her mother knew it bugged her but she kept doing it anyway.

It's not like she was going to run away. You ran away one time in the seventh grade when Billy Cooper tries to kiss you and it follows you around forever.

Men usually run away for me. But what really bugged her was her mother was always trying to hook her up with men. Parents! They never gave up trying to run your life.

A sly grin played across her mother's lips. "Isn't he a clever one, Saxony? Sharp as a pencil I'd say."

The man and the woman had finished their self-guided tour of the shop and they now approached the counter. The woman, a willowy blond, was model tall and thin and smelled of cinnamon toast. Her designer sunglasses were perched atop her head, and the arms of an angora sweater were tied loosely around her slender neck. Her male companion, also wearing designer clothes, looked three inches shorter than the woman. He was stocky like a fire hydrant. Dark sunglasses hid his eyes.

They not only look big city, she sniffed, they smell big city. Man, they're gonna be snobs, I see it comin', and I hate snobs.

Russ Crossley

"Are you done yet, Bryce? I want to walk on the beach before it gets dark," said the woman.

Bryce turned toward the blond woman. His blue eyes locked with hers and he smiled then wrapped one arm around her slender waist. "No hurry, Cinnamon, my love. There's lots of daylight left."

He shifted his gaze from Cinnamon to Sax. A slight smile played across his lips. "I'm sure Saxony here would agree."

The stocky man grunted. "Saxony? What kinda name is that?"

"Now, Pep, don't be rude," Bryce Kelly mock-scolded his companion. "This is Miss Saxony Edwards and her mother Bertie."

"Charmed I'm sure," said Pep, a sneer in his tone. As if it were an afterthought he added, "No offense."

His hands were stuffed in his tan Dockers and his expression was indicative of someone who didn't care who he offended. Sax had seen far too many tourists in Glad Beach like Pep. Summer residents were the worse. I'm a person too ya know, not your personal slave, mister. This used to be such a nice little town when they moved here fifteen years ago. Money was all people seemed to care about these days.

And the big city types were the worst. Sax sighed under her breath to hide her annoyance. The ultra rude arrogant visitors, who treated locals as if they were servants, were a pet peeve of hers. Sometimes ya just wanta kick 'em in the butt.

"None taken, Mr. uhhh...?"

Pep ignored her, preferring to stare out the picture window and at the traffic streaming by on Highway 101. He and the blond woman walked away to study the wall of mirrors. They whispered softly to each other and Sax couldn't hear what they were saying.

She looked at Bryce who rolled his eyes. He shook his head. "Sorry for my friend's bad manners. He's a New Yorker."

"Ohhh, I see. Pity." Sax covered her mouth and giggled. Oops. That was rude. She hoped her face wasn't too red. He could be from New York. Her face grew warm. "Sorry, did I say that out loud?"

Bryce laughed and it was like nothing she had heard before.

7

The joy in his laughter caused her heart to warm and she realized she would love to hear it again.

Cinnamon and Pep seemed oblivious to her and Bryce's conversation. Instead their attention was focused on the wall of antique mirrors.

Whew. I'm glad they didn't hear me. They might even buy some of her mom and dad's crap. Like her mom always said, never insult your paycheck.

Bryce held out one hand. "Let's reboot this conversation. I'm Bryce Kelly. That lady is my fiancée, Cinnamon Wolthorp and that is her brother Pep, my soon-to-be brother-in-law." Fiancée? Oh crap, he's engaged.

"You can call me Sax by the way." Sax took Bryce's hand in hers and was surprised how warm and soft his skin was against hers. Her fingers seemed to tingle, sending warmth through her body like nothing she'd ever experienced. She didn't want to let go. Until this moment she had never been comfortable speaking to, never mind touching, such handsome men.

Handsome men had intimidated her since high school when the football team's quarterback, Butch Arnold, made fun of her at the only school dance she ever attended. That memory was a source of pain that had tainted every man she'd ever felt any attraction for. She didn't want to be hurt like that ever again. Now the old painful feelings had surfaced again. This time with this man. Why now? Why him? She had to find to why.

She fought the urge to sigh. Butch Arnold was an idiot. Bryce, however, is so my type if only it weren't for the fiancé. Maybe their relationship wasn't that serious. You never know…oh my, what am I thinking?

Shaken by her drastic thoughts she withdrew her hand from his as if it were on fire.

Bryce frowned, his gaze appeared concerned. "Is something wrong?"

She shook her head. "No. Of course not."

Cinnamon interrupted them. "Let's get going, Bryce." Her tone was clipped. Cinnamon frowned at Sax as her cool gaze traveled up then down Sax's lean frame.

Wow! What was her problem?

"Uh yes, of course. I'll be back, Sax. I want to fill my new house with antiques and I think your shop is just the place I'm looking for."

Cinnamon wrapped a long arm around Bryce's and started for the door. Pep moved to the door and pulled it open. He held it for Cinnamon and Bryce as they exited to the parking lot.

"I'll be back! See you—" Bryce called out as the slamming of the shop door cut off his words. Gazing through the window Sax watched as Bryce held open the rear door of the silver and black Hummer for Cinnamon, who climbed into the back seat. The jealousy of watching him with another woman came as a surprise. She didn't even know him and yet wanted to claim him as her own. Bryce looked back at the shop. Quickly ducking at the fear of getting caught watching him caused her face to warm. Slowly rising, she could see a small smile on his handsome face before he climbed into the passenger side of the truck. As the massive Hummer merged with the flow of traffic, the sound of her mother's voice reminded Sax she was not alone in the room.

"Hmmm. He's a looker, eh, Saxony?" Her mother said, her tone amused.

"Uhhh, yes. I guess so...."

Now that they were gone Sax moved behind the comfort of the counter. She opened the accounts ledger again and tried to focus, but the numbers began to float around the page. Sax removed her glasses and blinked a few times. What's wrong with me?

She gasped in shock and her heart skipped a beat. Oh, crap! Did he say antiques? Her heart began to pound in her chest.

"Mom, did he say he wanted to fill his house with antiques?"

Her mother nodded. "Yes, I think that's what he said. Why?"

Sax groaned. "We don't have any antiques." Go figure.

She met an attractive, albeit taken, guy. He seemed like a nice man she'd be interested in, and now he wanted to buy "antiques" from her parents' store.

That is just my luck.

CHAPTER TWO

WHEN BRYCE ENTERED THE COFFEE SHOP early the next morning he found his father seated at his usual table. After getting a cup of coffee for himself he took a seat across from his father, who had his eyes closed. His lips were curled at the corners in a smile. On the table in front of his father was his usual cinnamon latté. The cinnamon scent made Bryce warm inside. The comfort of the usual was important to Bryce. The world was a crazy place and things like cinnamon latté were the anchors that made life worthwhile.

Bryce smiled to himself and raised his cup of black coffee to his lips and took a small sip. Dad sure loves his cinnamon lattés. The irony of him marrying a woman named Cinnamon wasn't lost on him. Especially since she wasn't the woman he loved and certainly not the woman he wanted to marry.

His father opened his eyes and they twinkled. "Good to see you, son," he said. The corners of his father's mouth twisted and laugh lines formed around warm blue eyes and grew deeper as he smiled.

"Hey Dad, can we talk about the wedding?"

His father's brow wrinkled. "Is there a problem?"

Bryce looked over the brim of his coffee cup at his father. He was such an idiot for thinking he could fool his father. Of course his father would think something was wrong. "No, of course not." I'm such a coward. "I thought we needed some alone time."

He knew he should tell her he didn't want to marry Cinnamon, but he was afraid. His father seemed to have his heart set on the wedding. "Ya know, some father and son time, like the old days."

His father smiled. "Good." His tone lacked any conviction. I wonder if he really means that?

Father and son looked away from each other across the sundeck of the Coffee Hut overlooking the white capped waves rolling into the beach far below.

After a few minutes of silence his father finally said, "We need to finalize travel arrangements for the guests." His father turned toward him and locked eyes with him. "After all, I did agree to pay for this wedding and I want to keep some of the expenses within the budget." He paused and grinned. "It's not like everyday my number one son gets married, is it?"

Bryce smiled and leaned back in the chair. "No. Especially when I'm the only son."

Bryce breathed in the salty air before he took another sip of his warm coffee as he took in the panoramic view from the coffee shop's sundeck. The seagulls swooped and cried as they rode the breeze above the restless Pacific Ocean, reminding him of his visits to the coast with his father and mother.

He had such fond memories of those days. The memories of Glad Beach flitted through his head and he realized he was at peace in this place.

Glad Beach had been his refuge from the bullies at school who picked on him because he was smart. The scars were still there hidden beneath the surface.

When his family vacationed at Glad Beach it was the one place in the world where he could be himself and not suffer from the constant bullying at school.

He'd shown those bullies when he developed a revolutionary software program for the U.S. Air Force.

He retired at thirty four. But having money and all the leisure time you could use wasn't all it was cracked up to be. You could only party so much and play golf so much. Sure, it was fun but he needed stability in his life. And he wanted a family.

A real family. Unfortunately, this was a big barrier between him and Cinnamon. She didn't want kids and he did.

But his father had his heart set on Bryce marrying Cinnamon. He didn't want to let him down. He loved his father too much to disappoint him.

"What are you planning for this morning?" his father said, breaking Bryce's introspection.

"I've had my sailboat moved to Pearson's Perch. I thought I'd take Cinnamon sailing."

His father pursed his lips.

Bryce's brow furrowed. "Bad idea, Dad?"

His father chuckled. "No. No. Of course not. It's just that Margaret told me she and Elizabeth were taking Cinnamon to the spa for an apple-cucumber-rose-petal-grape-juice treatment," he rolled his eyes, "Whatever that is. All I know is it'll cost me five hundred bucks. Minimum."

"Oh. Really? Cinnamon didn't say anything to me." Bryce drained the rest of his now tepid coffee. Of course, he thought bitterly. He had no say about anything around here. After the marriage he was convinced it would be even worse. He'd be the family puppet.

"How about you, Dad, you wanta go for a sail? We can talk about the wedding plans some more."

His father shook his head and waved him away. "No. The wedding stuff can wait. We're in no hurry. And besides I'm a landlubber by birth. Don't worry about me, I've got that new Cussler book to dive into this afternoon. That's as close to sailing as I like to get."

A thought occurred to Bryce. Sax Edwards. He wanted to see her again without Cinnamon and Pep tagging along. He really liked her. From the second he'd met her it seemed they had an inexplicable connection. It was like they'd known each other all their lives. He'd never been as comfortable with anyone so quickly. And he wanted to apologize for Cin and Pep's behavior toward her. It bothered him they were so rude to Sax. No one deserved to be treated rudely.

Sax certainly was cute. And he really loved her sassy attitude and great smile.

He hoped she'd agree to go sailing with him because she might know her way around the coastal waters. The last thing he wanted to do was end up smacking into a rock or something.

He frowned. Cinnamon didn't like sailing. In fact she didn't like most of what he enjoyed. They had very little in common. He doubted she'd even care if he went on a date with another woman. Not that he was going on a date with Sax. She was nice but he'd just met her and he'd never been comfortable being forward with women.

"Hey, Dad, maybe I'll ask that Saxony woman I told you about from the antiques store. She's a local so she'll hopefully know the coastal waters. And it'll give me a chance to talk to her about the decor for the house. That rattan stuff in the house now is really bad."

His father finished his drink with a loud slurp. He set the empty mug on the table with a click just as a sudden gust of wind swept over them.

Without waiting for his father's reply Bryce got up and started for the door to the parking lot where his truck was parked. As he opened the door the traffic noise on the highway filled his senses. Before the door closed behind him he thought he heard his father say, "You don't have to be a fortune teller to foresee rough waters ahead."

What was that supposed to mean?

CHAPTER THREE

BRYCE SLAMMED BOTH FEET HARD ON THE BRAKE PEDAL. He swerved off the highway as a beat up lime green pickup shot past him, narrowly missing his front bumper.

The heavy Hummer shimmied around him and he fought the steering wheel to stay in control until the truck came to a complete stop. His heart pounded in his chest and his breath came in gasps. Maniac. What the heck was that all about?

Bryce watched a white car appear from a side street. A siren began to wail as the red and blue lights on the roof of the car lit up as it sped away, obviously going after the pickup truck. The words on a gold seal on the door read GLAD BEACH SHERIFF in gold letters.

That was close. Adrenaline coursed through his veins. Clutching the skin above his heart, as if holding it would slow it down, he took slow deep breaths. At least I'm okay and no one was hurt.

He couldn't believe some people drove like that. He at least made the effort to be careful, not that it always worked out. But when you have bad luck all the time it wasn't entirely your fault.

Bryce blew out a breath then steered the Hummer back onto the highway and drove until he came to the parking lot in front of the Antique Virgin. He turned in, parked in an empty slot then shut off the engine.

He sat in silence for a few moments looking through the shop's front window at Sax's long medium brown hair tied into a pony tail that bobbed and weaved as she disappeared behind the beaded curtain.

Her tanned complexion dotted with freckles and the dimple in her left cheek was attractive and her eyes, the color of jade, intrigued him.

There was something different about Sax. Something that attracted him to her. His brow wrinkled. He didn't know why and it bothered him. He had to know more about her. Spending time with her was the only way.

He stepped out of the Hummer, and closed the door with a thump. The sound of cars rushing on the highway made a steady shush sound. The breeze carried the smell of the ocean. He took in a deep breath. He really loved it here. The air was so clean compared to New York.

He went to enter the shop, the bell hanging over the front door made a dull clunk when he opened it. Bryce frowned and looked upward at the bell over the door. It must be broken.

He closed the door and the traffic noises disappeared. The smells of the ocean were replaced by the mustiness of the shop. Looking around he spotted a wheeled step stool pushed against the back wall near the bead curtain. He decided to fix the bell to impress Sax. He enjoyed doing nice things for people.

He also hoped it would make up for Cin and Pep's rudeness.

Pep had left for New York already which pleased him. He never cared for his brother-in-law-to-be's stuck up attitude.

He retrieved the step stool, picked it up and carried it to the door. He set it up under the bell. He then scrambled to the top step of the step stool and leaned slightly forward on his toes in order to able to study the broken clapper inside the brass bell. The stool wobbled badly underneath him. But he wasn't worried. This wouldn't take long.

"Hello?" Sax called from behind the bead curtain.

At the sound of Sax's voice he turned his attention from working on the bell and saw her standing among the beaded strands, her arms filled with a stack of green and yellow striped beach blankets.

"Uhhh, hi, I thought I'd fix the bell...it doesn't work, you know."

There was a loud crack and the step stool began to sway under his feet like a drunken sailor on a Saturday night and began to wobble. He struggled to maintain his balance flapping his arms like a bird.

"Whoa!" Bryce's mouth formed an 'O' shape and he froze. His heart beat hard. "Look out!" He cried.

Suddenly the ladder began to fall to the right when the stool collapsed sideways, throwing him off. Oh crap! He closed his eyes when he saw he was going to fall into a pile of mismatched porcelain dishes. Everything happened so fast all he could do was close his eyes tight and brace himself for the pain that was sure to come.

Without warning someone slammed into him from behind and arms wrapped around his waist knocking the air from his lungs. He gasped for air as surprisingly strong arms wrapped around his midsection and held him tight as he and his savior flew to his right. A sense of panic came over him. Can't breathe!

His heart beat faster when he landed on his side, sending shooting pain up and down his back. The arms around him released him and they rolled away from each other. Bryce rolled onto his back and began to cough as spots danced before his eyes.

"Man, that hurt!" He finally gasped after he was able to draw in a breath. "I thought I was in real trouble there for a second."

"You can look now. But be careful."

Bryce opened one eye and looked to his right. His face was only inches from the red and gold face of a dragon. Its solid black eyes were angry and its mouth was open as if were ready to incinerate him. His hard skipped a beat and he swallowed hard.

I almost fell into that thing. That would have really not been good.

"Man! Good miss. Thanks." Bryce swiveled his head to see Sax sitting on the floor with her hands flat on the floor behind her, propping her up.

"You can say that again. Are you okay?" Sax was breathing hard and her features were flushed.

Bryce stood and winced due to a twinge of pain in his lower back. Good thing nothing's broken. "Yeah. Surprisingly."

He saw Sax cringe.

Bryce grinned. "Sorry. What I mean is nothing's broken. Thanks for saving me." He winced when there was another pinch in his lower back. He saw what looked like concern in her eyes. "Don't worry. I'll be fine."

Sax nodded and her features relaxed into a brief smile. "I'm glad you're okay." She paused and stood. "I'm fine too, by the way."

Bryce realized he'd forgotten to ask about her. Idiot. His cheeks grew warm. He was so selfish sometimes. "Good." He offered her what he hoped looked like a reassuring smile.

Good! That's the best I can do? Bryce looked around them in order to find something to change the subject. The beach towels lay sprawled across the floor where Sax had dropped them. He indicated them with a nod.

"Oh dear, the towels." Sax struggled to hold a strip of her torn pant leg over her bare leg.

Seeing her pants were ripped he decided he better help. "No worries. I'll get them." He knelt down and began to pick the towels up and throwing them over his right arm as went.

"Oh now, Mr. Kelly don't worry about those. I'll pick them up."

"It's the least I can do," said Bryce. A sharp pain in his back reminded him this was not a great idea. He gritted his teeth and kept going.

"But I almost committed ladder-cide," said Sax.

Bryce threw the last of the towels over his arm and stood. "Ladder-cide?"

"Yeah, I mean that ladder is a death trap. You could have died." Sax's eyes brimmwith tears. Oh crap, I must have upset her somehow. He didn't mean to hurt her feelings.

The sight of her crying nearly broke his heart. He didn't know why, but the sudden need to comfort her was overwhelming. He had never experienced this level of emotion for someone. He wrapped an arm around her. "Oh, now there, there, Sax," he whispered.

"No one was hurt. Besides it wasn't like I was going to break those mirrors on the wall over there. That would have really been some bad luck. About seven years times sixty I'd say."

Sax sniffled into his shoulder and chuckled. "No. I guess not. Besides, there are only ten mirrors on that wall."

"Who's breaking my mirrors?" Bryce swiveled his head and saw a man on the low side of sixty enter the shop from the back room. "What's all the commotion out here?" Now who was this?

Sax shoved Bryce away from her. Startled by her sudden shove he looked at her with his mouth hanging open. What the...? It's not like they were doing anything wrong.

The man's bushy gray eyebrows shot up when he stared at Sax's ripped jeans. His eyes came up to lock with Bryce's. "And what have you done to my daughter?"

CHAPTER FOUR

Sax let the strip of torn cloth drop away revealing her bare leg and smoothed her t-shirt. She shuffled her feet and pushed her glasses up her nose with her index finger. "Huh, Dad this is Bryce Kelly. He's a customer—"

Her father had to pick now to come in, just when she was getting her hug on. And Bryce was the best hugger ever.

"Customer? Of what? A brothel? This 'aint no house of ill repute, mister. We sell antiques. If you're lookin' for some whoopee you've come to the wrong place." Sax's cheeks grew warm. Her father acted so nuts sometimes.

Bryce laughed and held out his hand. "No, sir of course not. I was in the shop the other day and Saxony and Bertie were helping me pick out a few items for my new house. I recently moved to town."

Her father's hazel eyes narrowed as he studied Bryce's smiling features. Sax rolled her eyes. Her father thought Bryce was a pimp. Gross. Unbelievable.

"Well, you seem to know everyone around here except me. Name's Jack. Good ta meet ya." Her father grasped Bryce's hand in his and gave it one sharp shake then released it. Bryce winced in pain.

Her dad was showing off again. Would he ever lay off the protector role? Why was it whenever she was talking to a good looking guy he felt the need to go all barbaric?

19

"You're new here, eh? What're your intentions toward my daughter?"

Bryce grinned. "It's not what you think, Mr. Edwards. You see Saxony saved me when I fell off the step stoo—"

Her father spotted the collapsed step stool lying in a twisted heap near the front door. "What happened to my stool?" He gazed at the misshapen stool shaking his head, his fists balled on his narrow hips. "It's useless now. I was going to fix it."

Was he kidding? "When, Dad?" said Sax. "It's been sitting against that wall for a year."

Her father glared at her. "It's on the list." Nope, he's not kidding.

Her father's to-do list of chores now stretched from Glad Beach to the moon and back. A slight exaggeration, but not very far from the truth.

Not that her father was lazy, far from it, but he suffered from a bad case of procrastination-itis.

Sometimes she thought her father should have his own telethon. Distractions were the worst. Anything could suddenly catch his attention, drawing him away from whatever he was supposed to be doing.

"No worries, sir. I'll buy you a new one," offered Bryce.

Her father waved away Bryce's offer. "Naw, forget it. Accidents happen." He shifted his gaze to Sax. "Accidents happen around here all the time."

Sax's body tensed. He's gonna tell Bryce about my problem. Fear grew in the pit of her stomach. Bryce would think she was strange. And no guys she knew want to hangout with girls who were strange.

Instead, without another word her father scowled then spun on his heel and disappeared through the beaded curtain, accompanied by the clicking of plastic beads.

When Bryce looked at Sax his gaze seemed sheepish and sympathetic. "Does your father say stuff like that brothel bit very often?" She was relieved he didn't ask her dad what he meant about accidents.

She smiled. "You have no idea."

"Listen, Sax, I'm going sailing this morning and I thought you might want to come along."

Sax had never been sailing in her life but any chance to get away from the antique shop seemed like a good idea. "I don't know," she said, her voice hesitant. I can't just run off and leave Mom and Dad. Can I?

She looked into Bryce's eyes. His blue eyes were so inviting she thought for a second she'd dive into them. They were as blue as the ocean on a summer's day. She shook off the feeling of being lost in his eyes. He certainly made her juices flow.

"Oh, c'mon, Sax. It'll be fun." Is he asking me out? But that couldn't be right, he was engaged.

She needed a break from the shop. All she ever did was sleep, eat and work.

Mostly I want to because I like him and he's so handsome. She knew it was wrong to go out with another woman's fiancée. But this wasn't a date and she did want to go with him. And her Dad did hurt him.

She'd never been so riddled by indecision.

A crash and a yell from the back of the shop made up her mind. She closed her eyes and sighed. That tears it. She opened her eyes to the pleading smile on Bryce's handsome face. I must be out of my mind.

"Yeah. Sure, why not. What time do ya wanta go?"

Bryce's features broke into a wide smile and his eyes twinkled. "Great. How about right now? I was headed to Pearson's Perch where my sailboat is tied up. We can be hitting the sail in half an hour."

"But what about Cinnamon? Doesn't she want to go along?"

Bryce's eyes lost their twinkle and his smile dissipated. She wondered if there was something wrong with his fiancée. Hold it right there, girl. His impending marriage was way too personal and, she decided, none of her business.

He shook his head. "No. I'm afraid sailing isn't her thing."

It wasn't hers either but she was going sailing.

"Oh, well then I guess it would be all right." If he was my fiancé I wouldn't like it, but that's me.

"Can we stop at my house so I can change?"

Bryce looked at her torn pants and chuckled. "Of course."

Sax walked to the coat tree by the front door and grabbed her windbreaker. She knew it was a big mistake to go with him, but she needed to do something for herself for a change. She pulled the jacket on then zipped it closed. After opening the shop door Bryce walked out ahead of her. She paused and glanced over her shoulder at the bead curtain. She was leaving her parents alone in the shop for the first time ever. Guilt made her hesitate.

I better let Dad know I'm leaving. "Bye, Dad, I'm going sailing with Bryce." Sax called before she closed the door behind her. His muffled reply disappeared as she stepped outside and closed the door behind her. The cool ocean breeze in the parking lot washed over her. She smiled. She did it. She made it out the door.

This was a new day for her, the day she stepped out on her own for the first time in her life. Yeah, right. Like she was going to leave her mom and dad, ever.

Her mother would never be able to handle her father without her, he was too nuts.

She immediately chastised herself. That's not fair, girl. Her dad was sick. His strange behavior wasn't his fault. She would at least get a few hours of reprieve.

Bryce helped her step up to the passenger seat of his Hummer then he walked around the front and climbed in the driver's side. A few hours away from the shop would be fun. She never thought Bryce would come back. Now she was going sailing with him. It thrilled her to think a man was interested in her enough to come back for her and ask her to do anything with him.

After starting the engine, he steered the truck to the parking lot's exit and waited for a gap in the cars and motor homes that streamed by on the highway. Finally, he smoothly gunned the engine and blended into traffic headed south.

She smiled briefly at Bryce after he glanced at her then she shifted on the leather seat and looked out the passenger side window. I can't believe I'm this close to him. She thought about touching his arm but held back.

Instead she folded her hands in her lap but that didn't feel natural so she placed one arm on the door frame. The window was closed and the shiny door frame was smooth so her arm slipped off into her lap.

She shifted her bottom on the seat and the leather schussed to her movement. Her emotions were running high and her stomach was in knots. Though she'd tried to rationalize this it still seemed wrong. Bryce was engaged. She liked him and there was something about him that seemed different than any man she'd met before. Not that she'd met a lot of men but the way he looked at her was as if he'd known her all his life. She couldn't explain it but she had similar feelings about him. Another reason she'd agreed to go along was to find out why.

Bryce glanced at her. "You okay?"

"Oh, yeah. No worries. I'm fine."

The Hummer's interior smelled of coffee and cinnamon toast, a reminder that Bryce was engaged.

Her mom often said you could tell a lot about a person by how their car smells. He even smelled engaged. Sax sighed to herself. Girl, when you set yourself up for a mistake you at least make 'em big.

Bryce broke the silence. "I'm so glad you agreed to come along. I really need someone with local knowledge of these waters. I've never navigated the Oregon coast. And we can talk about some decoration ideas for my house."

Sax nodded and clasped her hands together. As if realizing what he just said her heart started beating faster and she took in a deep breath trying to calm her frazzled nerves.

Wait, what? Did he just say he expected he expected her to help navigate? Why would he even think she knew how to sail?

Maybe I should've told him I've never been sailing in my life.

CHAPTER FIVE

They stopped at her parents' house just long enough for Sax to run in and change into fresh jeans. She also put on a grey hoodie over her windbreaker. Bryce asked to wait in his truck.

The house was two stories high with five bedrooms, three bathrooms, and was painted royal purple. It certainly stood out in the neighborhood. Before she got out he said, "Boy, your parent's house sure is something, eh?"

"Huh, yeah," Sax agreed, pleased he had wanted to wait outside for her.

She didn't want to ask him in because he would see her eccentric parents' junk and he'd think she was as crazy as them. Everyone in town thought her parents were nuts. And as everyone knows nuts don't fall far from the tree.

She glanced at Bryce. He appeared calm and confident. Why should he be any different?

By the time they arrived at Pearson's Perch a rain squall had come and gone. The pavement in the parking lot above the dock was slick with rain and the puddles were like rainbows where spilled gasoline mingled with the collected rain water.

They got out of the Hummer and Sax joined Bryce in front of the truck's shiny grill.

"This is nice," said Bryce.

"Yeah, smells like the ocean. All salty and fishy."

Bryce looked at her and grinned. "Yeah. I like the smells of the ocean too."

Sax's nose wrinkled as he turned to look over the gentle swell of the waves beyond the stone breakwater that protected the docks.

She'd never cared much for the smell of fish. And the ocean was full of fish. A bad allergic reaction to fish certainly didn't help.

He started across the parking lot, the sound of gravel crunching underfoot as he walked toward the ramp to the dock. As they reached to top of the ramp the gray clouds parted and rays of brilliant sunlight streamed across the sea of boats of all sizes and configurations that surrounded the web of berths. There were fish boats, single and double-masted sail boats, some with wooden hulls, others with fiberglass hulls, and small motorized boats with open cockpits, and massive behemoths with flying bridges and multiple communication aerials and even satellite dishes. She'd never imagined the books her mom bought for the shop about sailing would ever come in handy. She smiled to herself. I may not know how to sail 'em but I do know what they look like.

All of the boats, regardless of size, rested in horseshoe shaped wooden berths that stretched across the manmade bay. A stone breakwater kept the boats safe from the open ocean.

Gulls, gray and white, some with black tipped wings, rode the ocean breezes above their heads, calling to each other in shrill voices.

Mom says they're flying rats who'll eat anything including small children or pets. Somehow I doubt that last part.

"C'mon, let's go," said Bryce leading the way down the ramp.

She followed Bryce to the ramp that dropped at a steep angle to the nest of berths. The ramp was covered in a Velcro-like covering, and they quickly made their way safely down to the dock. She gripped the railing so hard her knuckles were white and hoped she wouldn't slip.

The planks swayed beneath Sax's feet and her stomach protested with each side-to-side sway of the deck.

She stopped walking and waited for her stomach to settle. This idea gets worse and worse. Bile tastes good...not!

"Over here," Bryce called and started down one finger of the dock that was lined with boat-filled berths.

25

Antique Virgin

Sax swallowed hard, looking around at the people milling around the various boats, some loading groceries and fishing gear, others unloading small dogs and cats and children. They all looked so sure footed and confident, even the dogs and cats. She certainly didn't feel confident or sure footed. *Steady, girl. We'll be there soon.* The queasiness in her stomach increased when the dock swayed under her. *I hope.*

I would say I'm a fish out of water but that would be too obvious. She held back a laugh.

She watched in wonder as a small grey dog trot down the center of a side to side swaying dock. *How did he do that?*

Oh well, as Dad would say, head down and full speed ahead.

Swallowing hard again, she hurried after Bryce. She passed numerous sail boats in berths on both sides of the dock. Some were large with portholes above the water line. She wondered of Bryce's boat was as big as these others. She hoped not but if it was at least she'd have a chance of not drowning.

She was worried. *If she told him now she didn't know how to sail he might think she's a liar.* She tried to recall anything that she said that would make him think she knew how to sail. *Did I?* She shook her head. *No way. He assumed she knew how to sail.*

Finally as she neared the end of the dock a small sail boat bobbed in the water, and was nestled between the behemoths around it. Bryce's boat had a single mast. *I wish there was a backup mast.*

She was scared. *I am so going to drown.*

His boat was small. She swallowed hard. Her stomach flip flopped. It was very small compared to the other boats she'd seen. *Maybe he has a bigger one and this is the backup boat.*

"Say, Bryce, is this your boat?"

He nodded then squatted next to the small boat. "Yeah. Beauty isn't it?"

Sax's mouth dried. "Sure. Beauty."

He began unsnapping the cover over the cockpit area. She walked around to the back of the boat. The name, LUCKY STRIKE, was painted in stylized letters across the back. *Yeah, I have luck alright. All of it bad.*

26

"When I have the cover off jump in," said Bryce and smiled. "I'll give you the grand tour."

Sax smiled and her gaze rose and fell with the small boat as it bobbed on the light swells in its berth. Her stomach heaved again followed by the acidic taste of bile at the back of her throat. She covered her mouth to hide a burp and placed her other hand flat on her stomach. She wondered if she was sea sick. Looking up to see black clouds had begun to form on the horizon above the ocean swells that looked higher than before. That couldn't be good.

"Huh, Bryce. I think…" He disappeared inside the small cabin with the cover before she could stop him. I guess I'll find out if I get sick on the ocean the hard way.

He reappeared wearing a bright orange life jacket. He carried a matching life jacket in his right hand. "This should fit. You can never be too safe around the ocean."

He smiled as he handed it to her. Sax smiled weakly in return. He then disappeared below once again. Hefting the bulky life jacket she squatted next to the moving side of the boat and tried to figure a way onboard.

Do I jump, clamber, or fly? If she only had wings.

Sax stood then poised herself to leap aboard. She studied the movement up and down of the side of the sail boat. What am I thinking? I should just step on. It looked easy enough. After silently counting three ups and three downs she stuck one foot over the side. The boat moved down and she began to fall forward. Whoa! Crap!

Just then Bryce reappeared but he had his back to her when she stumbled aboard so he didn't see her face-plant into the seat cushions at the back of the boat. Pressing her hands against the cushions she managed to sit up gasping for air. Thankfully the life jacket was still looped around her arm. I'm never getting aboard a boat again, ever.

"Looks like bad weather out there," he called as he scrambled along the side of the boat leaning against the cabin shuffling toward the bow. I could never do that, she thought relieved he hadn't asked her to.

Before she could think about it Sax said, "Nonsense. We'll be fine."

She stood and the boat shifted underneath her. Stumbling forward she managed to stop herself before plunging over the side by gripping the edge of the cabin roof.

Why did she say that? What did she know about the weather? About as much as she did about sailing...it looks easy in the movies and on TV.

Bryce appeared shuffling along the deck like a real sailor his back pressed against the cabin. "You okay? You look a little green. Do you want a rain check?"

Say yes you idiot! "No, of course not. I'm fine."

"Good. I was hoping you'd say that. I'll go below and start the engine. You untie the stern rope." Bryce pointed to the orange life jacket with white straps hanging off it. "But put on your life jacket first." Bryce disappeared into the cabin as before.

She picked up the life jacket and studied it. There were two white straps held together by plastic clips across the front horizontally connecting the two sides.

She wondered how to get the straps apart to pull it over her head. Peering closely at the plastic clips that held the straps together and pressed down on the edge of the clip. The clip clicked and the straps came apart.

This wasn't going to be so hard after at all.

Pulling the ring over her head she pulled the straps across her chest. Her brow creased. That can't be right. She saw the straps were too long so when she inserted the clip the life jacket wouldn't be tight enough. I really have to take a boating course.

She looked around at the boats all around her. It was a little late for a boating course, wasn't it?

After several seconds she decided to tie the straps like shoelaces and tied them together and pulled them as tight as she could manage.

She gasped and coughed. Breathing must be optional in this get up.

Maybe Bryce wouldn't notice when she passed out.

A loud POP, as if a gun had gone off, caused her to jump with alarm. Her heartbeat elevated, and she realized the sound was the motor starting. Her heart leapt into her throat when she realized they actually headed out to sea.

That's it. I'm doomed.

The life jacket straps came undone and again hung limply down her front. Like I said, doomed.

Bryce stuck his head out of the cabin. He grinned and nodded at her life jacket. "You experienced sailors are all the same. Don't like to wear a life jacket, eh?"

He exited the cabin and came up to her. She stood. "Well, this sailor believes in safety first." He took the ends of the life jacket's straps snapped the clips closed across her chest then pulled the straps tight. Her grey hoodie was bunched up around her waist.

He smiled at her. "Sorry, salty, but my boat, my rules." She smiled sheepishly as her cheeks grew warm. I feel so stupid.

"You stay where you are." Bryce patted her pant leg, sending shivers though her unlike anything she'd ever experienced before. Her heart rate increased. She wanted to wrap her arms around him but held back. She didn't want to appear too forward.

"I'll get the stern rope," he said.

He moved to the stern and untied the rope wrapped around a steel stanchion. Sax plunked herself back down on cushion. He came back and sat down next to her then placed his left hand on a wooden stick that stuck off the end of the boat. It reminded Sax of a broom handle.

Next to the broom handle was a lever. Bryce pulled the lever gently back and the boat began to slowly move backward in the berth. He grinned at her then shifted his gaze to the front of the boat concentrating on steering. Unlike her Bryce looked so confident. She wished she could be as confident as him.

The engine's humming increased, causing the seat cushion beneath her to vibrate. The boat shifted as it lightly tapped the rubber tire affixed to the side of the berth. Whoa! This was going to be a bumpy ride.

Sax wrapped her fingers around the stainless steel rail behind her and held it tight.

She held on tighter hoping it might stop her from falling overboard. Her knuckles turned white from the pressure.

She grew more terrified with each bob of the boat. Her stomach heaved. She really didn't like boats. She glanced at Bryce, his eyes flitting back and forth as he steered the boat through the tangle of boats cruising among the berths.

The boat swayed in the gentle wake of other boats moving around the open areas on either side of the berths. Oh, crap-a-doodle. It crossed her mind if drowning hurts. This was such a bad idea.

She hoped she lived long enough to regret her decision not to tell Bryce she'd never been sailing before. But I have to find a way to make this happen. She didn't want to look like a complete fool.

She didn't know why but somehow she and Bryce had a connection. And she had to findout what that connection was all about. Or die trying.

CHAPTER SIX

ONCE THEY CLEARED THE STONE BREAKWATER they were clear of the artificial harbor and were quickly bobbing like a cork in the ocean swells. The ocean really began to undulate and the sail boat rocked side to side as it moved up and down over the swells.

Sax gripped the rail on the side of the boat with both hands. Her heart pounded in her ears.

Her body trembled and the knuckles of her hands turned white. I am so going to die.

Bryce steered the sail boat's bow into the waves that, as far as Sax was concerned, should have alerted the coastal Tsunami emergency network, but were probably classified as a light chop.

At least that's what the television weather man on channel three always said. The perfectly coiffed blond weather guy hadn't uttered the word Tsunami in her thirteen years of living on the coast, so she assumed this was probably normal.

Sax gripped the rail harder when the breeze in her face suddenly picked up speed. And the dark clouds on the horizon seemed closer than only moments before.

"Boy, look at those clouds. What do you think?" Bryce asked.

Sax smiled tight lipped and shook her head. She knew if she opened her mouth she'd throw up all over him. And she liked Bryce but if you had to blow chunks anyone in the spew zone was fair game. Her brothers learned that lesson the hard way when she came home from her high school grad party.

Bryce's blue eyes crinkled at the corners and he winked. "Yeah. Got it."

Got what? She looked over her shoulder. There wasn't anyone there but them, right?

"Should we steer north or south?" Sax nodded toward the north or it could have been south. What did it matter?

This was a death cruise after all.

"Ok. You're the boss."

Great.

"I'm going to let out the sail." Bryce crouched low to avoid the sail boom with his hand still on the steering stick. "Here, you take the tiller while I untie the ropes." He let go of the stick, his eyes focused on the mast. Reluctantly Sax unwrapped her fingers from around the railing then lay on her side across the cushion onto her belly, her trembling fingers outstretched trying to grab at the steering stick. The life jacket bunched up around her head covering her eyes. She waved her hands about until her right wrist struck the tiller. I'm an idiot.

"Owww," she said softly so he wouldn't hear.

She wrapped her fingers tightly around the stick then shuffled her bottom across the cushion until she was able to sit vertical again.

She let out the breath she'd been holding in. Made it.

She was determined to get the hang of this and now she may have proven this to herself.

She glanced casually at Bryce as he untied the straps around the sail on one of the arms of the mast. Once the last strap was undone the sail unfurled rapidly with a loud snap.

The boat leapt like a gazelle being chased by a lion, shooting forward and sending Sax off balance. In order to stop from falling she gripped the stick tight and pulled it hard into her belly. Her stomach heaved. Not smart. The boat turned sharply to the left and she was thrown to her back sprawling across the cushion grasping at air with her fingers. Oh crap!

She managed to sit up and slapped her hand over her mouth just as her mouth filled with vomit. Her eyes went wide.

I'm gonna spew.

Sax turned around on the cushion grabbed the rail with both hands and hung her head over the side of the boat. She heaved and tears streamed down her cheeks as her stomach emptied its contents into the sea. A wave caught the side of the out of control sail boat and shoved it violently to the right. She managed to hang onto the rail this time. There was a loud slap followed by a startled cry and a splash.

Oh, oh. That didn't sound good.

She finished heaving and looked up to see Bryce's head of brown curls bobbing in the waves behind the boat.

"Hey!" she called, "are you okay?"

He began to swim toward the boat but with each passing second he drifted farther and farther away. She realized he couldn't get back to the boat. Oh, oh....

He stopped and spat out sea water. "No! Help!"

Yup. What broken step ladders can't finish her curse always did. I've killed him.

~~~

Sax managed to steer the boat back to pick Bryce up.

"Hey, Sax! Stop the engine." She looked at him blankly.

"The lever under the tiller. Move it down!" He bobbed up and down spiting sea water with each new swell that rolled over him. What's a tiller?

She would never have been able to steer with only the sail and she had no idea how to stop the engine. The engine suddenly quit on its own. The only sound now was of water splashing against the hull of the sail boat. The boat eased closer to Bryce and as he floated up to the side he grabbed the side of the boat.

Bryce wrapped both arms over the side and with her help managed to pull himself back into the boat. He sat dripping and breathing hard on the deck. "Wow...that...was...weird...." he gasped. "You'd almost think you didn't know how to sail." He unclipped his life jacket and pulled it over his head. It landed on the deck with a wet smack. She sat down on the cushion the tiller behind her.

"I'm so sorry, Bryce. I, uhhh, I..."

33

Suddenly the boat rocked violently as the sky went inky black. Sheets of rain began to come down quickly soaking them. Sax grabbed the side of the boat to remain seated. Bryce shielded his face with one hand tilted his head back and squinted up at the sky.

A rumble of thunder sent shivers down Sax's spine.

Oh. Oh.

Bryce stared at her, his eyes wide. He got off the deck and sat next to her on the cushion. He's close. Too close. She shifted her bottom to her left.

The clouds had descended around them like fog. The shoreline disappeared. The waves came faster and larger now.

Bryce swallowed hard. His eyes betrayed his fear.

I guess poker isn't his game.

"Can you navigate at night?" he said his tone hopeful.

Sax shook her head slowly. I should tell him. She blinked as a flash of brilliant lighting lit up the clouds followed within seconds by the rumble of thunder. She knew if she counted the time between the flash and the thunder the lightning she'd know if the storm was right overhead.

She looked at the boiling clouds and decided her little problems could wait. Her heart beat hard in her chest.

The fear in Bryce's eyes disappeared and a slow frown came over his features. Finally he said, "Well then I guess we have three choices. We radio for hel—"

Another bolt of lightning lit up the sky. Sax's mouth fell open as a bolt of lightning hit the mast. A piece of shiny wire affixed to the mast lit up and sparked and crackled. It sizzled loudly, sparks flew then broke off and a sudden gust of wind carried it away. Fortunately the sail didn't catch fire.

Good sometimes follows bad. Only she wished it happened more often.

Bryce glanced at Sax, who smiled thinly. He cleared his throat and calmly said, "We have two choices: one we drop the sail, start the motor, and head in the direction we hope is toward the shore. Once we see the shoreline we'll follow it until we find a safe spot to land.

Or two we pull down the sail, leave the motor off, and ride out the storm below deck huddled together and wait for help or until the storm ends whichever comes first. You're the one who knows the coast better than I do, what do you think?"

Sax would have preferred the second option far more than the first, but Bryce was an engaged man and off the market.

That's just what she needed to be known for in Glad Beach, a home wrecker before there's even a home.

"Uhhhh...the first option?"

Bryce's easy smile returned. "Aye, aye there, skipper."

Bryce stood, his swaying body matched the motion of the boat as it bobbed up and down over the waves. Sax was impressed by his agility. He stripped off his sweater which had become heavy with rain water. His black t-shirt was soaked through as well. The skin tight shirt revealed his washboard stomach and his muscular chest.

Whoa! What a show! If I die now at least I'll die happy.

Bryce dropped the sweater at his feet and pulled the tee shirt over his head with both hands.

Wow! He was gorgeous!

He went to the mast and began to wrap the sail roughly around the mast's arm and secured it with the ropes then disappeared into the cabin.

"Sax! Push the lever all the way to the top."

She did as he said and blinked when the engine came to life again. Sax smiled as the humming and vibration of the engine shot through the cushion beneath her.

It sure beat the sound of salt water sloshing against the hull, and the thunder. She grabbed the tiller and steered the boat's bow into the waves.

Up and down beat side to side any day. She smiled to herself. Wow. I'm really getting this sailor-speak down.

Bryce stuck his head out from the cabin. He had on an orange water-proof coat and a similar coat stuffed under his left arm. He stepped out of the cabin and slid the door closed behind him. He handed her the coat. "Here, take off that wet life jacket and the hoodie and put this on."

35

Sax smiled and undid the clip on her life jacket and soon had it off. Next she took off her hoodie that was soaked through with rain and dropped both to the deck in a heap. She then slipped one arm then the other into the arms of the orange coat. She zipped it up to her neck, but began to shiver due to the cold water that had managed to seep through her windbreaker and her t-shirt. The orange coat was at least dry inside. The jacket had a hood which she pulled up to cover her head.

Bryce sat down next to her, and before she could shuffle away, he wrapped one arm around her shoulder. He smiled at her then turned his attention to the cloud bank surrounding them.

"So. Which way?" he said.

Sax looked at the dark clouds around them.

I wonder where we are? This had to be what it's like for astronauts in orbit. No up, no down, and no north, south, east, or west.

"Ummm..." she began.

Bryce laughed. "Just kidding." He pulled an object the size of a pocket watch out of the right pocket off his jacket. He flipped it open with a flick of his wrist. It was a compass. At the moment they were traveling south.

She sighed and the tension eased out of her shoulders. We're saved. My hero.

Bryce frowned. "I'll head east...that way we'll come to the coast. These clouds should lift near the coast." He looked up from the compass. "At least I hope so. Or we might hit the rocks and sink." He smiled wanly.

Sax trembled as her heart began to beat faster again. Sink? Her mouth dried. She'd never thought of that. I think I may have spoken too soon.

"Why don't you go below and get some rest?" suggested Bryce.

She nodded. Good idea. She was more tired than she first thought. Her eyes were heavy with sleep. "Yeah, okay."

I hope I wake up alive.

CHAPTER SEVEN

AFTER SAX FELL ASLEEP IN THE CABIN below Bryce tied off the tiller with a piece of rope he kept in the compartment under his seat cushion to secure the tiller when he had to go below.

Once he'd helped her into the cabin she immediately turned on her side and curled up in the fetal position. She was shivering so he got a blanket out of the storage locker and covered her. She murmured and pulled the blanket up to her chin and sighed.

He smiled to himself. She was cute when she was asleep.

The boat swayed hard under him. He only remained standing because he placed both hands flat on the bulkhead next to the cabin door.

Now what? He stole one last look at Sax sleeping soundly and couldn't help but smile. Then he raced top side.

Once back on deck he saw the rope had been torn loose from the tiller. How did that happen? Movement in the corner of his eye made him look to his left. His jaw dropped and his heart beat faster.

Traveling away from the sail boat was a wall of black water some twenty feet high. I hope that's the only one out here. He shook his head. That was one big wave.

Like he often was, his father had been right about coming out here. Bryce worried his father knew when his bad luck was going to strike. This time though could be the end of everything. He steeled himself. He wasn't about to let this happen. "No way," he muttered.

Bryce moved to sit on the cushion and grabbed the out of control tiller. The sail boat rocked back and forth but he managed to steady the boat and turned the bow into the waves. He reached into the pocket of his floater jacket planning to retrieve is compass but it wasn't there.

"Oh, crap." My bad luck is holding nicely.

Suddenly the engine sputtered and died along with the wind. The boat drifted in the silence and the ocean became calm like glass. "Now what?"

Looking to his right he saw a wall of water building. His heart began to pound in his chest and his fingers tightened around the tiller.

"That is so not good."

~~~

The Coast Guard cutter Axelrod appeared out of the wall of fog, it's name in black print against the white hull. The coast guard cutter was the most beautiful thing he'd ever seen. Thank the heavens for the U.S. Coast Guard.

The sail boat's mast had been torn off by that last massive wave and Bryce expected the little sail boat would end up in Japan before they could be rescued.

He loosened the rope he'd tied around his waist when he saw the cutter headed for them and breathed a sigh of relief. He stood up and waved his arms over his head. "Hey! Over here!"

The cutter had a spotlight scanning the ocean from the bow to lead it through the darkness created by the black clouds. The beam of light swung around and soon captured him in its glare. He closed his eyes and dropped down to sit on the wet cushion that squished out excess water.

Did they have to blind him with the light? Really?

"Ahoy! How many are you?" It was a man's voice. A high-pitched man's voice.

"Two!" Bryce held up a hand to shield his eyes from the fierce white light and blinked. "Can you get that light out of my eyes?!"

"Sorry." The spotlight beam swung away from him. "Do either of you need medical attention?"

"No!" If he means other than a seeing eye dog that is. He blinked to clear his vision. "Okay. I'm going to throw you a line. Tie the line to the bow and we'll pull you to a safe harbor. Do you understand?"

Bryce blinked rapidly until his vision finally cleared. "Yes! Let me get to the bow!" Bryce stood and moved to one side of the cabin. He climbed up to the thin edge next to the cabin and edged along until he was standing on the bow.

He eyed the ocean swells nervously. He looked around, worried another giant wave would catch them before he and Sax could be saved. He wasn't about to let Sax down. This was all his fault and he had to keep her safe.

"Ready?" called the man from the cutter.

Bryce nodded. With a swoosh a thick rope appeared out of the gloom. It struck him on the head then landed at his feet. "Owww! Watch it! That hurt!"

He rubbed the spot where the rope hit him. He frowned and glared into the darkness at the beam of light.

"Sorry."

He says that a lot. Bryce bent over and picked up the rope then tied it to the stainless steel cleat in the center of the bow deck.

He stood up straight and waved his right hand over his head. "Okay!"

The deck suddenly lurched beneath him and he slipped and fell hard on his tail bone, knocking the breath out of him. "Owww!" He tried to take in a breath but couldn't. He couldn't breathe. Not good.

The deck lurched again and the sail boat was jerked violently around and began to cut through the water. The bow was pulled upward.

Bryce opened his mouth to yell but nothing came out. The wind had been knocked out of him. Without warning he slid across the deck headed for the edge. "Oh, crap!" He was going over the side and there was nothing he could do about it.

As he fell over the side he managed to grasp the stainless steel railing with both hands and dangled over the side. He was up to his knees in the cold sea water and he was being dragged along.

The water was very cold. His legs and arms immediately began to tingle as the cold penetrated his clothes. He gritted his teeth. His strength was waning due to the cold and he had no idea how long he could hold on.

Suddenly the pulling stopped and the sail boat came to a stop. Bryce coughed and took in a breath. He could breathe again. He grunted and managed to pull himself over the railing.

He rolled onto his back on the deck, his arms out at his sides, gasping.

"Sorry."

"Okay!" he called then rolled over and stood up. He looked at the search light. "This time wait until I get to the stern."

"Sorry."

Bryce waved one hand to show the coast guard crew where he was headed, shook off the pain of the rope hitting his head, then crawled back along the side of the cabin again until he was at the back and seated on the wet cushion next to the tiller. Looking at the closed cabin door where Sax slept he sighed.

He was glad Sax hadn't woken up. If she saw what a klutz he was she would discover his secret and then she'd never be his friend. He rubbed the spot where the rope struck him and winced. It hurt. He wondered why he cared what she thought of him. He frowned. It did seem strange that she didn't know much about sailing.

He hoped she didn't lie to him. I really don't like people who lie.

He decided he would ask her about it later. His immediate problem was saving them.

Suddenly the clouds broke, the fog lifted and the sun came out. He looked around and realized he was less than fifty yards from the breakwater. He could see the plethora of boats safe in their berths.

I don't believe it. They were back where they started.

CHAPTER EIGHT

IN HER DREAM SAX WAS GARDENING on a sun drenched morning outside a cute little bungalow with a white picket fence, married to the most perfect man in the world. Her husband had just called to her when she jerked awake out of her nice, very silly dream.

She blinked away the haze of sleep and opened her eyes to the sight of Bryce.

"Oh, okay. Bryce. Good." He smiled at her. I'm not dead and he's still handsome. In her dream it seemed her husband was Bryce. She suppressed a groan. It was a ridiculous thought.

"Are we there yet?" she murmured.

Bryce chuckled. "Yes," he said simply.

She raised her head and peered around her uncertain where exactly they were. But the world had at least steadied itself. Then she noticed the door of Bryce's Hummer.

Are we in his truck? She was confused. Last thing she remembered they were on the sail boat lost at sea.

"How long was I asleep?"

"Long enough."

"Oh" She blinked. Her head felt like it was stuffed with cotton so her thoughts were fuzzy.

"You okay?" Bryce frowned.

"Yeah. I'm fine. Just a little disoriented is all." She cleared her throat. "Are we in your truck?"

"Yes we are."

"And?"

Bryce laughed. "Sorry. I'm trying to be funny. And obviously not succeeding. When we made it back to the dock you were sound asleep so I decided to bring you home so you could change out of your wet clothes."

"Huh?" C'mon, girl, get it together.

"Okay then." Her brow wrinkled. "Did you call my folks? To let them know I'm okay."

Bryce chuckled. "Yes. I called the shop."

"Did my dad answer?" Sax sighed. I so hope not.

"Yes, but then your mom took over and she told me to bring you home. She says one of your brothers came home from school today. Does that make sense to you?"

Sax snorted. "Yeah, all too well. My brother Winnie was due home from college in Portland today." Her father's odd behavior had to be explained. She wasn't about to tell him her father was ill, she barely knew the guy. "Dad's quite funny, don't you think?"

Bryce raised one eyebrow. "Yes. Quite," he responded without elaborating. A sense of relief washed over her.

Good God, what did her father say to him? She looked out the window to hide her embarrassment from him.

The truck came to a stop at the top of the winding dirt and gravel driveway in front of her parents' house. He shut off the engine then opened the driver side door of the truck and got out closing the door behind him.

Sax got out of the truck. The gravel driveway crunched under her wet runners.

This was the first time she had ever brought a man home with her. She hoped no one was home but she knew her brother would be here. She really didn't want to explain to Winnie why Bryce was with her. If her brother stayed true to form he'd tease the crap out of her.

You can do this, Saxony Edwards.

This was the second time he'd seen her parents' house. But it was the first time she would invite him inside. Wait'll he sees the crazy stuff Mom and Dad have.

She fully expected Bryce would think they were all nuts.

If Mr. Welch ever painted a house, this was the color he'd choose. A grape house.

Bryce whistled softly. "Like I said before, that's some house." The two white window frames on the second floor, and the one matching window frame on the first floor in the middle of the purple-painted wood made the house look like a giant face with a nose and eyes peering at them.

Sax's face grew warm. She smiled weakly at him then turned away. Her thighs rubbed against each other as she shushed across the gravel leaving a trail of water behind her.

It dawned on her his truck's seats were probably expensive. Oh, crap. She feared her wet clothes must have ruined his leather seats.

She walked up to the front door and pulled the screen door open. She tried the door but it was locked. Her brother must have locked the door when he came home.

Sax reached into the pocket of her blue jeans and realized she'd left her house keys on her dresser. She'd ridden with her father to the antique shop this morning, expecting to spend the day at the shop and come home with her father.

"I don't have my keys," she said.

"Where's your brother?"

"I don't know." Sax knocked on the door. The echo of her tap-tap-tap against the solid wood door was followed by silence.

She knocked again only harder this time. A cloud passed over the sun momentarily causing Sax to shiver. She glanced at Bryce and smiled weakly. He nodded, his expression unreadable. Her brow wrinkled. Where was Winnie?

"Mom said Winnie was home right?" Bryce nodded.

Stepping back Sax looked up at the two upper windows. Her mother and father's room was to the right of the front door but both windows were closed.

Her mother enjoyed fresh air. When Mom was home she left one window open day and night. Good thing the coast was never as cold as other parts of the country. Sax recalled the winters in Indiana and shivered.

"Wait here," she said.

Moving to the side of the house, the two windows there were also closed. Sighing she walked down the side of the house until she was at the back. The tall wild grass ran from the back door to the edge of their property that was bordered by a forest of pine, fir, and birch trees.

The high grass and the forest afforded them privacy and meant Mom and Dad could play their royal processional marches as loud as they liked.

One of the windows on the second floor at the rear of the house was partially open. The room was her brother Winnie's bedroom.

Why wasn't Winnie answering?

When her younger brother was home he usually slept until two in the afternoon. When they were kids her youngest brother was a light sleeper. Now all he did was sleep. She often wished she could sleep as much as he did, she could use the rest.

Not that she blamed Winnie, actually. He burned the candle at both ends at college. Classes, two part-time jobs, and studying were all Winnie had time for. Time at home he spent decompressing.

She cupped her mouth with her hands and called his name.

Nothing. She snorted in frustration. I'm cold, I'm wet, and I'm hungry and my lazy brother's not answering.

Looking on the ground she spotted three small rocks. She squatted on her haunches and picked them up.

Sax tossed one in the direction of the window and it struck the siding well below the window with a snap. Instinctively she ducked as the stone rocketed back over her head. Sax grunted her disappointment at missing the window and nearly hitting herself. She was so bad at throwing anything, even pebbles.

Scanning the ground she found a larger rock took a step back, the tip of her tongue sticking out the side of her mouth, then wound up and used all her strength to toss the rock with a grunt of exertion. Pebbles were for wimps.

The rock missed the window again only this time it hit the metal gutter along the roof line with a clang then fell straight at her.

Sax screamed, crouched down, and covered her head with her arms. Her eyes were shut tight waiting for the rock to strike. After a couple of seconds she opened one eye and saw Bryce's pant legs standing over her.

"Lose something?" he said.

Rising to her full height Sax let her arms drop to her sides. Bryce had the rock in his left hand. "I snatched it out of the air," he said with a grin.

"Thanks," Sax said. "You're timing is impeccable."

Bryce chuckled. "It's not always I assure you."

"Hey! What's the big idea? I'm trying to sleep," said a man's voice from overhead.

Sax looked up to see her brother Winston, his head stuck out the window with his arms resting on the windowsill. At least she thought he resembled her youngest brother. His dark eyes were angry. And his hair...his hair was the color of a ripe banana gelled into a row of spikes that ran down the center of his shaved head.

"Oh, my," she said. Banana and grape do clash. What has Winnie done now?

CHAPTER NINE

"UHHH, WINNIE?" Sax said with a gulp.

A smile spread over the younger man's face. "Hey, Sis! You forget your key again?"

"Yeah. Would you let us in? Please?"

"Okay. I'll meet you at the front door." Winston's elaborate, colorful 'do disappeared from the window.

Sax looked sheepishly at Bryce. "Sorry about this. My brother is a college student and he's...he's a little bit of a rebel."

Bryce smiled. "No worries. It wasn't that long ago since I was in college. I remember doing some crazy stuff in those days."

Together they rounded the corner of the house and walked side by side toward the front door. "Really?" she said hopefully. At least one of us did some crazy stuff in college.

"No. Not really. I was pretty much in the computer geek class at college. We lived more like moles in the below ground computer labs."

"My brother is an art major." Sax paused to consider what she should say next. She liked Bryce but didn't want to appear too nosy.

Fortunately, Bryce must have sensed her discomfort because he offered more about himself. "I graduated with a Ph.D. in computer science. Then I started my own company. You may have heard of it. Ask_me_stuff.com."

46

Sax had heard of ask_me_stuff.com. In fact she'd used it to find knock off antiques for her parents shop. Suddenly she realized Bryce was going to probably ask her about antiques at some point.

What am I going to say? I can't lie. Friends don't lie to each other. And I may have just met him, but I really want to be his friend. I know what it's like being the new kid in town. Making friends was very important to her.

True to his word Winnie met them at the front door wearing black Nike shorts and nothing else.

"Sorry to wake you," said Bryce before Sax could speak.

"No worries. I was gonna get up soon anyway."

"I'm Bryce Kelly by the way." Bryce held out his hand.

Winnie grabbed Bryce's hand and shook it. "Wow! Not THE Bryce Kelly? The guy who sold AMS.com?"

Bryce smiled weakly as Winnie stepped back and beckoned them inside. Visible behind Winnie was the flight of stairs that led to the upper floor. To the right of staircase stood a cardboard cut out of Queen Elizabeth and Prince Phillip dressed in their royal finery.

Oh, no, not again. She'd hoped she'd convinced Mom to get rid of that thing.

Seeing the horrified look in Sax's eyes Winnie nodded at the cardboard Queen and her majesty's ever smiling consort. "Don't mind them. They don't talk much."

Bryce chuckled. "It's okay, guys. It was kind of hard not to notice your parents were a little obsessed with all things England."

Winnie's eye brows rose up his forehead. "You've been to the folks' trinkets shop I take it?"

"If you mean their antique shop, then yes, I have. Some pretty cool stuff in there."

Sax rolled her eyes as she saw the mischievous look in Winnie's eyes. "Yeah, cool is one word to describe their collection of crap."

Bryce laughed easily. "Yeah, I guess that's another way to look at it. But I'm going to take Sax to a late lunch and talk to her about buying a few things for my new house. I just moved to Glad Beach."

Sax looked at Bryce. Lunch?

47

"Oh, really?" Winnie's eyes traveled up and down Bryce. He stroked his stubble coated chin with long fingers as a slow frown spread over his face. "Why are you guys all wet?"

"Long story, Winnie," Sax said. She grabbed Bryce's arm and nearly dragged him up the stairs. She had to get him away from her brother or he'd spill the beans about her bad luck curse.

Once upstairs, Sax led him down the carpeted hallway to one of her brothers' bedrooms. There were several doors off the hallway and they were all closed. She really didn't want him to see the living room downstairs so after they were changed into dry clothes she had to get him out of the house. If it meant agreeing to going to lunch with him then so be it.

No doubt Mom had her Princess Di collector plates on display, along with the busts of every King and Queen of England in history. And they were no doubt on the display shelves her father had installed along one wall of the room. And then of course there was the framed picture puzzle of the map of the British Isles hung over the brick fireplace.

One person's nut was another's eccentric.

They stopped outside a closed door. "You can change in here." She swung open the door to the main bathroom, looked in and immediately yanked it shut again her back against the door. Her mother had put out the royal family toilet paper again.

Unbelievable!

"Sorry. Out of order," Sax said as she dragged him farther down the hall to another door. She opened it a crack to peek inside. Good. Her brother, Nelson's bedroom looked almost normal.

His collection of ship models would seem normal to most males, even if they were positioned strategically around the room to fight the great sea battle of Trafalgar. Dad played Napoleon while Mom was Admiral Nelson. Not that Napoleon was at Trafalgar, but Mom and Dad didn't let facts get in the way of a good English win.

"In here...change in here. Nelson will have some dry clothes that should fit you."

She swung the door wide and stepped aside. Bryce looked at her with an eyebrow arched but he stepped in to the bedroom anyway.

She worried her erratic behavior was scaring him. Great, he must think I'm flighty, or off my nut, or both.

When he saw the ship models a slow grin spread across his features. Before she closed the door behind him Sax said, "I'll be back in fifteen minutes." She smiled weakly. "Then we can go to lunch."

Bryce nodded as she closed the door.

Sax turned to go to her room and saw Winnie leaning on the door frame of the room he shared with their brother Brit. He leered knowingly at her. "So, sis, why're you hangin' with Bryce Kelly? He your boyfriend or sumthin'?"

Sax glared at her brother as she rushed past him to her room. She hesitated, spun on her heel and before she moved to slam her bedroom door she said, in a low voice. "Mind your business, Winnie."

"Don't you know who he is?" Winnie whispered quickly.

"I don't care." Sax slammed the door cutting off their conversation.

~~~

Fifteen minutes later Sax opened her bedroom door. A pair of dry blue jeans, a forest green t-shirt, and her leather sandals made her feel refreshed. After finally using the bathroom she toweled her hair dry and combed out her hair. She usually wore it tied in a bun or a pony tail so her hair wouldn't get caught on anything at the shop. But since she was going to a late lunch she thought it might be nice to wear it hanging loose about her shoulders for a change. Sax had considered wearing makeup but this wasn't a date, just lunch with a new friend, so she dismissed the idea. Sure she'd dabbed a little perfume behind her ears hoping it would mask the fishy smells of the ocean she assumed had permeated her pores.

After she closed her door she started for Nelson's room which was closest to the stairwell. Before she could knock familiar voices drifted up the stairwell from downstairs.

Oh no, Winnie was talking to Bryce! He better not be messing up this whatever it was.

Other than a possible friendship, of course.

After talking to her brother with the crazy hair Bryce would think they were all a bunch of weirdos. Racing down the stairs she entered the kitchen to find Bryce seated at the kitchen table with a glass of water in front of him. Winnie stood by the sink leaning back against the counter his arms crossed over his narrow chest. Her brother and Bryce were both laughing. They hadn't noticed her yet.

"Ha, ha, ha, you thought Sax was a sailor?" her brother was saying. Bryce was laughing harder than her brother. What was so funny?

Bryce was grinning but it was the same goofy grin her father had when he watched Manchester United beat...beat anyone. Ever since her dad found BBC America on cable he'd been fixated on any soccer match involving his new favorite team. Funny, when they lived in Indiana it had been no-holds-barred basketball. Her grandfather claimed he had Hoosier blood in his veins so Sax concluded long ago sports was a genetic affliction. This meant her father couldn't help himself. But Bryce...Bryce had no excuse for laughing at her.

Bad luck was her curse. It wasn't her fault.

It was time to interrupt this tea party.

Bryce raised the glass to his lips and took a sip. "Hey guys, I'm ready," she said. He choked, then spewed the water across the table. His eyes shifted to hers and his cheeks flushed crimson.

Satisfied she'd caught them in the act she said as innocently as possible, "Ready?" Under her seemingly innocent gaze she saw the color drain from Bryce's handsome features and his shoulders tense.

Bryce looked down at the water he'd spewed over the table. "Uhhh, sorry about the water." He pushed the chair back from the table. "I'll clean it up."

"No worries, B. You run along with sis. I'll take care of this," Winnie said. Her brother wore a bemused expression on his face.

"You sure?"

Winnie waved him off. "You kids go have your fun."

Bryce stood, the chair squeaking on the linoleum floor.

He walked out of the kitchen to the foyer without looking back.

Sax smacked her brother across his left arm with the back of her hand and mouthed, "What did you say?"

"Nothing."

From behind her Bryce called from the foyer where he was putting on his shoes, "Everything okay, Win?"

"Everything's great, B." Winnie grinned at her.

Sax gave her brother a withering look and headed after Bryce and exited the kitchen.

"Is something wrong?" he said with apprehension in his voice when she joined him in the foyer and began to put on a dry pair of Nikes.

"No, of course not." Only my brother outed me as a non-sailor. Bryce must think she's a liar.

"Ok, let's go." Bryce opened the front door and walked toward his Hummer. She stomped her foot forcing it into her second shoe, then grabbed a dry windbreaker off the coat tree and rushed out slamming the door behind her.

He went to the passenger side of the truck and opened the door. He held it open for her and held one of her hands as she climbed in, albeit awkwardly because her shoe was still loose.

Whoa! Cool. Her first real gentleman.

Bryce walked around the front of the truck and got in the driver's side. He smiled at her then started the engine. It roared to life then dropped to a steady hum.

I guess that's why they call it a hummer.

Putting it into gear Bryce drove down the hill to the junction where the gravel road met the paved highway. As usual the traffic was heavy so they had to wait.

"Ummm, Sax..."

"Yes?" She glanced at him then looked back at the steady stream of cars. Here it comes. Sax dumped again. 'I forgot I have a dentist appointment. Or it's his mother birthday.' Men always found a reason to disappear from her life.

"Ummm, I know I upset you back there and I'm sorry."

"Do you know why I'm upset?"

He glanced at her. "I said something?" She shook her head. "I did something?"

"Maybe."

"You're not going to tell me are you?" Sax shook her head and looked away to hide a grin. They were going to lunch. No need to discuss spilled milk under the bridge.

"Anyway, I'm sorry for whatever I did or said that hurt you. Okay?"

"I'll think about it." He's sooo forgiven.

Bryce sighed. "Is the Fish Monger okay for lunch? I hear they have the best seafood chowder in town. I've been eager to try it since I hit town."

Sax nodded. She would have agreed to any restaurant. Her stomach protested with a grumble, it needed to be fed.

Hold on. Did he say the Fish Monger? All they serve is seafood. But she was allergic to seafood. She was going to tell him she forgave him over lunch, but if she bloated up like a plague victim she wouldn't be able to talk because she'd be dead.

Crap-a-doodle. I should tell him I'm allergic to fish. She looked at him. But she didn't want to be the party pooper. He said he enjoyed seafood. Who was she to spoil his fun? She slumped in her seat. She had the sinking feeling this lunch would end badly.

CHAPTER TEN

ELIZABETH WOLTHORP RAN HER INDEX FINGER across the oak mantel over the stone fireplace in the living room of Bryce's new house. She looked at the dust on her finger and smirked. Her gaze drifted to her daughter who sat on the rattan loveseat flipping the pages of a June 1992 issue of Cosmo magazine. It had been gathering dust on a rectangle shaped rattan basket that served as a coffee table. The right side of her mouth curled in disgust.

"Not much of a place, Cinnamon."

"Yes, Mother. Like, I know." Cinnamon emitted a bored sigh, closed the magazine and let it drop into her lap. Her gaze shifted to her mother.

"But Bryce seems to like this town. He says he used to come here on summer vacations with his parents." She rolled her eyes. "Like, can you believe it? Who in their right mind would vacation here when there's Martha's Vineyard or the French Riviera or Monaco? Those I understand. But Glad Beach, Oregon?"

She stuck out her lower lip and slumped lower on the squashed flat cushions on the creaky rattan loveseat. It snapped loudly under the sudden increase in weight. A single tear rolled out of Cinnamon's left eye and down her pale cheek.

Elizabeth moved to sit beside her daughter and wrapped one arm around Cinnamon's shoulder. "Now, now, dear. Remember what your pageant coach told you about slouching."

53

Cinnamon flipped her waist length blond hair across her right shoulder, straightened her head and shoulders then dropped her head to one side until it rested against her mother's shoulder. "But Mommy, this place is awful. No clubs. There's no decent shopping. There are no decent cafés where I can gossip with my girlfriends. Besides, all my friends are in New York. How am I supposed to breathe in a hick town like this?"

Elizabeth patted her daughter gently on the side of her face with her open hand. "Not to worry, my little pookie. It won't be long till you and Bryce are married. Then you'll insist you and he move to New York. He'll have no choice then."

Elizabeth chuckled. "How do you think I controlled your father all those years?"

Cinnamon's features brightened and a mischievous grin played across her thin lips. "Oh Mommy, you always know just the right thing to say."

"What are you filling the girl's head with now, Liz?" Elizabeth's sister Margaret entered the room carrying a Safeway bag in her right hand.

Cinnamon moved down the couch from her mother, her eyes burrowed into the worn grey rug. Elizabeth Wolthorp stood and crossed her long arms across her chest. She shifted her weight over her left leg.

"Hello, my dear sister." Elizabeth raised one perfectly plucked eyebrow as she eyed the Safeway bag. "I see you've been shopping."

"Yes, Liz, you may have heard of that rare animal sighted around here."

Both eyebrows rose up Elizabeth's forehead to register her surprise. "Really?"

"Why yes, Liz," said Margaret, sarcasm dripping in her voice as thick as cold pea soup. "It's called the wild chef, often seen in home kitchens."

"She's just kidding, mother," said Cinnamon, rolling her eyes.

Margaret feigned a 'who me?' look. "Moi?" She laughed and then disappeared into the kitchen.

Elizabeth's lips formed a thin line and she glared at her daughter then mouthed the B word.

Margaret returned from the kitchen with a red and green apple in her left hand. She rubbed the apple along her right pant leg. "Anyone want an apple?" She held up the clear plastic bag of apples in her other hand.

Holding the open bag six inches above the basket she abruptly turned it upside down to let the fruit drop into the basket. The apples landed with a thunk. She released the empty bag and it floated to land in a crumbled heap on the counter between the living room and the kitchen, next to the basket.

Cinnamon glared at Margaret then ran for the bedrooms down the short hallway off the living room. Margaret stared after the fleeing younger woman. "What's the matter with her?"

Elizabeth grunted and glared at Margaret. "Oh, for heaven's sake, Maggie. What's the matter with you?"

Maggie smiled and took a generous bite of the apple. Her right cheek was distended with the generous piece of fruit. It crunched loudly as she began to chew.

"Really, Maggie do you have to be so common?" Elizabeth's eyes narrowed. "You know what's at stake."

Maggie rolled her eyes and swallowed. "Yes, yes dear sister, I know. I know."

"We need Cinnamon to go through with the marriage to Bryce if we're going to..."

Maggie raised one hand that made her sister pause. "Don't tell me again, Liz. I know. For goodness' sake, do you have to keep reminding me?" Maggie moved to stand over a wicker waste basket then dropped the half eaten apple into it dead center.

"Where's Bryce?" asked Liz, changing the subject. She walked to the basket of apples on the counter and studied the fruit.

"His father took him to that coffee shop near the outlet mall. I begged off to get some fruit and coffee for the house." Liz snatched a fresh apple in her long fingers. She bit into her new prize.

Liz mumbled around the generous bite of fruit. "Smart, dear sister. We might as well be comfortable while we're in this backward berg."

Her brow furrowed and she looked disapprovingly at the apple.

Maggie grinned. "Yes, my dear Liz. Comfort is our middle name."

Liz tossed the remainder of the apple across the room in the direction of the waste basket. It struck the rim then rolled end over the edge and fell in.

"Two points?" said Liz with a chuckle.

Maggie grinned then they both began to laugh.

CHAPTER ELEVEN

SAX SAT ACROSS THE TABLE FROM BRYCE, an uneasy smile on her face. Her fingers were intertwined on the table in front of her. On the blue and white checkerboard table cloth sat a glass of water with a wedge of lemon floating amongst the ice chips. Beside the glass was a set of cheap nickel-plated Wal-Mart cutlery lying on a thin paper napkin.

Bryce's grin was infectious. "You come here much?" he said.

"No. Not really."

His brow wrinkled. "Yeah. Cinnamon took one look at the place and refused to come in. She said it looked too touristy." His features brightened. "But I hear the food is great."

Bryce picked up the wine bottle with a white candle stuck in it, secured by thick melted wax.

Sax fought the urge to roll her eyes. She said, "Yeah. I hear that too." Rumors were the Fish Monger used frozen seafood from an unnamed European country. Another rumor told the seafood was cheaper because it was unsafe for human consumption. Personally, Sax doubted the truth of any of these rumors. Instead she suspected the fish just wasn't fresh.

Fortunately, there was a vegetable soup on special today so she would avoid the seafood. Relieved that her narrow escape meant she could relax, until Bryce ordered the seafood chowder and insisted she try some.

I should tell him I want to be friends. She was worried because she was allergic to seafood. In fact, if she ate any she might die. But the last thing she'd wanted to do was put all of her faults on display. Bryce would think she's a whiner.

She opened her mouth to speak but before she could say anything the waitress arrived with two steaming bowls on a plastic tray with a cork liner. She was a plump woman sporting a wide been-a-waitress-too-long bottom. Her bored expression seemed permanently fixed to her ruddy complexion.

She placed the seafood chowder in front of Sax and the vegetable soup in front of Bryce. Maybe I should say something smart or funny before we eat.

She decided it could wait. Besides she was terrible at telling jokes.

Bryce looked at her then smiled at the waitress and thanked her.

The waitress acknowledged him with a nod then turned and walked away. She disappeared through the swinging western-style doors.

There were two other couples in the restaurant. The other customers included an elderly couple slurping their soups loudly, and two men both eating fish and chips with an eagerness that made Sax feel queasy.

Bryce reached across and switched the two bowls. Immediately Sax's nose wrinkled. Something stinks.

She leaned forward to sniff the soup. It had a slight metallic odor. Her brow furrowed.

Great. Supermarket canned soup.

"Is it ok?" said Bryce.

Sax smiled weakly. "Yeah. Sure. I love canned soup."

"You should have ordered the chowder. I hear it's homemade."

Who's this guy's source? Homemade? In this tourist trap? Get real.

"I don't like seafood much." He must have had his heart set on the clam chowder.

Sax picked up her soup spoon. She eyed a piece of carrot floating on the oily surface of the lukewarm soup. She dipped her spoon and in and started to raise it to her open mouth. Like a jet interceptor another spoon popped into her mouth. The warm cream infused with oregano and clam juice hit her tongue.

Her eyes widened and she looked up from her soup at Bryce grinning as if he were a kid with his hand caught in the cookie jar. "Well? What did I tell you? I couldn't let you miss out on the best clam chowder on coast. Good, huh?"

Sax's tongue swelled and her head began to spin as spots danced before her eyes. She was going to die. Bryce Kelly's killed me. Oh well, at least he's a handsome murderer.

Her head sagged to the table and the world disappeared into blackness.

~~~

When Sax woke up her head was being pounded by a soul splitting headache. Bright lights above her forced her to shield her eyes with one hand.

"Miss Edwards? Can you hear me?" It was a man's voice. A soft voice she recognized.

The light dimmed and she blinked three times to clear her vision. A man with handsome ebony features and hair the color of oil, with traces of grey at the temples, came into focus. His eyes were gentle and he wore an easy grin on his lips.

"Dr. Parks? Where am I? What happened?"

"You're fine, Sax. You're at the clinic. You're going to be fine. Bryce and I knew each when we lived in Boston. Good thing he brought you to the clinic as soon as he did. If it had been much longer the shot of epinephrine I gave you wouldn't have done much good."

His grin morphed into a frown. "Why did you eat seafood? You know better."

"I know, doc I know, but it wasn't me." He eyed her skeptically.

"Really! It was…didn't Bryce tell you?"

Dr. Parks shook his head. "It was him. He shoved a spoonful of seafood chowder into my mouth before I could stop him." Dr. Parks left eyebrow rose up his furrowed forehead. "I know it sounds ridiculous, but really! I should call a cop. He nearly murdered me." Sax's lips narrowed and her brow furrowed.

"Did you tell him about your allergy?" said Dr. Parks.

"No. But people shouldn't go around shoving spoons into others people's mouths. I mean if everyone did that there would be anarchy."

"Hello?" Bryce strode through the door to the examination room carrying a large bouquet of flowers. The room was immediately filled with the scent of the fragrant flowers. "Oh, there you are." Bryce glanced at Dr. Parks. "Hey Doc, how's she doing?"

"She'll be fine." Dr. Parks smiled amiably. He picked up a clipboard off a small dresser across the room. "Why don't I leave you two love birds alone?" He patted Sax on her shoulder. "I'll be in my office if you need me."

Sax watched as Dr. Parks beat his hasty retreat from the room leaving her alone with Bryce.

Awkward, uncomfortable moment number forty-seven. Her face grew warm.

"Sorry about that, Bryce. The doc clearly has the wrong idea about us, uhhh, I don't mean us exactly...oh, my." Sax snorted in frustration. "You know what I mean."

Bryce cringed as he handed her the flowers. "Sorry. I had no idea. I just thought you didn't like fish. I feel so stupid."

She eyed him. "How do you know I'm not allergic to flowers?"

His face paled and his eyes widened. "You're not...are you?"

Sax let her shoulders droop and chuckled. "No. I'm not. But I could be."

Bryce sighed with relief. "I'm so sorry. How can I make it up to you?"

"What time is it?"

He glanced at his watch. "Almost seven thirty."

"Really? Oh boy, Mom and Dad are going to think I dropped off the edge of the planet. Do you have time for dinner?"

Bryce rolled his eyes. "Sorry. I should have been more exact. It's seven thirty in the morning."

"Oh." I missed the better part of a whole day. Her neck hurt. No wonder she had a kink in her neck. She had to call her mom and dad. They were sure to think something terrible had happened to her. She looked at Bryce. "Did you call my parents?"

"I called your house. Win said he'd tell them you were okay."

Winnie? Her brother was the biggest practical joker on the planet. Who knows what he told Mom and Dad to embarrass me. She loved her brother but he was a real pain in the butt sometimes.

"Did you want to get some breakfast, then?"

Bryce appeared to hesitate. She smiled. "Don't worry, I've lost a day before."

"Actually, I was going to go for a hike up Mount Mockingbird. Do you want to come with me?"

"What about Cinnamon?"

"Don't worry about her, she's gone for a couple of days. She left this morning for Portland with her mom and her aunt to do some shopping. She's not the great outdoors type."

Even though he'd nearly killed her, Sax didn't miss the tinge of sadness in his voice and in his eyes. She determined she would do everything she could to cheer him up. They say a near death experience changes a person.

Let's see if it's true.

Sax slid to the edge of the bed and hopped down to the floor. One foot landed on Bryce's foot. He yelped. "Oops, sorry, buddy." She looked into Bryce's eyes. "We are buddies, right?"

Bryce winced as he yanked his wounded foot from beneath Sax's running shoe. "Yeah, right."

Sax smiled triumphantly. She had a new friend. "Good. Let's stop at my place. I'll whip up a quick breakfast and then we can head for Mount Peck."

"I think it's called Mockingbird."

Sax laughed. "Not if you're a local. We call it Peck, after Gregory Peck, the actor who played Atticus Finch in the movie To Kill a Mockingbird."

"Movie?"

Sax looked horrified. "You've never seen To Kill a Mockingbird? You must have read the book. We all did when I was in school."

He chuckled and shook his head.

Sax smiled. I think he's pulling my leg. "We're just going to have to educate you about the finer films and books of the twentieth century. The film is about the evils of discrimination in the deep south during the depression."

"From the title I thought it was about how to hunt mockingbirds."

Sax's jaw hung loose. Then a slow smile spread over her lips. "Now you're just pulling my leg." She slapped his right shoulder playfully.

He grabbed his shoulder in mock pain. "Okay. Okay. I'll check it out. You don't have to beat me."

~~~

After breakfast, a shower, and a change into fresh clothes and her favorite boots she kept in her closet for hiking, they headed for the mountain in Bryce's Hummer.

What a great idea. A good hike would clear her head and help her forget the awful boat ride and the killer chowder. If they were going to be friends she needed practice at forgiveness, something very important to her.

The Hummer had four-wheel drive so it was an easy ride along the dirt road that led to the parking lot at the base of the mountain. A sign by the side of the road showed there were several trails that led up and around the mountain. It was still early in the hiking season so they probably wouldn't see too many people.

Bryce said they were going to take the easiest trail. He joked it was the bunny hill of hiking.

She nodded and grinned. She often hiked these hills and knew them well. It was the one hobby that relaxed her and one where nothing bad had ever happened to her. Nothing would go wrong today.

They arrived just before ten o'clock and found there was a single green and white pickup truck parked in the lot. On the door was the state seal, indicating it was a park ranger's vehicle. The parking area was bordered by tall pine and fir trees, some over sixty feet tall. The tops of the trees swayed in time to the wind.

Sax got out and had to hold her Tilly hat on her head with one hand or it was sure to blow away. She took it off, flipped it over, and used her fingers to loosen the chin tie and put it back on, adjusting the tie underneath her chin.

"Kinda windy," said Bryce. The trees swooshed and shushed as branches brushed against each other. The smell of pine, fir, and oak filled the air.

Sax strapped on her waist pack she'd brought to carry her wallet, sunglasses, and suntan lotion. She'd forgotten her allergy medicine, but wasn't worried. There wasn't any skunk cabbage up here the last time she was here. This was not, after all, a mountain swamp, was it?

"Hey. Nice fanny," said Bryce. Sax froze and glared at him. I don't believe it. Bryce was talking about her butt like she was a piece of meat. And she hated that attitude from men.

"Is something wrong?"

"That was an incredibly crude thing to say. I may not be a fancy New York model but I'm not one of your football buddies either."

"What're you talking about? What did I say?"

"You know exactly what you said, mister." She held up one hand to stop him from speaking. "I'll let it go this once. But you better mind your manners if you want to remain friends."

"But your fanny pa—"

She silenced him with a stare.

Bryce nodded. There would be no further explanation. "Okay. Sorry."

He wore walking shorts, a black t-shirt and hiking boots. Over his shoulder was a navy blue nylon day pack.

He pointed to a trail entrance not far away amongst the trees. They walked side by side to the trail head and stopped. The trail led away and upward on a gentle slope. "According to the map sign in the parking lot we should be at the lower summit by two o'clock. We'll be back here before it gets dark."

Sax smiled at him then adjusted her waist pack. Peering at the pack she saw the brand name read Fanny Pack. "Oh, that's what you meant," she said. "I thought you meant—" Her face grew warm. If she could crawl under a rock she would.

"Yes?" he said.

"Nothing. I made a mistake. Sorry, Bryce."

He smiled. "Never mind. Stuff happens. Let's go." He started off up the trail.

Sax started off after him, whistling her favorite work song from Snow White. Should be fun. Giddy up.

CHAPTER TWELVE

THE BLACK BEAR SAT ON ITS HAUNCHES licking its paw with its long pink tongue. Bryce, frozen like a statue by fear, stood on the other side of the path from Sax. His eyes were wide and beads of sweat dotted his forehead.

Sax stood as still as she could, afraid to breathe. No matter what she did to try to control them, her knees trembled. She never thought she'd end up as bear kibble.

Her foot still itched from the skunk cabbage. Her nose wrinkled. I swear I can still smell the stuff.

She knew as soon as she suggested it that the short cut through the woods was a bad idea. How did skunk cabbage get into the woods anyway?

Just when her bad luck seemed to have taken a day off it struck again. She would cry but then the bear would eat her.

After ten minutes, which seemed like ten days, the sleepy bear yawned and flopped on its side. Within seconds the large animal began to snore like an old man with a deviated septum.

Sax's brow creased. Just her bad luck a bear decided to make his bed at a bend in the trail.

Bryce caught her attention with a small wave of his hand and mouthed he was going to walk into the woods behind him. He nodded slowly to indicate she should do the same on her side of the trail. Sax looked over her shoulder into the dark woods beside her. There was no way to determine what was on the other side of the trees.

The way her luck was going today there would be a cliff and she'd fall to her doom.

Oh well, it has to be better than death by bear.

Looking back at him she nodded.

He made a circular motion with his index finger.

Had he gone loopy? "What?" she whispered.

The bear snorted and used one massive paw to scratch its long snout. Bryce placed one finger over his lips to indicate she shouldn't speak. She nodded she understood. Obviously charades wasn't his game.

Bryce swung his arm in a sweeping motion his index finger pointing at the trees. She nodded she understood. They would circle around the clearing and meet in the woods. Good plan, there, guy.

Bryce counted to three silently then disappeared into the woods behind him. Sax did the same on her side of the trail.

The forest was dense with thick undergrowth and moss covered logs. There were scratchy vines that seemed determined to reach out and catch on her clothes and nick at her jacket. There were ferns so large they must go back to the Jurassic period.

I hope the dinosaurs are sleeping like that bear.

The ground beneath her feet was soft and squishy and covered with pine needles. She stumbled along, her shoes kept getting caught in hollows every few feet where the needles had accumulated.

Very soon she lost her sense of direction in the dim light that managed to make it through the heavy tree branches. After fifteen minutes of stumbling she stopped and leaned back against a large, moss coated log. Her breath came in gasps. At least it was better than being bear chow.

This stuff is like walking through pudding.

She surveyed the forest around her. Where am I?

Then she remembered her cell phone in the waist pack. She unzipped it and found the phone.

Thumbing the red button the phone lit up. The happy wake up tune she'd programmed sounded, making her start. She covered the phone with her hand.

It was loud. Too loud. She feared the way it echoed in these trees would wake up the bear. And that would be sooo not good.

I don't remember it being so noisy.

Finally the music stopped and the tiny screen came to life. She looked at the signal strength bar, there were no bars. None.

The phone's screen showed it had switched to roaming mode.

Finally it changed and indicated it had found a signal. She sighed, "Houston we have contact."

Quickly she dialed 911. She wished now she'd written down the number for the ranger station on the map sign back at the parking lot. Thankfully the one piece of advice her dad gave her before his illness was when you were in trouble always call 911. Her lips formed a small smile. She loved her dad even when he drove her nuts.

It rang once and a woman answered. Her tone suggested boredom. "911...police, ambulance, or fire?"

Sax wasn't sure. "Uhhh...none of the above?"

"Ma'am, this line is for emergencies only. Please get off the line."

"No! Wait! I'm trapped by a bear."

"A bear?"

Sax nodded. That got her attention. "Yes. You see my friend Bryce and I went for a hike, and we came to a sleeping bear at a bend in the trail. That was after I stepped on some skunk cabbage— I'm allergic to skunk cabbage—"

"So you need an ambulance?" interrupted the woman.

"No, no. I'm fine. Besides it's not as bad as yesterday when I ate that clam chowder Bryce shoved in mouth." Sax snorted. "Ya know he almost murdered me."

"So you need the police?"

"No. No. I'm fine." Sax chuckled. "Do I sound like I've been murdered? If I was dead how could I be talking to you?" She shook her head. "Anyhow, we got away from the bear—"

"So you're not trapped by a bear?"

The woman's constant interruptions were getting annoying. Stay calm, girl.

"No. I mean yes...I mean...oh, never mind about the bear. He's asleep back on the trail. Or maybe he's a she? I didn't look that closely. I'd be a real weirdo if I spent my time looking at bears genitalia wouldn't I?"

"Yes, ma'am."

Sax didn't appreciate the amused tone in the woman's voice. But what am I gonna do? She's the 911 operator. You can't criticize the 911 operator. "So we went off the trail into the woods and now he's huh, somewhere. And I'm here." Sax frowned. But where was here?

The operator sighed. "So you went on a hike with your friend, stepped on skunk cabbage, that you're allergic to, but not as bad as clam chowder, then you met a sleeping bear at a bend in the trail, then you ran into the woods, now you don't know where your boyfriend is and you're lost. Is that about it?"

She gets it! "Yes. Exactly. Lost. All except the boyfriend part. Bryce is not my boyfriend. We just met the other day."

"Ok. Where are you calling from?"

Sax rolled her eyes and her hand formed a fist at her side. Her cheeks warmed. She gritted her teeth and spoke slowly, "The woods. I'm in the woods. I don't know where the freak I am."

"Ma'am, there's no cause to yell at me." I didn't yell! Sax's heart beat faster.

"I meant where is the hiking trail?"

"Oh. Sorry. It's one of the trails on Mount Peck."

"Mount Peck?"

"Yeah."

"Ma'am there is no Mount Peck. I'm going to let you off with a warning this time because I'm going to win jackass-caller-of-the-month. If you call this line again to waste our valuable time when someone who is in real danger may die we will charge you with public mischief and you will go to prison. I'm going to hang up now. I'd suggest you go back to bed and sleep off the booze from the party last night."

There was a soft click and the line went dead. Lowering the phone she stared at the tiny screen. 911 hung up on me.

I'm definitely losing it. Sax realized she must have sounded like a crazy lunatic. She was so embarrassed. No wonder she hung up. She dropped her hand holding the cell phone to her side and sighed. *I would have hung up on me.*

"Problem?" said a voice behind her. Startled she dropped the phone. It struck a dead branch and flew into a hollow where it disappeared into the brown pine needles.

"Hey!" She swung around and saw Bryce standing atop a log. A wide grin split his handsome features and his blue eyes sparkled. Standing there he reminded her of Robin Hood, or at least the Robin Hood who wore shorts and hiking boots.

The guy just looks too good. It was no wonder he was engaged to a model.

"Sorry," he said and jumped down to the forest floor and was immediately on his knees feeling around for her cell in the pit of pine needles.

"Here it is!" He raised the phone triumphantly but the backing of the phone had fallen off. He stared at the phone. The battery was also gone. "Oops."

"Let me," Sax dropped to her knees beside him and stuck her hand into the needles. She felt around until she made contact with what had to be the back. But something moved across her hand, or more correctly slithered. "Oh, MY..."

She screamed and jumped to her feet and began running her hand frantically up and down her pant leg. Her heart pounded hard in her ears. "A snake! There's a snake in there!"

Bryce's face paled. His eyes fluttered then rolled up in his head revealing the whites then he collapsed on his side with a muffled thud. He was out cold.

Great. My hero. Now what am I going to do?

CHAPTER THIRTEEN

T<small>HE PHONE ON THE COUNTER AT</small> A<small>NTIQUE</small> V<small>IRGIN</small> rang three times before Jack picked it up.

"Antique Virgin, good evening. Jack Edwards, antique specialist speaking."

Good thing Bryce kept his cell phone in his pocket. And I caught Dad before he left for the day. She hoped her luck was finally turning for the better.

"Dad, it's me."

"Me who?"

"Dad! Stop kidding around. It's me, Sax. I'm lost in the woods. I need help."

"So? Call 911."

"I tried them already."

"So why do you need my help then? They're the professionals."

Sax closed her eyes and suppressed a scream. He was so frustrating. She took in a deep breath then puffed her cheeks as she let gradually it out. She spoke slowly. "Dad. I'm off a trail in the woods on Mount Peck. I'm here with Bryce and he's passed out. There's a bear and a snake and we're lost."

"Is that the same Bryce who was in here looking for a brothel?"

Sax shook her head and her face grew warm from embarrassment. It was no use. Why fight crazy? She gave up.

70

"No Dad, it's another Bryce. He's a friend." She paused. "I need you to look in the phone book and find me the number for the Oregon State Forest Service. Can you do that?"

Jack snorted on the other end of the line. "Of course. I'm not a complete idiot ya know."

"I know, Dad. Can you please give me the phone number right away?"

"Hold on." The line went dead. He must've hung up to look for the phone book.

Unbelievable.

Sax counted to ten then hit the redial button. As before the phone rang three times before he father picked up.

"Antique Virgin, good evening. Jack Edwards, antique specialist speaking."

"Dad, did you find the number?"

"For what?"

"For the Oregon Forest Service."

"Why?"

"Daaaaaad!"

"Settle down, girl I'm kidding." He gave her the number then made her promise to come for dinner the next evening. He said her mother would really appreciate it. Since she lived at home, didn't have a boyfriend, and was always home for dinner, Sax readily agreed.

Dad's eccentric but his sense of humor is still intact. She smiled to herself.

Sax pressed the red button to end the call then quickly dialed the forest service number. It rang once then an answering machine kicked in.

The message said if it was an emergency she was to call a different number. She cut the connection then dialed the emergency number.

It rang twice then a man answered.

"Oregon Forest Service, Maxwell Pithy speaking."

Since the call to 911 hadn't gone so well Sax decided to take a different tact. I'll try really, really nice. I'll turn on the charm. She grinned hoping it would add cheerfulness to her tone.

"Hi, Mr. Pithy. My name's Sax Edwards and I'm with my friend Bryce. We're in the woods off a trail on Mount Mockingbird. We need help."

There, that should be clear.

"What's the emergency?" said Mr. Pithy. "This line is for emergencies only ya know."

Clarity, Sax. Clarity. "Like what?"

"Well, let's see...forest fires, floods, wild animal attacks...ya know emergencies. Which one is your emergency?"

"All of the above."

"Ohhh, really?"

"Yup. All of 'em." There, that should bring the cavalry. Sometimes you need to add a little pepper to a recipe if you want to add heat. I'm sure multiple disasters will light up the emergency boards.

"A flood on a mountain trail?"

"Well, not exactly a flood, but a fire and wild animals are involved."

"Wild animals?" He paused. "What kind?"

"A giant snake and a bear."

"Giant snake? An anaconda maybe?"

Anaconda? What am I, a National Geographic Special? "Yeah, sure I guess so. I didn't actually see it."

Mr. Pithy chuckled. "Believe me, if it was an anaconda you'd see it."

He wasn't taking her seriously. "Mr. Pithy, please I really do need help."

"That much is obvious. Listen. I know it's still early in the day but take my advice, go to bed and sleep it off."

"But—"

"Oh, and by the way we locals call it Mount Peck, not Mount Mockingbird. Nice try." He hung up.

"Great." Anger burned in her belly. Sax threw the phone as hard as she could deeper into the thick forest. "Take that!"

Throwing your only life line away was probably not a good idea. But what did the pioneers do when they were lost in the woods? Simple. They died.

Sax sat down heavily on the pine needle covered forest floor and wrapped her arms around her knees. She gazed forlornly at Bryce. Maybe she shouldn't have thrown his cell phone away.

His chest rose and fell in time to his breathing. Who would've thought a giant snake would cause a big, strong guy like him to pass out?

"Hello?" Sax started when a woman's voice echoed through the woods.

Sax jumped to her feet. "Hey! Over here!" she called.

"Okay. I'm coming. Stay where you are. Keep talking so I can find you."

Sax scanned the woods for any movement. Nothing, but she heard the rustle of branches and the snap of twigs being broken.

Sax started to talk rapidly. "I'm so glad you found us. I thought we were doomed. I mean first there was the skunk cabbage, then the bear and then the giant snake. That 911 operator was rude. I'm gonna file a complaint about her. And Mr. Pithy, he was just stupid. I was perfectly clear—" Sax stopped when it suddenly occurred to her she didn't know who the woman headed their way might be. She could be one of those survivalist nuts, or an axe murderer from one of those B grade horror movies.

I mean who knows what's in these woods? Maybe she'd kill them then feed their bodies to the bear and the snake.

A tree branch in front of her began to shake violently. Sax began to tremble. She held her breath, her heart in her throat.

A red headed woman stepped into the clearing. In her right hand she held a machete. Pine needles stuck to her red and blue checkerboard shirt and her blue jeans were dirty and stained. Her hiking boots were scuffed and worn. She was breathing hard and her blue eyes seemed to pierce Sax's soul.

"Hi. I'm with the Oregon Forest Service. Name's Argula. Tiffany Argula."

"Uhhh, hi...I'm Sax Edwards."

"Yes, I know."

Sax cocked an eyebrow. "I don't understand."

"Your father called my boss. He asked me to find you."

Her dad called this lady's boss? What surprised her most was her dad knew a normal person. Assuming her boss is normal. Wait a minute, how did she get here so fast?

Sax turned away at the sound of a groan coming from Bryce. He was at last waking up.

I guess fainting due to snakes last just long enough to wake up in time for the rescue. She was relieved he looked unharmed. She fought the urge to hug him. She took a step then stopped. No, too much, too soon. They were friends. That's all. But how she wanted so much more.

"What happened?" he said rising up on his elbows.

"Is he ok?" asked Tiffany, one eyebrow rose up her pale forehead.

"Yeah. He's fine. We were attacked. He fainted."

"Really?" Tiffany knelt at his side burying the point of the machete in the forest floor. From a waist pack she pulled out a small packet. She tore off one end then shoved the open packet under Bryce's nose.

He coughed and pushed her hand away. "I'm awake already. I don't need smelling salts."

She rose to her feet. Tiffany lifted the machete and used it as a pointer into the woods. "We'd better get out of here. The sun is setting in about an hour this time of year." A cruel looking smile twisted her lips and her eyes narrowed. "And we don't want be caught out here after dark."

Sax swallowed hard. Monsters. I knew it. "Okay. Let's go." Tiffany turned and led the way to a wall of thick undergrowth.

Sax helped Bryce to his feet and together they followed Tiffany as she hacked at the low hanging branches and the tangled bushes. She grunted as she chopped them into mulch. Sax was shocked how fast the woman was able to clear a path. She was a human bulldozer.

"Who's jungle Jane?" whispered Bryce.

"Oregon Forest Service. She's our rescue party." She glanced at him. "Do you think we'll make it out of here by dark?" She scanned the undergrowth around them looking for any monsters that were ready to pounce out of the deepening gloom.

"Yeah." He added, "Probably." He glanced at her from the corner of his eye. "But don't worry. She's just trying to scare us tenderfoots."

Sax nodded her stomach in knots. "It's working."

Bryce frowned. "I thought forest rangers wore uniforms. Besides, she's going the wrong way." He nodded over his shoulder. The trail is that way."

Crap-a-doodle. This is my fault. They were soooo dead.

CHAPTER FOURTEEN

AFTER AN UNEVENTFUL HIKE DOWN THE MOUNTAIN they arrived at the parking lot just as the last rays of the sun disappeared behind a hill. The sky was a deep indigo color dotted with the first stars of twilight. The wind's strength increased, causing Sax to shiver as the temperature suddenly dropped several degrees. The tall fir and pine trees shushed and swayed like mythical giants in fairytales.

Seeing her shiver Bryce put an arm round her shoulder and pulled her close. His warmth felt good against her. She smiled weakly at him and mouthed a thank you. He winked. She could get used to this. He likes me. Cool.

"Here we are," said Tiffany. The trail she led them to, she said, was a short cut. It turned out to be true. Tiffany was a park ranger, and a botanist. It was her work truck in the parking lot. She'd been collecting toadstool samples when she received the call from her supervisor about two lost hikers.

At first Tiffany thought her boss was drinking when he said they were trapped by a bear and a snake until she came across the bear sleeping in the clearing. She realized immediately his improbable story was in fact true.

Broken branches, and depressions made by Sax's shoes in the soft earth led her in their direction until she heard Sax's cries.

Sax's face grew warm as Tiffany explained that a flying cell phone just missed her head when she finally tracked the boot prints to the clearing where she found them.

"Thank you, Tiffany," said Bryce. "I don't know how we're going to repay you."

The corner of Tiffany's mouth curled in a smile. "All in a day's work."

"Can we at least take you to dinner?" Bryce offered.

She hadn't thought to bring money. There weren't any restaurants on hiking trails.

Which reminds me, who paid for lunch? Sax made a mental note to ask Bryce about it later. She wasn't about to let an engaged man pay for her meal. They were just friends. Strictly plutonic. If only he wasn't so nice.

The look in Tiffany's eyes said she had dropped the lumberjack persona. Sax was impressed, Tiffany was all-woman. And she rescued them which made her Sax's new official hero. She had a lot of heroes because she had a lot of bad luck.

As if to emphasize her transformation Tiffany unbuttoned her work shirt, took it off and tossed in the back of her pickup truck. Underneath she wore a sleeveless form-fitting gray t-shirt. Her arms were toned, her waist slim and athletic.

Whoa! Good thing I'm not letting Bryce hit on me or I'd be jealous for sure. And then who would be her hero of the day?

"Sorry, but my boyfriend is waiting for me." She climbed into her pickup, rolled the driver's window down then started the engine. "Rain check?"

Bryce chuckled. "Yeah, next time we're lost in the woods we'll all go to dinner."

Tiffany smiled put the truck in reverse then backed up. She put the truck in gear and was quickly gone in a cloud of dust and a goodbye tap on the horn.

"Nice girl," said Bryce. "And quite attractive, don't you think?"

"Yeah. I guess so. If you like that type."

Bryce walked to his Hummer and opened the passenger door. He helped Sax climb in. "And what type is that?" he said playfully.

"Oh, I don't know, the red-headed-body-by-Nautilus-type."

Bryce laughed and shut the truck door once Sax was seated with her seatbelt fastened.

He then went around the front and unlocked the driver's door and got in.

The truck's engine rumbled to life. It was dark enough already that the Hummer's automatic headlights snapped on. He drove out of the parking lot and they were soon on the highway headed toward Glad Beach.

Bryce's nose wrinkled. "Whew! We smell like rotting rain forest. Let's go to my place, have a shower, then go to dinner."

Sax's heart sank. She really enjoying being with him but she couldn't spend money she didn't have.

She needed to come up with an alternate plan. But there wasn't much time. They'd be in Glad Beach inside fifteen minutes. She fidgeted in her seat.

"I've a better idea," she said after thinking about the problem for several seconds.

"Oh?"

"It's Tuesday. Right?"

"Yeah. What about it?"

"Tuesday is barbecue night at my house. How about you come over to my place for dinner?"

Bryce grinned. "Great. I love a good barbecue. Is it okay if I call my father to join us? He's the legendary barbecuer of Elmore, Connecticut."

"He is?" Her heart rate increased and she felt sick. What had she done now?

Bryce nodded. "Oh, yeah. Dad even has a cookbook and those big shot chefs on the Food Network consult with him all the time."

What am I saying? Girl, when you dig a hole you use a back hoe. Sax chuckled uneasily. Why was she acting as if she was still a high school girl with a crush? I hope he forgives me later. "Sure, more the merrier."

"Fantastic. I'll drop you off at your place then go home, have a shower and pick up Dad. We should be back in about an hour." He looked thoughtful. "Is there anything we need to bring?"

Yeah, how about the food and the barbecue grill? "Maybe some beer, English of course, and wine. Preferably champagne. My parents read somewhere that the English drink more champagne per capita than anyone in the world."

"Sure."

They rode in silence the rest of the way to Sax's house. Sax's mind was in overdrive working on her plan for the great barbecue caper. Maybe I can borrow the neighbor's barbecue? She'd seen them use it a few times and it didn't look that hard to grill on a barbecue.

She crossed her arms and grinned. This would be simple. What could go wrong?

~~~

The Buttsman's barbecue grill was best described as ancient, practically civil-war-era old. Her mother would love this thing for the shop.

Her mother could tell customers it was used by Henry the Eighth. He must have loved barbecue, he was certainly fat enough. Too bad Mr. Buttsman wanted the grill returned. She wanted to cook on it all the time. Cooking outside seemed fun.

Sax placed several Tiki torches around the circular gravel driveway. Her mother purchased the torches a year ago at the local Goodwill store. She wanted to use the backyard but the grass was too high.

The grass could catch fire and that'd be dangerous. But danger was her middle name.

She chuckled. Not really. Bad-luck-putting-me-in-danger is my way too long middle name.

She embedded one of the torches in the soft ground next to the barbecue grill. Since the sun had set the driveway was usually cloaked in darkness, the flames from the torches gave the front of the house and the surrounding tress a soft, golden glow. On a different occasion it might even be described as romantic.

Sax sighed. If only Bryce thought of me that way. She shook her head.

What am I saying? He was engaged. Who am I kidding?

She was pining for a man who was impossible to attain. He was way out of her league and she knew it.

The forty foot high Norfolk pine, her father's favorite tree, was right behind the grill. Her father insisted on calling it a Cook pine after Captain Cook's failed attempt to make ships masts out of the tree in the eighteenth century. The arborist who moved it from their home in Indiana to Oregon insisted it was definitely a Norfolk. Ever since, the rest of the family dubbed the tree Cook's folly, but not when their father was within earshot.

The handle on the grill's lid rattled when she used it to flip the lid back. It was loose. She decided to tighten it later.

The smell of burnt charcoal assaulted her senses. The grates were coated with thick, black charcoal. Burnt charcoal must add flavor.

She looked around the grill. That's funny, I thought these things came with a brush? The smiling dad in the Home Depot flyer always seems to have a brush. Sax snorted at the image of her father wearing an apron with the words World's Greatest Grillmaster stenciled in cartoon letters across the front, and a funny looking chef's hat on his head. Dad wouldn't be caught dead dressed in an apron and a chefs hat.

"What's going on?" It was her father. The screen door slammed behind him. Tucked under his arm was a month old copy of the Times of London newspaper.

She let go of the grill's lid and it closed with a clang. She smiled. "Ummm hi, Dad. I'm making dinner tonight."

Her father's gray eyebrows rose up his forehead registering his surprise. "Really? Why do you have that here?" He pointed to the sagging grill.

"To make dinner?"

"But it's bangers and mash night. I don't think you can cook mash on a barbecue."

"No, Dad. I thought barbecue chicken would be nice for a change." She'd been lucky to score a couple of whole frying chickens in the freezer. They were past their expiration date, but she was sure they'd be fine.

Right now the two freezer birds were in the microwave defrosting.

Her father looked thoughtful for a second then said, "Ok. Why not? Chicken would be better than bangers and mash." He turned away and headed back into the house. The screen door rattled after it slammed shut with a loud bang behind him. Sax thought about reminding him it was actually Cornish pasty night, but decided against it.

If she reminded him it would reset the conversation to the beginning. She snorted again. No way was she going to start over after the phone call from the forest. Her father was a life long learning experience.

Bertie Edwards stuck her head out a window on the second floor. "Sax? What are you doing, dear?"

"Isn't it obvious? I'm barbecuing."

"I know that, dear. What I meant is what are you making?"

"Chicken." She snorted. Her mom and dad didn't know anything about barbecue. She studied the barbecue grill. I hope this thing works right.

"Good. You're a life saver. Nelson, Brit and Wallace, and the children are coming for dinner. And of course, Winston too. I'll set the table for nine." Bertie started to withdraw from the window.

"Eleven, Mother."

Bertie stuck her head back out the window. Her brow furrowed. "What was that, dear?"

"Eleven. There'll be eleven for dinner. You better set the table for eleven."

"Why, dear?"

"Because I invited someone. He's my guest and he's bringing his father."

"He?" Her eyes lit up and a smile brightened her features. "Not that handsome Bryce Kelly?" Sax's face suddenly seemed to be on fire.

Before she ducked inside again Bertie added, "And don't snort, dear, it's undignified."

Ignoring her mother, Sax kept her eyes focused on the two black plastic knobs on the front of the grill.

Beside the knob on her right was a red button. The printing on the panel had long ago faded so she had no way to tell what any of them did, but she'd figure it out. Mr. Buttsman said it was easy. His instructions seemed simple enough. It couldn't be that difficult. Could it?

Her mother yelped after she disappeared from the window. Her shouts echoed through the house. "Jack! Sax has a guest coming for dinner. Did you know?"

"No, dear, I'm not reading," came her father's reply. Her father was a voracious reader. Naturally, he only read what was recommended by the Times of London.

If her mother didn't question him several times a day he'd have his nose in a book instead of doing whatever job he was supposed to be doing, which was never reading. Whenever she asked him, and especially when he was reading, he'd stuff his book in his back pocket and answer her truthfully that he wasn't reading. Sax thought it was a neat trick and played along whenever she could. It was the one of the few things she enjoyed about still living at home with her parents.

"Jack!" Bertie shouted. "Forget about the book. Guess who's coming to dinner?"

"I know! I know!" Sax's father shouted back, "It's the guy from the brothel!"

Sax let her head fall to her chest then slapped her forehead with the palm of her hand. How did he know Bryce was coming over? She thought she only told her mother. Does he have ears in the back of his head? Her dad was far smarter than he acted sometimes.

Unbelievable. Great, just great. She liked Bryce and her father thought he's a pimp. She shook her head. He is so nuts.

CHAPTER FIFTEEN

THE COOK'S FOLLY PINE WAS SHEATHED IN A PILLAR OF FLAME. The smoking remains of the Buttsman barbecue grill rested high in the branches of the furiously burning tree.

The fire department's report would later state that the fire started when concentrated propane gas in the air was ignited by the Tiki torch next to the grill.

Doing as Mr. Buttsman instructed, Sax turned on the propane tank using the tap on the top of the tank. The instructions didn't say to open the lid of the barbecue so she didn't.

Then, also as instructed, Sax pressed the red button which was followed by a sharp clicking sound. Satisfied the burners were lit and ready, she went inside to check on the thawing chicken.

What she didn't know was all red buttons on gas barbecues stop working after three uses. When the button fails you have to use a portable barbecue lighter to light the burners. If the gas was on and the burners weren't lit the build up of gas could be very dangerous. It fact if the gas built up it would explode if there was the slightest spark. Mr. Buttsman forgot to mention the button was broken.

Once the air was filled with propane gas the Tiki torch's flames started a chain of events that resulted in the Cook's Folly bursting into flame. Naturally a burst of superheated air caused the remaining propane in the tank to explode.

And of course a forty foot high flaming pine tree tended to attract attention.

From the wail of multiple sirens in the distance it sounded like the entire volunteer fire department, the sheriff, and the town's ambulance were headed their way.

Sax, her face covered in soot, and coughing from the acrid smoke, looked up from the charred azalea bush she'd just doused with a bucket of water.

Bryce's truck! Oh, crap! Bryce! And his father. She looked down at her soot covered clothes. I look like a chimney sweep. Her eyes brimmed with tears. Her dirty clothes and face made her want to weep. She was a mess.

Bryce's Hummer sat at the entrance to the circular gravel driveway. From inside the truck, Bryce and his father watched dumbfounded as Sax and Winston ran around with water buckets dousing spot fires then running back to the tap to refill before repeating the process. Not that their efforts were doing much good. The front yard looked like a war zone after a bomb had been dropped.

She let go of the bucket. It landed on her foot. Ignoring the pain she pasted her best how're-you-I'm-fine-smile on her face and limped toward the truck. Bryce got out and walked toward her to meet her halfway. His father remained in his seat his eyes fixed on the burning pine tree.

"You okay?" Bryce said.

Look calm. Act as if nothing's wrong. "I'm fine. How're you?"

"Uhhh...better than..." he paused and glanced at the tree. "A Norfolk pine?"

"Oh...really, you know the Norfolk?"

"Yeah, sure. I like trees and I've seen Norfolk's in New Caledonia."

Sax stopped in front off him and placed her hands on her hips. She wanted to appear as casual as possible under the circumstances. Fire? What fire? "You've been to New Caledonia?" she said. He nodded as his eyes alternated between her and the burning tree. "Really? Isn't that something?"

She turned toward the house. "Hey, Dad! Bryce has been to New Caledonia!"

The screen door swung open the hinges protesting loudly. Her father walked out, his concentration on a book he was reading. With his eyes locked on the pages of the book he stopped just short of running into his daughter. "Hi, Sax. What was that about New Caledonia?"

A slow smile curled the edges of Bryce's mouth. He winked. Her cheeks grew warm and she offered him a weak smile. She relished his support, it would make what was about to happen easier to take.

When her father saw his beloved pine burning she would be dead meat. She trembled with fear.

"Hi, Mr. Edwards. It's me, Bryce Kelly." Wally Kelly walked from the passenger side of truck and now stood next to Bryce. Bryce laid one arm across his father's shoulders. "And this is my Dad, Walter."

This finally unglued Jack's eyes from the pages of the book.

"Jack! Are you reading?" It was Bertie doing her scheduled check.

Her father slapped the book closed then quickly shoved it in the back pocket of his Dockers. He said, "no, dear!" after the book was shoved in his back pocket.

He eyed Bryce up and down. "Now, what was that?"

"I'm Bryce Kelly and this is my dad, Walter."

"Yeah, yeah I know who you are." Her father dismissed him with a wave of one hand. She watched her father apprehensively. She knew her dad was going to say something inappropriate again.

Mom says he's never been right since he left that asbestos mine in sixty-three.

"So, Dad, who is he?" said Sax she pointed at Bryce. Please don't say he's a pimp.

"He's the brothel guy." Oh, no. The curse struck again.

"You have a date with him." Her embarrassment meter had officially gone off the scale. No wonder I don't have a boyfriend.

Walter's jaw dropped and Sax snorted sheepishly. Her father's eyes narrowed and he glared at Bryce. "Young man, you've made a mistake. My daughter is not a lady of the evening."

Bryce grinned and a playful look appeared in his eyes. Oh, oh... "How do you know?"

Her father frowned. He looked doubtful. C'mon, Dad you know the answer. Finally, her dad turned his head toward the house and yelled, "Bertie, is Sax a prostitute?"

"I'll be right out!" Came Bertie's muffled reply from inside the house.

They waited in silence, interrupted intermittently by the sizzle of water poured on flames and permeated by the smell of smoke. Her brother Winston continued to run around the yard dousing hot spots with water. This was super awkward. She shuffled her feet back and forth, avoiding Bryce and her father's eyes by staring at the blackened gravel.

A bright yellow fire truck appeared at the top of the driveway behind the Hummer. When the large pumper truck came to a halt the driver honked the horn. "Hey, fella!" called the driver, his head out the window. "We gotta get to the fire! Move that truck!"

Her dad's frown deepened in intensity forming ruts in his pale forehead. He marched head down toward the fire truck like an enraged bull. His steady glare made the driver recoil.

"There's no fire here, young man. Now why don't you get that thing out of my driveway. I have guests coming. And my daughter's new boyfriend is coming for bangers and mash."

The driver pointed past her father. "Yeah, okay, sir but what about that?"

Her dad turned his head until his eyes settled on the burning Norfolk pine. "That?" He crossed his arms over his chest and chuckled. "You call that a fire? You shoulda seen the great fire of London in 1666—"

Her father abruptly stopped talking and the color of his face changed to pure whitefish. His features morphed into a glare. "Well don't just sit there! My tree's on fire!"

~~~

After Bryce moved his Hummer out of the way the pumper truck rumbled onto the circular driveway in front of the house.

Unreeling the hoses the firemen quickly doused the remaining fire. But all that remained of the Norfolk pine was the smoking trunk and the blackened branches where the barbecue grill, or what was left of it, landed after the explosion. The tree looked like the pipe cleaners used in Kindergarten to make stick men.

As if reading her mind Bryce, standing beside her said, "Ya know, that looks like Paul Bunyan's pipe cleaner." Sax laughed. He glanced at her and winked.

He's not only handsome, he's funny too. She smiled. His presence made her feel better. He must be good for me. She felt safe with him around. It was almost as if they had something in common. It was something just on the horizon of her mind. Something she couldn't quite see. And it frustrated her.

She pushed away those thoughts when it suddenly dawned on her she must look a fright. Sax ran her index finger down her right cheek then looked at her finger coated with black soot.

"See," he added, "not all is lost." Bryce picked up one of Tiki torches that had been blown over by the force of the water from the fire hose. "You could use this again."

She snorted. "Not on your life."

He chuckled and let the spent torch drop to the ground. His smile disappeared to be replaced by a serious expression. "Listen, Sax, I feel somewhat responsible for this." He held up his hand to stop any anticipated objections.

Not that Sax was going to object. If he was willing to take responsibility she would let him. After all, he did stick a spoon of deadly chowder in her mouth

"So how about I take us all to dinner? My treat," Bryce said.

Sax snorted. Big city people. "You know this is a small town right?" He nodded, looking slightly perplexed. "Well, in small towns like Glad Beach we roll up the streets by seven o'clock this time of year, sometimes even earlier if business is really slow."

"Oh? Really?"

"Yes. The only place open late is an awful country bar called The Cowboy Way. The food's horrible, the servers surly, and the décor early cattle drive."

Bryce shook his head and a wistful smile pulled across his lips. He's up to something. "I don't think so, Sax. I think there's a very famous seafood restaurant on Highway 101 that stays open later than you think."

"Oh? Really?"

He nodded. "I know the head chef. My dad called him and he's holding spots for all of us. And don't worry. Albert is making a special chicken dish for you." He frowned thoughtfully. "Is anyone else in your family allergic to fish?"

Sax shook her head. "But, my brothers are coming for dinner, and my brother, Brit, his wife Wallace, and their two kids. There'll be eleven of us." Sax's words dropped off into silence.

Whoa, girl. You're being waaaayyy too forward. I must sound awful.

Bryce smiled then said, "No worries. Albert said he could accommodate up to twenty. Do you want to invite the Fire Department?" Just as he finished speaking the charred ruin of the Norfolk fell over. With a loud crash, tree branches landed in the remains of the burned out bushes with a loud thud. At the same time there was a sharp crack and the charred tree trunk split in two. The remains of the grill were thrown from the branches, the blackened parts scattering and rattling across the gravel driveway.

"No, but we better invite Mr. and Mrs. Buttsman." She nodded toward the shattered barbecue. "After all, the grill was theirs."

CHAPTER SIXTEEN

Hugo and Wilma Buttsman glared at Sax all through dinner. The chicken offered a welcome distraction from the embarrassment of blowing up their grill and burning down her father's favorite tree. *I've gotta make this right.*

Bryce is right. The chef was amazing. The sauce...a hint of heat and subtle oregano was like a taste explosion on her tongue.

I better stop thinking about explosions. She was certain she'd have nightmares filled with exploding trees for weeks to come.

She stole a glance at Hugo and Wilma and smiled weakly. One eyebrow rose up Hugo's tanned forehead, while Wilma harrumphed over her seafood stew. Thankfully Hugo turned his attention back to his halibut. *Man, if looks could kill I'd have been dead so many times.*

Bryce was the life of the party. It seemed a little arrogant when he ordered for everyone, even the children. But everyone seemed more than happy with the food. Even her niece and nephew. They were six and seven respectively, and usually fussy eaters, but they were eating their fish and chips with unbridled gusto.

To her surprise Bryce defended her. He placed a hand on Hugo's shoulder to get his attention. "Hey there, Hugo, why don't you and Wilma forgive Sax? After all it was an accident, don't you agree?"

How did he know it was an accident? True, it was an accident but Sax hadn't told him the details of what happened.

89

Can he read my mind? That'd be cool but a little creepy too.

Hugo mumbled through the piece of fish he'd just stuffed in his mouth. "Well...yeah...I guess so...but I had that barbecue grill for a long time. I used it a lot when my kids were young."

"Oh? How old are your kids?"

"Maury's thirty eight and Sheila's thirty five. He lives in Houston Texas, she's in New York."

Bryce's blue eyes crinkled at the corners. "Then I guess your grill really is an antique."

"Antique? Where?" Her father said from his seat farther down the long table. On his left side was Wally Kelly. Up to now they'd been engrossed in a lengthy review of the latest Cussler novel.

She and Bryce sat side by side on one side of the long table. Next to her was Winnie, who sat next to Walter who was next to her mom and dad. On the other side of the table were Brit, Wallace, and Nelson. And at the end, next to their Uncle Nelson, were her niece and nephew.

Before Bryce could respond her mother spoke up. "Why don't we pay for a new one? Surely they can't be that much. I mean thirty year old barbecue grills must grow on trees."

Trees? Why did she have to say trees? The bad luck curse was ruining her life. My dad's gonna kill me! She buried her face in her hands. Wake up, girl. This was a nightmare. Spreading her fingers she snuck a peek at Bryce who had a wide grin on his face. Huh? What gives with him?

"You know, Bertie I agree. Though how about I pay for the new one?"

"Huh, Bryce," said Wally, "I'm tired. It's past my bedtime. Can we go home?"

Bryce looked at his watch. "But, Dad it's barely nine-thirty."

"Bryce?"

"Yeah, okay Dad. Well, everyone, I guess we have to call this a night. I left my Amex Card number with Albert. I've taken care of everything so continue on without us." Before he rose from his chair he promised the Buttsmans he'd call them the next day to go barbecue grill shopping. His eyes locked with Sax's as he stood up.

"Thanks for wonderful evening, Bryce," she said. "This is the best dinner ever." Bryce eyes twinkled and he winked.

She hoped he'd forgiven her for the stuff that happened on the hike. The few men Sax had dated usually ran for the hills when her bad luck curse caused bad things to happen. But there's something different about Bryce.

She planned to ask him at the first opportunity. There had to be something they had in common that made her feel so attracted to him. He was the first man who forgave her faults. And he seemed to accept her bad luck. That's just too weird.

Wally shook hands with her dad, and promised to drop by the shop soon so they could continue their conversation.

As Bryce and Wally neared the exit her father called after them, "Your son is a pretty good guy, Wally, even for a guy who frequents brothels." Wally wore a bemused smile on his lips when he shook his head as the door closed behind them and they were gone.

Sax let her head and shoulders sag, closed her eyes, and slapped her forehead with the palm of her hand. Her dad's craziness gave her nightmares and she hated nightmares.

Sax's head snapped up when she heard Winnie's chuckle. "Are you about to add to my embarrassment, dear brother?"

"You bet, sis." She didn't like the evil looking grin on his face. "I think you've got a crush on that man."

"Who? Wally?"

Winnie laughed. "No, silly. Bryce. You really like him don't you?"

Oh, man is it that obvious. Was she really falling for Bryce?

He continued. "And don't try to deny it. I saw the puppy dog look in your eyes when he first came in."

Sax leaned forward to rest her elbows on the table on either side of her empty plate. She had to nip this loose talk in the bud before it got out of hand. They lived in a very small town. Rumors had a way of spreading like wild fire in small towns. "Ok, smart guy. I was going to deny it, but not for the reasons your dirty little mind conjures up. I can't be anything more than friends with Mr. Bryce Kelly."

"Really, sis? Tell us why." Winnie shifted in his seat and leaned back then crossed his arms over his narrow chest. The spikes of hair atop his head bobbed in time to his movements.

I'm gonna wipe that smug expression off your face, clown boy. Her family had suddenly gone too quiet. They were hanging on her every word. Even her young niece and nephew seemed interested in her response.

"He's engaged to a fancy New York socialite."

The sparkle in her mother's eyes disappeared. "What's her name?" asked her mother.

"Why, Mom? Are you planning to have her bumped off?"

"Don't be silly, dear. For heaven's sake, it's not like I'm asking for the name of an undercover secret agent."

She decided it would be okay to tell her mother about Cinnamon. After all what harm could it do? "Okay, okay. Cinnamon Wolthorp. Her family is old money from New York."

"I know them," said her dad.

Her mother looked skeptically at her dad. "How would you know them?"

"I read about them in the Times."

Sax stared at her father expecting him to say more. When he didn't she had to ask, "So? What did it say in the Times about the Wolthorps?"

"It was in the financial section."

Sax nodded. "And?" It's like he pulled every tooth out of her head.

"It was in Max Scott's column."

I'll take the bait. She never knew what he'd say next but sometimes she had to let him say whatever it was now or he'd blurt it out in the local supermarket. Who knew what he would say this time. She loved him but he drove her nuts. "All right, Dad, I'll bite. Who is Max Scott?"

"He writes a column called Rumors."

Sax frowned. "So, Dad..." Focus, old man. "You read in Max Scott's column, called Rumors, something about the Wolthorp family." Jack's attention drifted to a stain on the tablecloth.

She worried that eccentricity ran in the family and in the future she might become turn as weird as her dad.

"Dad, pay attention," she said sharply.

Her mom took her dad's hand in hers. Her father looked up and smiled when she gently patted it with her other hand. "Jack, your daughter asked you a question."

His gaze shifted to his daughter.

"Now, tell me about the rumors involving the Wolthorps?" Sax asked.

"Wolthorps? What's a Wolthorp?" he said.

Sax snorted and buried her face in her hands.

"Now, dear, don't snort, it's undignified," admonished her mother.

CHAPTER SEVENTEEN

AFTER BRYCE HAD THE TRUCK HEADED NORTH away from the restaurant he glanced at his father in the passenger seat beside him. Bryce's mind whirled with questions. He had to know why his father wanted to leave so quickly. Maybe he didn't like Sax? Maybe her father embarrassed him? Was his father ill? Had he said something wrong?

I should be tactful. "So, Dad."

"Yes?" His dad leaned forward and adjusted the radio knob, tuning to his favorite country music station. Willie Nelson's mellow voice came through the speakers.

"What's the real reason you wanted to leave the restaurant?" He nodded at the clock recessed into the dashboard. So much for tactful. "It's nowhere near your normal bed time."

"Can't a man go to bed early sometimes?"

Bryce cocked an eyebrow. "You sick or something?"

"No, no. I'm fine. In fact my doctor says I'm healthier than I've been in years." He sighed. Bryce was relieved his dad wasn't sick.

Since his mother died way before her time he'd always been conscious of his father's health. His dad's job had been killing him with stress, and fast paced days and long hours. His doctor said Wally added twenty years to his life the day he retired.

Bryce worried the marriage to Maggie had started to adversely affect his father's health. I know she certainly adds to my stress level with all her game playing.

94

All Maggie had to say was hello and he thought she was playing a mind game with him. Bryce hated mind games. It was such a waste of time and energy.

"I had to get you out of there," his father said finally.

"Me? Why?"

"Because you're getting too close to that Saxony girl."

Bryce steered off the main highway onto the gravel road leading to his house on the lake. "She's a friend. Nothing more."

His father smirked. "If you say so, son."

"Yes, I say so." Why would he think I'm interested in Sax? More than as a friend I mean. It was bad enough he was worried his feelings for her were confusing him, now they were showing.

The truck bounced as it crunched the gravel under the tires. They were soon parked in front of the dark house. The women were still on their shopping trip in Portland. Bryce shut off the Hummer's engine.

"What're you going to do now, Dad?"

His father smiled. "I'm going inside to read. Margaret and Elizabeth are still away and I'll have some peace and quiet for a while. And I'm going to enjoy it." He opened the passenger and stepped out. He looked back at Bryce who remained seated behind the steering wheel. "What about you?"

"I think I'll take a walk along the lake. I need some me time." And time to think about things. He had begun to care about Sax more than he should. He'd never felt so close to someone so fast in his life. He wished he knew why.

The smile disappeared from his father's features. "Okay, but be careful."

"Dad, I'm not five anymore, you know."

His father closed the passenger door and started walking away toward the house.

He opened the truck door and stepped out onto the gravel driveway and closed the door. The gravel crunched under his sneakers as he walked to the grassy strip that ran along the lakeshore.

There was no wind and the moon now cast a white glow across the flat water. In the distance a fish jumped, followed by a splash.

Captured in the glow of the moonlight a pair of loons floated on the calm water. Suddenly one of them emitted a mournful call that echoed across the lake. The other bird made a matching sound before the echo died.

Looks like someone's in love. Bryce squatted and picked up a flat rock. He rifled the rock side arm across the water. The stone skipped ten times across the lake then sank out of sight.

Too bad I don't love Cinnamon. But he knew he had to marry her anyway. The plans had been made and his father wanted him to marry her. Cin and he had been friends since grade school. They dated briefly in high school but there was no spark between them. He liked her so when his stepmother suggested the match he went along with it. Being married to a friend isn't a bad thing, is it?

Stuffing his hands in the pockets of his blue jeans he began to follow the grass strip along the edge of the water. He had his head down, his eyes focused on the ground.

Sax and I seem to have a lot in common. They both liked the outdoors and she had a great sense of humor. And she had been a good sport about the disasters his problem caused them. At first he wondered why she accepted all the trouble he caused but she seemed to take it in stride. It was to him strange how she accepted him even with his faults. And she even forgave him for almost killing her with clam chowder.

Cinnamon had never accepted his problem. She thinks everything should be perfect. What's ever perfect anyway?

He kicked a rock he thought was loose but it was like an iceberg. Most of it was buried below ground. "Ouch! That really hurts!"

He stumbled and dropped onto his butt with a cry of pain. He raised his injured foot and grabbed his sneaker and gritted his teeth. "Owww. Crap."

He froze at the sound of footsteps somewhere in the shadows. His heart beat faster and the moisture in his mouth evaporated. The echo of the footsteps off the lake made it impossible to determine where they were coming from.

"Hello?" No answer. I hope it's not a bear. Not again.

Maybe I should call out for help? His dad might hear him if he yelled for help. Making a lot of noise when a bear is around was not a good idea. I'd be bear chow before Dad got here.

He decided to lie on his back and not move a muscle and play dead. He read somewhere playing dead worked. At least he hoped it worked. Bryce lay on his back and held his breath straining to listen for more footsteps.

Quiet. The loons made two more calls followed again by silence.

He lay on the grass for what seemed like an eternity listening to his heart beat in his ears. He couldn't lay here forever.

"Bryce?" It was his father. He sighed as he released the pent up air in his lungs.

"Dad. It's you. Thank goodness."

"Why are you on the ground?" His father stepped out of the shadows carrying a steel bucket in one hand.

"I thought you were a bear."

"A bear?" His father looked around nervously. "Where?"

Bryce chuckled as he stood up. "Oh, c'mon, dad. It was you walking around out here."

His father's brow wrinkled. "How long ago did you hear the bear?"

Bryce slapped his father's shoulder. "I don't know, fifteen minutes, maybe ten."

"I just came outside. I was going to gather some dandelion flowers to make tea."

Bryce looked at his father for several seconds and his face was cool with fear. Oh, crap, maybe it was a bear. "Oh, well then I guess we better go inside."

His father looked around. "Yeah, I'd say you're right."

Father and son started off toward the house. "Something's wrong isn't it?" said his father as they walked side by side.

"Yes." His father could read him like one of his favorite books. He'd always been able to read Bryce's emotions but more so after his mother died. It was time to confess his growing feelings for Sax. He'd always trusted his father and valued his opinion.

"Tell me about it."

Bryce stopped and buried his hands in the pockets of his pants. "I think I'm beginning to have feelings for Sax, but I'm not sure."

His father stopped beside him and nodded. He placed one hand on his Bryce's shoulder then gazed into his eyes. "So, son, do you love Cinnamon?"

Bryce looked at his father. It was time to admit the truth. "No, Dad, I don't."

CHAPTER EIGHTEEN

AFTER HUGS AND KISSES ALL AROUND, Sax drove her father and mother home in their 1982 Toyota Corolla. Winnie left with Brit, Wallace, and the kids. Nelson excused himself shortly after Bryce and his father left, saying he didn't want to miss the PBS special on Napoleon. Coward.

She knew he owned a TiVo. Her brother wanted to get outta crazy town while the gettin' was good. Not that she blamed him. When Dad gets on a roll it can be too much for my brothers.

She on the other had had gotten used to his off kilter view of the world a little more than her siblings.

The dilapidated made-in-Japan automobile shook, popped, and rattled around them. Not surprising since the car had four hundred and fifty thousand miles on the odometer. Sax wouldn't be surprised if the odometer had been turned back by that used car dealer—who was busted for fraud shortly after her father purchased it. At least it still got them from A to B, and it stopped when you pressed on the brake, which is always a nice feature in a car.

"Dad, you're sooo cheap," Sax groused, her eyes fixed on the dark, winding highway ahead. But her life was mixed up right now with Bryce and all the crazy bad luck she'd had lately. Her bad luck seemed worse than ever. She didn't need him going all nuts on her right now.

I swear if he wrecks my friendship with Bryce I'll—I'll do nothing as usual.

Her parents were a little nuts but she loved them too much to abandon them.

"No, I'm not," protested Jack, accompanied by a grunt.

"Let's see, you guys don't own a barbecue so I had to borrow a faulty one from the neighbors. And it blew up. And you own this wreck that seems to run on hungry squirrels. And you didn't pay for a new barbecue for the poor Buttsmans, you let Bryce pay. And you didn't offer to pay for dinner. Dad, you could have at least left the tip."

"Ya know, Jack," said her mother. "You are cheap. I just never noticed before."

"Yeah? So what?"

"Nothing. Just wanted you to know I never noticed, is all."

Sax rolled her eyes and snorted. Unbelievable! She hated family meetings.

Sax waited but her mother didn't say anything about her snort. Good, they may finally be accepting me.

I can be just as eccentric as the best of them. She slowed the car as they came to where their driveway met highway 101. Oh, man what am I saying?

~~~

The next morning Sax was busy in the back of the store when Bryce dropped in unexpectedly. Thankfully, her father was at the Goodwill store in Newport hunting for more antiques. Her mother was up front taking inventory and humming "God Save the Queen" as she counted the Prince Charles ear warmers and the Henry the Eighth smoking jackets, her back to the door, when Bryce entered.

"Hey, Mrs. E."

Sax's ears perked up when she heard his cheerful greeting and her mother's equally cheerful response.

I know what you're up to, you old matchmaker, you. Not that it was a bad idea but she knew she had to stop her mother before she got carried away. She was pleased Bryce had stopped by the shop.

100

She'd been worried he would never come by again after yesterday's disaster and having to pay for the Buttsmans new barbecue.

Sax dropped the Prince Harry swim thong into the box. She'd tried to explain to her mother how inappropriate a thong was for the royal personage, but her mother insisted the wholesaler told her the royal grandsons wore identical ones when they were on the French Riviera. It wasn't entirely impossible, but highly unlikely with the paparazzi dogging their every move. Wouldn't the Queen be impressed if the papers had a picture of Prince Willie's willie splashed across the front page?

Sax came through the bead curtain, her eyes focused on Bryce. "Hi!" she said using one arm to hold the bead curtain back.

"How're you doing?" he said.

"Okay, I guess. Other than that I'm still coughing up smoke from the fire."

His brow wrinkled so she added, "Just kidding."

He smiled. "Listen, Bryce, it was an accident. If you haven't noticed accidents happen a lot around me. I have a curse."

"Really?"

"Not a real witch-poisoned-apple curse, but it seems things just go wrong around me. Been that way since I was a kid."

Bryce nodded. "I guess we have a lot in common."

"Yeah, right. You're a millionaire and I'm…" No need to emphasize they were not in the same league. He already knew she wasn't rich since she worked at a junk store.

"Not?" he finished for her.

She smiled. "Yeah. Not. So, what can I do for you today?" Her heart beat faster. She felt anxious and hoped he came to see her and not look for antiques. He'd never find antiques in here anyway.

He smiled. "I came to see you, actually. If that's okay with you."

"Yes, of course," she replied quickly. Too quickly, she thought. Her face grew warm and she averted her gaze to hide her embarrassment for being so obvious.

Antique Virgin

"Listen," he said, changing the subject. "How about we do something? I heard those famous sea lion caves aren't too far from here. I really want to see them. Want to come with me?"

"Do you think we should take the risk?" she asked.

"Sure. Why not? After all we've survived every disaster so far, what's the worst that can happen?"

The worst thing that could happen is they'd be eaten by hungry sea lions, or Cinnamon Wolthorp would have her killed for going out with her fiancée...again.

CHAPTER NINETEEN

THE FLAGS ATOP THE FLAG POLES THAT SURROUNDED the parking lot of the Sea lions Preserve were sticking straight out. The breeze had grown stronger on the way here.

It's a bad omen, but like Bryce said, we've survived worse.

Bryce steered the truck into the gravel parking lot. Thick black, rain-filled clouds crowded the horizon. Two gray and white seagulls rode the wind off the cliff overlooking the restless ocean beyond.

A sign stood next to a rusted steel railing where stone steps cut into the rock cliff that led to the caves below. It warned that the Sea lion caves were at the bottom of a steep incline.

The parking lot was filled with motor homes, some the size of people's houses, and cars stuffed to overflowing with luggage, sleeping bags, coolers and other flotsam of life on the road.

Maybe we should go home.

"Looks like fun, eh?" said Bryce as he turned off the engine. He threw open his door accompanied by a blast of cold wind that sent shivers down Sax's spine.

Sax steeled herself and pulled her hoodie over her head before she got out of the warm truck. The wind that hit her in the face was raw, salty, and made her stagger slightly due to the force. She stumbled to the front of truck.

"C'mon!" Bryce cried over the wind when he appeared from round the front of the Hummer. He had one hand pressing his own hoodie on his head as he ran for the top of the stairs.

Sax lowered her head and ran after him.

They started down the stone steps. Bryce led the way taking each step faster than she was able. Sax gripped the cold steel rail tightly as she stepped carefully, afraid she'd be blown into the next state by the fierce wind.

At the bottom of the steps Sax could see Bryce standing, watching her from under the cover of a cave opening carved into the black volcanic rock. It looked so far away, she wondered if she'd make it in one piece. You're not in Kansas anymore, girl.

Just as she reached the last two steps the ink-black clouds opened up, pelting her with rain. "Hey!" Sax yelled and flew down the last two steps, anxious to get undercover. It was better to be cold than cold and wet.

"Whew, that was close," said Bryce. He pushed back his hood to reveal his head of dark curls. "Let's hope it stops before we finish the tour."

"Oh? There's a tour? Like Disneyland?"

"'Fraid not. No little cars to ride in. It's a walking tour."

The cave was lined with yellow light bulbs in steel cages set equi-distance into the ceiling. The lights cast a soft glow over the cave walls. Footsteps echoed from out of sight ahead in the tunnel.

Sax's nose wrinkled. Yuk. Not fish again.

Bryce started down the gentle slope as the tunnel took them deeper and deeper down the Cliffside. After fifteen minutes of walking her feet hurt. The passageway began to widen. The sound of pounding surf and dog-like barks mingled and grew louder with each step.

Must be the sea lions. They didn't smell so good either.

Finally they arrived in a large cavern, the jagged, uneven stone ceiling rose about twenty feet over their heads. A chain link fence was cemented into a wide public viewing platform. The platform was carved out of rock and the fence prevented visitors from falling over the edge.

That's what she called a good sign.

A gaggle of tourists with cameras hung round their necks jostled for positions to snap the best pictures of hundreds of sea lions that lay across the rocks.

An Oregon State Park Ranger in her green uniform and brown Stetson was explaining the eating habits of the large mammals as they approached.

The massive cavern ran from just below the viewing area to where the sea came in through a wide opening in the cavern wall. Waves roared into the cave in great swells to smash against the rocks.

Water splashed over some of the sea lions who bellowed their objections. Whoa, they're so big. But the baby seals were certainly cute. I should have visited these caves way before now.

Finally, something had gone right. They'd made it down the steep stairs safely. She looked at Bryce who caught her eye and winked, one side of his mouth curled in a half smile.

He was so handsome and so nice. Somehow though, she'd always fallen for the taken men. The ones who were available disappeared quickly when her bad luck scared them away. Bryce was the only man who never ran away. That made him even more special in her book.

He turned his attention back to the view of the sea lions.

I should tell him I like him. There's no harm in saying you like someone. "Uhhh, Bryce?"

"Yeah?" he said absently, his gaze on one of the larger creatures who was shuffling across the rocks headed for the ocean.

"I'm sorry. I just can't. It's none of my business." I almost told him how I feel about him. She had to be careful not to upset his marriage plans. It wouldn't be right, not to him, to herself or to Cinnamon. She knew she shouldn't even be here right now.

He turned and bracketed her shoulders in his strong hands. He looked into her eyes. She fought the urge to squirm but was unable to force her eyes from his. She was lost in his soulful blue eyes.

Suddenly his eyes narrowed slightly and she held her breath. He was about to ask her something important. Could he want what she wanted? Could he be about to tell her he loved her?

"Sax, please tell me. Do you have a boyfriend?" Okay. So why would he want to know that?

"No. Why?"

Bryce let his arms to drop to his sides and looked away. Oh, oh. Now she'd done it. If only she wasn't so pushy. She hoped she could hitch a ride home with one of those motor homes in the parking lot.

"You okay?" The gentleness in her voice surprised her.

Bryce turned to face her. His eyes brimmed with tears. She wanted to wrap him in her arms to comfort him but held back fearing she would only make things worse. She hoped he still liked her at least.

"I'm not upset," he blurted loudly. Too loudly.

The tourists turned to stare at them. The Park Ranger even stopped her speech mid-sentence and glared at them. Sax offered them a weak smile then wrapped her arm over his shoulder and led him to a spot as far away from the others as she could on the rocky platform. The chain link fence here was partially collapsed and coated in thick rust.

"Keep your voice down," she whispered. "You're attracting attention." He nodded, his eyes on the ground.

Sax looked back and glared at the gawkers. They looked at each other, then turned their attention back to the Park Ranger who continued with her talk.

She whispered, "Tell me what's wrong. Maybe I can help."

"Cinnamon..." he paused, his words caught in his throat. He blew out a breath then continued, "Her mother's been hounding her about our wedding date. We haven't set a date because..." he hesitated and his eyes drifted toward the surging waves that roared into the cavern not very far away from where they stood.

Spit it out, man. Her heart beat faster as her anticipation heightened. "You're gay?" He snorted.

"You're older than you look?" He shook his head.

"Your parents forbid you to marry?" Nope.

"Am I getting warm?"

"No. Cold as an iceberg."

Ah-ha. "She's frigid?"

His cheeks reddened. "That's just silly."

Her voice increased in volume. "Then c'mon, tell me."

106

Sax glanced at the crowd of tourists but their attention was elsewhere. Thank goodness for small gifts.

"Cinnamon comes from an old money family. They were once one of the top five wealthiest families on the East Coast. Her great-granddad was a rum runner."

"Were?" Her stomach muscles tightened and her heart skipped a beat. Cinnamon and I may not be so different after all.

His eyes dropped to the cave floor. "Yeah. They lost their money. You know, with the bad economy and all."

"Oh. I'm sorry." Cin was a poor little former rich girl. Interesting.

"Anyway, Cin and I planned to marry to restore her family fortune, and get the Wolthorp family name back on the society registry of who's who."

"Planned?" Sax crossed her arms over her chest. "Don't tell me you two lovebirds are having problems?" I hope. I hope. I hope.

"Yeah. That's why I need your help."

Oh. She gazed at him expectantly. Her heart rate increased. I may have a chance with him yet. He asks me if I have a boyfriend and I say no. He's gonna ask me something important. She knew it in her gut.

Finally he said, "You don't have a boyfriend so I was wondering if you'd pretend to be in love with me. Cin will get jealous then she'll want to marry me, even if she doesn't love me and I don't love her."

Sax's heart froze. Bryce was going to marry someone he didn't love when standing in front of him was a woman who loved him with all her heart. But she couldn't say anything, not without betraying everything she believed in.

She stared at him, uncertain what to say. I want to tell him I'm falling for him but I can't do that. She knew she was going to regret this. "Uhhh, yeah sure. When?"

Bryce chuckled. "She desperately wants to go back to New York and I can't stand the place. When she called me last night I told her you'd love to go with her. You can tell her about our undying love for each other during the trip."

CHAPTER TWENTY

HER FACE GREW WARM AND HER ARMS DROPPED TO HER SIDES. She hadn't seen that coming. He expected her to fake love him when in reality she did love him? She felt like a fool.

I'm such an idiot. Disappointment fell over her like a dark cloud. She looked into his eyes and recognized fear. Now what was wrong? How could this situation get any worse?

From behind her came a throaty grunt followed by a loud snort. Then her back was sprayed with water.

Oh, oh. I think things just got worse.

Since her back was to the rocks she ever so slowly turned her head until one large oval shaped, ink-black eye was staring back at her. Sax turned back toward Bryce who was edging his way back away from her. She squeezed her eyes shut tight and waited for her inevitable doom. Fear made her unable to move.

Born to be bait. The curse had finally caught up with her. It's a wonder I lasted this long.

The large sea lion's hot breath wafted over her causing Sax's heart to pound in her ears and sweat to trickle down her face. She had never been so scared.

What's taking it so long? Does he think I need tenderizing before he eats me? Then again he might be a she. Whom she assumed might be a mommy.

Maybe what little meat there is on these bones might help raise a future generation of woman eating sea lions.

She decided running was her only hope of escape. After counting silently to three she decided to make a break for it.

Before she could take off a sudden high pitched whistle rattled her nerves and she trembled. She quickly covered her ears with her hands as the harsh whistle sounded right next to her. The creature behind her bellowed loudly and she heard its heavy body shuffle as it moved away.

Bryce stepped to her side. He wrapped an arm around her shoulders and guided her away from the bellowing animal. His eyes were gentle.

She smiled. He must care for me. Wow. She could get lost in those eyes.

The blond ranger rushed past them blowing on a brass colored whistle hung around her neck on a lanyard. The ranger ignored them and kept blowing into the whistle again and again as she ran. Sax titled her head to one side and slapped one hand against her ear to try and clear her hearing. Why can't I hear the whistle? It must be broken or my ears must be plugged.

They stopped and Bryce smiled as he turned her to face him and gripped her shoulders in his strong hands.

"Yeah. I think I'm okay." Strange. Why do I sound like I'm underwater? His lips moved, but no words came out of his mouth. Now that was weird.

"I can't hear you," she said. His lips moved again and his eyes narrowed. It looked like he said yes.

His worried expression was reflected in his eyes and his brow furrowed. He held up one hand. "Yeah, I'll stay here."

She shoved an index finger into one ear and twisted it and yawned repeatedly, hoping to clear her ears. Still nothing. No sound at all.

This is too weird.

Bryce turned away toward the rocks.

Sax saw the sea lion's massive black and brown head bobbing in the swell. Its mouth was opened and it looked like it was bellowing but she heard nothing. The waves still pounded the rocks but she didn't hear them anymore either.

The realization of what had happened struck her like a thunderbolt.

Great!

I'm deaf!

But at least she wasn't dead.

~~~

Bryce's cell phone buzzed, causing Mrs. Parks to remove the Otoscope from Sax's ear to stare at him. Her husband, Dr. Parks, was in Newport. Bryce had read the sign at the reception desk that all cell phones were supposed to be turned off, but he was waiting for an important call from Sax's father.

Sax seemed physically okay, but her hearing had been damaged by the ranger's whistle. I should never have taken her to the sea lion caves. This is all my fault.

But no matter how he tried to ignore them, his feelings for Sax were growing stronger. Asking her to pretend to love him was a ploy to keep her near him. But he knew it was impossible to fall in love with Sax. If he fell for her it'd complicate things worse than they already were.

Besides, she didn't love him, so what was the use even thinking about such romantic nonsense?

He offered Mrs. Parks a thin smile and his face grew warm. He had to take the call. Bryce stepped out of the examination room.

After he drove Sax to the clinic he thought about calling his father to meet him. Something in his gut told him time was growing short.

He knew he had to talk to his dad about his growing feelings for Sax. His father would know what to do. His father and he had been very close after his mother's death, that was, until his father married Maggie.

Not that he could blame his father. His father was lonely and at first Maggie seemed the perfect remedy. Once the "I do's" were exchanged it quickly became evident Maggie had designs on his money more than him.

Maggie's divorced sister Elizabeth moved in and the two women began extensive shopping trips into Manhattan. It was like a cougars Sex in the City episode. Bryce really didn't care much for Elizabeth Wolthorp. But he did care about Cinnamon. They'd known each other since they were in high school. Even if she wasn't the love of his life, she was a good friend.

Things were different now. Meeting Sax had complicated his life. Bryce never dreamed when his company achieved such success that his life would get so complicated. In business, the more successful you become, all you did was trade up for a new set of problems.

Business problems were relatively straightforward compared with the people you could potentially hurt with your careless words.

Dad had plenty of cash to spare, but his dream of being a wealthy benefactor and philanthropist had taken a backseat to Maggie's free spending ways.

After three years of marriage to Maggie, his father confided in him that he was wounded to his core by his new wife's greed and excess. "I could divorce her, but I really believe in until-death-do-us-part. I'll try to work it out with her. I love her and deep down I know she loves me."

Unfortunately his father hadn't brought up his issues with her behavior. Bryce wondered if his father was afraid of Maggie or maybe Elizabeth.

Bryce lifted the phone to his ear. Thank goodness Jack Edwards had called him back. He hated to leave Sax alone but he had to be elsewhere and Sax needed a ride home from the clinic.

Her father was still under the misconception he had something to do with brothels. Jack was delusional but it was hard not to like the guy. He cared for his family as much as he did his. "Hi, Jack. This is Bryce Kelly. I'm at the clinic with Sax."

"Who?"

"Your daughter Sax. I'm at the clinic with her."

"Oh, that Sax. Why didn't you say so?"

Bryce grinned. Jack was such a funny bird. "Don't worry, Jack. She's fine. Mrs. Parks says her hearing will come back in a few hours."

"Good. Glad to hear it." The line went dead. Bryce pulled the phone away from his ear and stared at it. Unbelievable! He pressed the redial button.

Sax's father answered after one ring. "Jack Edwards, antique specialist."

"Jack. Don't hang up."

"Who is this?"

"Bryce Kelly. I'm at the clinic with Sax." Silence. "Your daughter?"

More silence, then, "I know she's at the clinic and her hearing is coming back. So?" Jack snorted.

What's with this family? The family that snorts together stays together?

"Can you come to the clinic and pick up Sax?"

"Yeah, sure." The line went dead again.

Bryce removed the cell phone from his ear and stared at it for several seconds. Something isn't right.

He hit the re-dial button. After two rings Jack answered again.

"Jack Edwards, antique specialist."

"Jack. Are you leaving for the clinic?"

"Why?"

"To pick up Sax."

"Why?"

Bryce sighed. "She needs you. The brothel guy left her here."

"Really? I'm on my way."

Bryce turned off his phone and put it in his pants pocket. That should do it. But I really must ask Sax about her dad's strange behavior.

He shook his head then went back into Sax's room.

~~~

Sax's father walked in the front door of the clinic. Mrs. Parks, who was the little clinic's nurse, sat behind the reception desk. She nodded at him as he walked up to her.

112

Jack smiled warmly at her, his hands buried in the pockets of his shorts.

"Hi, I'm Jack Edwards."

Bryce stepped into the hallway from Sax's room and waved Jack over.

"Are you the brothel guy who left my daughter here?" said Jack.

CHAPTER TWENTY-ONE

THE NEXT DAY, AFTER MRS. PARKS CLEARED SAX TO GO HOME, Cinnamon Wolthorp called and asked if Sax would like to come with her to New York. She explained Bryce wanted them to be friends, and besides, she loved New York. Cinnamon said sharing it with someone who loved to shop would be fun.

Why would Bryce tell her she loved to shop? Oh, brother.

Now two days after being released from hospital she sat shivering in the damp air on a cold cement bench under the canopy next to the lobby doors of the hotel where the bus to the airport picked up passengers.

Sax agreed to meet Cinnamon in the parking lot of the Glad Beach Hotel. Sax knew she had to tell Cinnamon she was in love with Bryce but she decided to wait for just the right moment.

No matter how much mental gymnastics she played with herself she'd been unable to convince herself this trip had an upside. But she'd promised Bryce and she didn't want to disappoint him.

If Cinnamon gets angry and leaves me in New York I'm gonna have to hitchhike home.

A light drizzle had begun to fall from the steel gray sky pre-dawn sky.

She hated early starts. Too dark. Too cold. Too wet.

She pulled her jacket tighter around her to protect her from an assault by the cold breeze coming off the crashing surf on the other side of the highway.

She detested being cold. How did I ever let Mom and Dad convince me to move here? The daytime highs were lower than Alaska.

After what seemed like an hour of shivering under the canopy, Bryce's Hummer finally appeared. He stopped under the canopy.

Cinnamon stepped out from the passenger side. As usual she was dressed in designer fashion that would have made a Ford model jealous. Bill Blass, Pierre Cardin, and Liz Claiborne's jaws would drop if they saw this leggy beauty wearing their clothes. Her long, full hair shone in the low light of the first rays of daylight in the eastern sky, and the single bare bulb on the roof of the canopy.

Sax gazed forlornly at her Levi's, ten-dollar-made-in-China Wal-Mart shirt, and Nike knockoffs. She felt so out of her league next to Cinnamon. She was a very beautiful woman.

Cinnamon gave her a dazzling smile as she walked around the back of the car to retrieve her overnight bag from the trunk. Bryce had popped the trunk from the inside.

Bryce stepped out and hurried around the back of the car to lift Cinnamon's bag out of the back for her. She smiled warmly and pecked him lightly on his right cheek.

He sure plays the part of the gentleman around her. And gentlemen deserve their rewards. Her life was crap. Maybe Bryce loved Cinnamon after all. Maybe she'd been fooling herself into believing otherwise.

Her heart skipped a beat at the sight of his dimple-cheeked grin. His eyes sparkled. She turned away and dropped her gaze to the wet pavement. Oh, man, he is too handsome. I hope he treats me like he treats her someday.

"Hi, Sax," Cinnamon said, with too much cheeriness in her tone.

Why was she smiling? She'd treated Sax like the maid at the shop. What changed? "Huh...hi." Oh, brother, do I sound lame or what?

Cinnamon's tiger print bag had wheels but Bryce carried it to the sidewalk. Just before he got to the curb he stumbled as his boot caught the edge of the cement.

"Oops…" cried Bryce, who managed to stop himself from falling on his face by using his arms as windmills. Sax thought he looked like he was dancing the funky chicken.

Sax stifled a snort by covering her mouth with one hand. Bryce teetered and danced trying to regain his balance but he kicked Cinnamon's bag across the cement pad accompanied by a loud scraping sound. Sax winced. She hoped he didn't damage her bag, it looked expensive.

Cinnamon chuckled and winked at Sax. "Don't take him grocery shopping unless you plan on having scrambled eggs for dinner."

Bryce's swarthy features had taken on a distinct reddish hue. He finally righted himself and retrieved the bag. "Sorry, Cin."

Cinnamon stepped up to him and ran one hand down the sleeve of his brown leather aviator jacket. "It's okay, lover."

He grinned sheepishly. There was something in his eyes Sax hadn't seen before. He's embarrassed. Sax frowned. Interesting.

Bryce shifted his gaze to Sax. "I'm so pleased you two are going on this trip."

"Trying to get rid of us?" said Cinnamon with a laugh.

Bryce chuckled. "No, of course not. It's just that you two will get a chance to know each other better is all."

Cinnamon gave Sax a grin. Sax offered her a tight thin-lipped smile in return. This was going to be the hardest day of her life. Her heart beat hard in her chest. She scares me. When I tell her I love her fiancée she's going to yell at me and I'm so not good at confrontation.

Just as an awkward silence was about to descend over them the shuttle to the Portland airport roared into the parking lot and pulled up to the curb, forcing them to step back. It rocked back and forth as it came to a stop.

Bryce loaded Cinnamon's tiger print bag first, then stopped and stared at the lumpy green garbage bag, the top of which was tied into a knot. It lay lopsided on the ground at Sax's feet. "Huh. Is this your luggage?" he asked.

Sax rolled her eyes. Great. I'm a bum.

Bryce looked up from the bag and smiled at her. "No worries. Cin will buy you a proper suitcase when the airport shuttle gets to Portland." His gaze shifted to Cinnamon. "Right?"

Cinnamon smiled thinly and nodded.

Bryce looked back at Sax and grinned. "See, no problem."

"I'm not a charity case, you guys," said Sax her face growing warm. Country mouse and city mouse go on a trip. "I can get by with this bag."

Bryce eyes went wide with horror. "No. No. No. Of course not. I'd never think...I...." He hesitated and looked at Cinnamon.

Cinnamon sighed and chuckled. "Oh, Bryce you are a dear, silly, sweet man," she said with a dismissive wave of one hand. "Sax can pay me back later." She grinned at Sax. "Right, Sax?"

Since when had she become so familiar? "Of course. Cin."

Cinnamon's brow wrinkled slightly then she grinned.

Sax smiled in return. Cinnamon turned away. We're gonna be friends? She must be kidding.

The driver came round from the driver's seat. She was the largest woman Sax had ever seen. At least six feet tall, with arms like oak tree trunks and a neck the size of Cinnamon's waist. Her dark eyes and coffee colored skin were accented by the snow white shirt and navy blue pants she wore. A shiny steel ring hung off her belt filled with jangling keys.

"PDX?" she said.

Bryce's brow wrinkled in puzzlement. "Huh?"

The woman rolled her eyes and grunted. "Sorry," her wide mouth formed an I'm-not-being-at-all-sincere smile, "I forget sometimes. Portland airport?"

"Yes," chimed Cinnamon in a cheery tone.

Sax rolled her eyes. Oh, brother. This is gonna be sooo much fun.

CHAPTER TWENTY-TWO

THE BUS BROKE DOWN THREE TIMES BETWEEN GLAD BEACH and the Portland Airport. It was normally a two hour trip to the airport but had become at least three hours. So Gilligan's Island.

She wished they had been lost on a desert island. It had to be better than wrecking someone's life by telling them the man they're about to marry doesn't love them. Why did I agree to help Bryce? For the tenth time since they started on this trip she thought he should tell Cinnamon he didn't love her and didn't want to marry her. She winced. But I said I'd help and I really want to prove to him I'm his friend, so I'll play along for now.

The very large, very angry driver had begun to eye Cinnamon and Sax suspiciously. Sax squirmed under the woman's gaze. She must think they were on the FBI's most wanted list. Every time the driver looked in her rearview mirror, her dark eyes glared at them like they were responsible for breaking the bus. Which, in her case, with her curse, could be true.

Sax avoided the accusatory stares of the driver by staring out the bus window.

The last breakdown of the airport shuttle wasn't technically what you'd call a breakdown. The driver suddenly steered off the road, very nearly tipping the bus over, and into a gas station in Ferretville. The bus came to a stop with a jerk. The driver yanked the exit door open then ran holding one hand over her bottom for the washroom screaming for help from Jesus, and something about the mother of God that Sax couldn't quite make out through the window glass.

Russ Crossley

Sax glanced at Cinnamon across the aisle. She had to sit beside a Mr. Hopkins while Cin sat next to a sleeping woman. The leggy blond looked at her with a tight smile on her lips then turned back to study the New York restaurant guide she'd been reading.

She considered now might be the time to tell Cinnamon about her fake love for Bryce. But I'm worried how she'll react. She decided it was better to wait because Cinnamon looked so happy, laughing and prattling on to her seat mates about how wonderful New York was and what a wonderful time they were going to have. If Sax told her now it would only ruin her trip. I'll tell her when we get to New York.

As Sax saw it there were two possible outcomes; I'll be her shoulder to cry on, or her punching bag. She really preferred a wet shoulder over a sore face.

"These windows are certainly well constructed," she said to Mr. Hopkins who was seated beside her. He boarded the bus in Capital town and, after he introduced himself, he told her was off to visit his nephew in Cincinnati. Mr. Hopkins's pale gray eyes regarded her dispassionately. He had to be at least a hundred years old with a fringe of gray hair around his freckled head. His lean body was slightly hunched at the shoulders.

"I know your type," Mr. Hopkins said in his gravelly voice.

"Huh?"

"Cursed, right?"

A twinkle appeared in his eyes. "Don't worry, young lady. I make this trip every month." Sax stared at him. "I have a lot of nephews," he explained.

"Oh."

"Anyway," he continued, "there's one like you every couple of months on this bus. Ya know, cursed people."

Sax looked at him. Her heart seemed to stop. How does he know I have a curse?

Her mouth dried and she stared at him. He sighed and a wistful expression came over his gray features. "I've lived a long time and seen a lot of strange things. There are a lot of you folks." He shook his head sadly. "It's not your fault. It's just the way things are."

119

He thumbed in the direction where the driver disappeared. "The company can't keep drivers. They lose one every couple of months." He looked out the window and a frown creased his already wrinkled brow. "Glad Beach attracts a lot of your kind. Something special about the place." He looked at her and a sad half-smile crossed his lips. "You're special, you know?"

Special? I don't think so, old guy. He's screwy.

Sax shifted her gaze to Cinnamon, who sat composed and stiff-backed in her seat looking straight ahead, seemingly unaware of Sax's conversation with Mr. Hopkins.

"I can hardly wait until we get to New York," Cinnamon said to the old woman next to her who was obviously asleep. The old woman's head rested against the window. "We're going shopping and to the theater and Central Park and The Statue of Liberty. I'll show Sax my city. All of it." She reached across the aisle and grasped Sax's hands in hers. She looked over into Sax's eyes. Her own eyes were wide with excitement, her grin was infectious.

Sax grinned sheepishly and her cheeks grew warm. This is awkward.

"But what about the curse?" Sax whispered.

The grin on Cinnamon's face disappeared and her eyes narrowed. She released Sax's hand. "What are you talking about?"

"Mr. Hopkins said—"

"Who?"

"The man sitting beside—" Sax turned to find Mr. Hopkins had been replaced by an old woman with yellow teeth, snoring softly, her head also resting against the window. A streak of silver drool ran from the left side of her mouth then down her cheek. Okay...where did he go?

"Never mind. It must have been a dream." She scanned the bus for the missing Mr. Hopkins. Seated a few rows back sat a "businessman type" dressed in a chocolate brown suit, repeatedly glared at his watch. A young couple sat on the very rear bench seat locked in a passionate embrace.

Opposite them sat a Hispanic man in blue jeans and a black leather jacket and white t-shirt, his eyes hidden by sunglasses. He looked in her direction when her eyes locked on him.

She looked away quickly and hoped he hadn't noticed her staring as him. You never knew when some weirdo would take objection and do something not-so-good.

Where has Mr. Hopkins gone? She thought she must be losing her mind. Bad enough she was cursed, now people were disappearing. I must be going screwy now. Scanning the gas station outside for any sign of him, she saw an obese man wearing a plaid work shirt and stained blue jeans pumping gas into a Pontiac Firefly.

Until now she thought the only weird person in the world was her. I guess not. Mr. Hopkins was definitely weirder than her. Like all the cursed people live in Glad Beach? As if.

She turned to face Cinnamon and grinned. I must have a sign on my forehead that reads sucker. She'd fallen for way too many scams in the past. But not anymore. Like that time she opened a bank account and they said she'd get a free shotgun. Yeah, right. She snorted at the memory. But no bullets. Read the fine print, they said. Give me a break.

"Something funny, Sax?"

"Yeah. I had to buy my own bullets."

"Oh. That in your dream, too?" Cinnamon said innocently.

Sax looked at Cinnamon, dumbfounded, then laughed. "No. No. Sorry. I just remembered something is all." She waved one hand in the direction of the gas station. "It's not important."

Cinnamon cocked one eyebrow at Sax then shifted her gaze to the gas pumps.

Before Cinnamon could ask anything else the driver climbed the stairs and sat down heavily behind the bus' steering wheel. The bus sank on its suspension with a sigh, leaning slightly to the left under the driver's ample weight. "Sorry for the delay, folks," she said. "Mr. Hopkins tol' me ta go ahead without him."

"What? Where?" She peered out the bus window, frantically searching the gas station for any sign of Mr. Hopkins. The Firefly pulled away from the gas pump island leaving a puff of black smoke in its wake. No Mr. Hopkins.

Before Sax could ask about the old man the driver turned the key in the ignition and pushed the starter on the dashboard with the toe of her black leather boot rather than her finger.

The diesel engine roared to life, filling the passenger compartment with engine noise and the slight odor of carbon dioxide. Conversations were impossible over the sound of the engine.

Cinnamon indicated the driver with a slight nod of her head. She leaned over and cupped Sax's ear and whispered, "Some move, eh?" Sax grinned.

"I heard that, miss beauty queen," said the driver her dark eyes visible in the rear view mirror. "You wanta walk the rest of the way?"

How did she hear us when I can't hear my own stomach growl? "No," Cinnamon said with a shake of her head, "I'd rather ride. Sorry, I didn't mean anything."

A sly grin spread across the driver's dusky face and the corners of her eyes crinkled. She grunted and turned her attention to the parking lot and stepped on the gas. The bus lurched forward forcing Sax to grab the steel rail over the top of the seat in the front of her. Cinnamon dropped her black leather handbag.

Crack.

Oh, oh, something broke.

"Next stop, Portland airport," shouted the driver as she steered the steel beast onto Highway Eighteen. A small white car beeped its horn as the bus driver cut it off. The driver smirked and pressed the gas pedal to the floor. The massive diesel roared and they were off, the bus swaying side to side before it settled into a straight line and gradually began to pick up speed. The bus came to a steady speed and the diesel's growl leveled off so they could hear each other again.

"What broke?" said Sax, looking at the handbag lying on the floor, leaking something onto the floor in a growing puddle of shimmering, strong smelling liquid. Sax's nose wrinkled. Phew! That's strong stuff, whatever it is.

Cinnamon rolled her eyes. "My opium."

Opium? "Isn't that a drug?" Sax whispered.

Cinnamon sighed. "Yes. In all the finest restaurants and theatres in New York."

"Huh?"

Cinnamon chuckled and patted Sax's shoulder. "Sorry. That's not what I meant. It's my perfume. Very French. Very expensive." Her eyes drooped at the corners. "It's my last bottle."

"Oh. Don't worry," said Sax, "I'm certain there's more where that came from. Sure, there's a recession but I'm pretty sure France hasn't run out of perfume yet."

Cinnamon looked at Sax dumfounded for several seconds then burst out laughing. "You are the cutest thing! We're going to be BFF's for sure."

Sax laughed nervously. BFF's? I hope that's not something painful. When she had a minute she'd Google BFF's to find out what it meant. It must be a new word for murder in New York.

For now, all she hoped was they were going to survive the trip. Or at least me. When she told Cinnamon about her fake love for Bryce she'd be really angry. Then she'll probably BFF me.

Sax turned to look back at the gas station receding into the distance. Just before the bus rounded a bend in the road and Ferretville disappeared, she thought she caught a glimpse of Mr. Hopkins standing beside the highway waving, then he was gone, blocked by a stand of pine trees. There he is. Why didn't he get back on the bus?

She turned in her seat to face front once again and crossed her arms over her chest. Too weird.

CHAPTER TWENTY-THREE

THE HUMMER DEFINITELY LOOKED OUT OF PLACE amongst the Volvos, SUV's, motor homes, and pickup trucks of the tourist crowds that flocked to the coastal towns like Glad Beach on the weekends. Bryce steered the expensive truck around a mustard yellow Volvo that pulled off the highway in front of him into the local pancake house parking lot.

In the Volvo were two adults, two kids—a boy and a girl—and a bright eyed Golden Retriever whose alert brown eyes followed the Hummer as it passed.

Bryce glanced at his father, Walter, sitting in the passenger seat, and grinned. He stepped harder on the gas pedal causing the powerful V8 engine to send a rumble through the car's frame. He caught a glimpse of the smiling man in the driver's seat of the Volvo before he shot past them.

That guy sure looks happy. He sighed. One day I'll have a family. Just not with Cinnamon Wolthorp.

Suddenly there was single blast of a siren from behind. He glanced at the rearview mirror. Oh, crap. A cop. What had the curse done now? "Oh, Oh, Dad, I think we have company." Great. The locals would never accept him if he broke the laws around here. "Cops," he said simply.

He eased back on the gas pedal and the white and silver police cruiser came up quickly behind him, the blue and red roller lights bright in the mirror.

Bryce looked at his father who held up his hands in surrender. "How many times have I told you not to go so fast, son?"

Bryce laughed and steered the Hummer to the shoulder and came to a stop. "Yeah, I know, Dad. You just love saying I told you so."

His father chuckled. "That's because I'm right so often."

Bryce turned off the engine and pushed the power button to roll down the driver's side window. He glanced into the rearview mirror and frowned.

The woman officer was out of the car, the cruiser's door still open, and she had her pistol out.

I think she's aiming that thing at me. He squirmed in his seat. What did I do?

He glanced at the side mirror on the passenger side and saw her male partner moving up the side of the car cautiously, like he and his father were armed bank robbers or something.

"Dad, did you do something I should know about?"

"Like what?" His father looked at him a puzzled look in his eyes.

"Put your hands above your heads and get out of the car," shouted the woman officer in a gruff tone.

"What is she talking about?" said his father.

"I don't know. I guess speeding is a capital offense around here. We better do as she says."

He glanced into his side mirror and saw the grim expression on the woman's angular features.

Bryce opened his door as did his father then they both raised their hands above their heads and got out of the Hummer. Bryce stumbled when he bumped against the door. He almost fell face first but managed to maintain his footing. He was bent forward as he stumbled away from the car his hands held straight out in front of him. The gravel on the shoulder crunched under foot. When he finally managed to stop he was standing on black top. A loud air horn split the air making him jerk his head to the side in time to see a semi truck bearing down on him.

"Oh, crap!" he yelled after dropping his hands to his sides. I'm dead.

Without thinking he dove for the gravel shoulder. He landed with a crunch, on his belly, which was followed by searing pain across his stomach where the sharp gravel tore at his skin through his golf shirt.

"Owww!"

He lay on the ground breathing hard, his body trembling, his stomach queasy as the truck raced past him and the driver blew two more blasts of the horn.

"Don't move!" screamed the male officer over the roar of the truck.

The man's rough hands gripped his right arm and forced one hand then the other behind his back as the officer slapped handcuffs on his wrists with ratcheting clicks. "Hey! Owww!" The officer pressed a knee into the middle of his back, pressing his face into the pavement. Man, these cuffs are tight.

"What's going on?" Bryce mumbled from the side of his mouth. "Can't you see I was nearly run over?" He raised his head at the sound of a second set of footsteps crunching the gravel. The female officer had his father's back to her and she was handcuffing his wrists as well.

"Hey!"

"Quiet, scumbag." Something hard jabbed him in his side. Scumbag? Me? He thought they must have mistaken them for someone else.

"Whoa, listen, officers! I was speeding. I admit it. I'm guilty! Please don't shoot!" Bryce closed his eyes and head-to-toe his body began to tremble from fear.

He didn't think his life would end this way. Why me?

Bryce opened one eye when he heard tires crunching over the gravel. Another car had stopped. Another police car. A sense of relief washed over him.

Good. He hoped whoever it was would stop these mad cops before they shot them.

"We got 'em, Sheriff," the woman said, pride evident in her tone.

A car door slammed.

"Yeah. I can see that, Izzy," said a deep man's voice, accompanied by the crunch of gravel as the man came closer.

A man wearing brown leather cowboy boots was coming toward him. The boots were well worn with ornate designs of miniature horses sculpted into the leather. Nice boots.

"Only problem is, who have you got?" said the man.

"The terror suspects the Homeland bulletin said were headed our way," she said, as if it were obvious.

The boots moved away out of his line of sight. "Have you checked license and registration?"

"Huh. No?" Her voice was uncertain. He's got ya there.

"Ok. While Dobbs here checks that, and radios in the names, etcetera, why don't we get this guy to his feet so we can have a nice chat." There was a brief pause, then he added, "Okay by you, Izzy?"

"Yes, sir," she said.

A sense of relief washed over him and his shoulders relaxed. He may get shot someday, just not today.

She holstered her gun, then she pulled on his handcuffed arms to help him to his feet. "Ouch! Stop that! It hurts!" Bryce protested as the handcuffs cut into his wrists. Tiny pebbles embedded in his cheek hurt where the skin had been pressed into the pavement.

With her help he managed to regain his feet. He leaned back against the hood of his car and winced from the scrapes on his belly and the pain in his wrists.

The sheriff stood over six feet tall, his wide shoulders and narrow waist suggesting a powerful man beneath the mocha brown uniform. He could take care of himself in a fight. Aviator sunglasses hung off his left side breast pocket underneath a shiny gold badge. A brass name plate over the right breast pocket read CONSTITUTION.

They sure loved their bling around here.

The sheriff's calm expression on his tanned features made Bryce uneasy. Now I know what an amoeba feels like under a microscope. He shivered. There was no emotion behind the eyes. A toothpick hung out the left side the man's wide mouth. It twirled in his lips as he studied Bryce as if he were a lab specimen.

His arms were crossed over his chest, emphasizing his bulging biceps. "What's your name, sir?" said the Sheriff.

"Bryce Kelly," he nodded to his father who leaned against the driver's side of the hood looking confused. "And this is my father, Walter."

"Yeah. Okay." Sheriff Constitution took a step back and his eyes shifted to study the Hummer. "Nice wheels." His eyes shot up to lock with Bryce's. "Yours?"

"Yes." Bryce sensed the sheriff was stalling, waiting for something, but what?

"Uh, uh." The sheriff turned away to look at the cruiser parked behind Bryce's car. "What ya got there, Dobbs?"

The reddish blond man stuck his head out the open door of the cruiser. "DHS says to bring 'em in. They match the profile of the two they're lookin' for. But the truck doesn't fit."

Profile of who? He doubted they had a profile of a son and his father on a coast highway. This stinks.

The Sheriff nodded and uncrossed his arms, hooking his thumbs in the polished leather gun belt bristling with tools and compartments. He frowned. "Any wants or warrants?"

"No, sir."

The Sheriff looked thoughtful for several seconds then he said, "Okay. Let's take 'em to the station and hold 'em. I'll call the Feds myself."

"Izzy, you wait here. I'll give Harv a call and ask 'em to tow the car to the station. You ride back with the tow truck." The woman's gray-green eyes reflected her disappointment but she nodded.

"Sheriff. I must protest," said Walter. His face flushed bright red. You go, Dad.

Sheriff Constitution regarded Walter with deadpan eyes. The toothpick in his mouth twirled faster. "Yes, sir?"

Walter hesitated. Oops. I guess he expected an argument. "I'm a tax payer, sir." Walter stuck out his narrow chest as best he could. "And a veteran."

One eyebrow on the sheriff's rose upward slightly. "Oh, yeah? Me, too. What unit?"

Walter looked at Bryce. His eyes lowered to gaze at the ground. "1st base Post office, Korea."

A sardonic smile crossed Sheriff Constitution's face. "1st Brigade—1st Cavalry Division, the Ironhorse Brigade myself. Iraq in '90." He moved to Walter's side and took out his handcuff keys. Walter's cuffs were off before he could say anything.

"Uh, sir. Sheriff. Do you think it's safe to let a dangerous prisoner loose?" The sheriff looked at Dobbs. "Sir," added the officer.

"No worries, Dobbs. I don't think Mr. Kelly's going to try anything. Right, Mr. Kelly?"

Walter rubbed his reddened wrists with his fingers. "No, sir. Of course not."

Constitution smiled at Dobbs with a gleam in his eyes. "See, Dobbs, what'd I tell you?"

"But what about my son?" Walter said indicating Bryce with a nod of his head.

Constitution laughed again and shook his head. "Nope. Sorry. No can do. He's a terrorist."

Walter eyed Bryce with a wry grin on his lips. "He is, eh?"

Bryce rolled his eyes. Oh, brother. He's enjoying this.

CHAPTER TWENTY-FOUR

SAX SHIFTED UNEASILY ON THE HARD PLASTIC SEAT in the row of chairs at gate 12C. The seats were so uncomfortable.

The two magazines Cinnamon had bought Sax to read on the plane were surprisingly heavy. When Cinnamon bought The New Yorker and Vogue at the newsstand she told Sax they would educate her about New York, both its charms and its dangers.

"What did you mean danger?" said Sax.

Cinnamon had just returned carrying a cup tray with two grandee lattés from the Starbucks at gate 48D. While there was a Coffee Spot outlet across from gate 12C, she explained New Yorkers only drank Starbucks or a coffee from one of the most trendy cafés.

"Oh, now don't you worry, all will become clear once you start studying." Cinnamon sat, leaving a seat between them, and placed the tray on the empty seat. "I bought us skinny lattés with a twist of lemon."

Sax's brow wrinkled. I'm not sure getting on a plane with a crazy person is such a good idea. Lattés with a twist of lemon? That's what I call nuts.

Cinnamon took one of the lattés from the tray and brought it to her lips. She took a sip, closed her eyes and made soft purring sounds that reminded Sax of her friend Alice's cat Scruff when he went into the litter box.

"Uhhh, why?" said Sax. "I like fat in my coffee."

Cinnamon lowered the Starbucks cup, her eyes wide with horror. Oh, oh, I think I said something bad.

Cinnamon glared at Sax, reminding her of Mrs. Bixer, her ninth grade English teacher who had a crooked nose with a large wart on the tip.

Ouch. I hope that memory gets wiped when the aliens invade.

"Don't. Ever. Ever. Ever, say that word again." Cinnamon had the look of a zealot in her eyes. Scarrryyyy.

"Fat?" said Sax meekly.

Cinnamon stood and picked up the tray and moved it to the seat she'd been sitting in, and sat down next to Sax. Sax leaned back as far as she was able while still remaining in the chair.

If I go back any further I'm gonna be in a different zip code.

Cinnamon leaned in and whispered, "Sax. There are four things you have to know about me before we can be BFF's."

Sax forced a tight smile to her lips. BFF's again? I really gotta Google that.

Cinnamon held up her right hand then began counting off reasons on her long fingers. "One, we never discuss our weight. Two, we shop and shop and then, shop some more. Three, night clubs are not places to meet men. And four, we never use the F word." Fat must be the new F word.

She lightly tapped Sax's arm. "That will guarantee our happiness and," she looked around the gate, "the happiness of others around us."

Others? "Yeah. Okay. I think I understand. We never say the F word." Sax made a check sign with her index finger.

"Excuse me!" said a woman's voice behind them. Sax looked around at a woman with dark curly hair wearing a heavy wool coat and flat Wal-Mart tennis shoes. In her right hand she held the hand of a young girl with blond pig tails and black framed glasses. The little girl's blue eyes were wide.

"There are children present," said the woman, nodding toward the little girl. The woman glared at Sax, her right foot tapping out what sounded to Sax like "America the Beautiful".

Oops.

"No...I...no...I meant...something else," she said finally, avoiding the woman's eyes that bore into her.

The woman finally harrumphed and walked away, her feet stomping loudly across the tile floor. Sax looked up to watch them go. The little girl looked over her shoulder at Sax and grinned. They sat down on the other side of the waiting area in an empty row of hard plastic seats.

Sax winced. Oh, crap-a-doodle. I put my foot in my mouth, but it's not my fault. Embarrassment was her new middle name.

"Sorry, I didn't mean that F word," Sax called to the woman who frowned and turned away to look out the window at the planes moving to and away from the gates that stretched into the distance. The little girl smiled and waved.

Cinnamon chuckled as she reached for the second latté, which she offered to Sax. "Ah, the uninitiated. Good thing you're with me."

"Yeah. Good thing." She accepted the offered cup. "Ouch! It's hot," Sax jumped in her seat. She shifted the cup back and forth in her hands blowing on her fingers as she did. "Why didn't you get me a sleeve?"

Cinnamon ignored Sax's discomfort. Cinnamon's cup had a paper sleeve. "Don't worry, Sax," shaking her head she nodded at the woman and her daughter. "They hate us because we're too perfect." Cinnamon brought her latté to her lips and took a sip.

An unseen speaker crackled to life. A man's voice said, "Attention passengers of Albatross Airlines flight eight non-stop to New York. We will be boarding by row number after our super great, and extra great reward, and elite passengers board. Then we will board the wheelchairs and persons with children and babies. Next, all passengers who paid the ultra discount special rate. And lastly, everyone else."

Scanning the gate seating area she saw besides them there were six other passengers, including the woman with the little girl.

A stout Hispanic man wearing gray coveralls with a patch over the left breast that read Cleaning Staff came around a corner pushing a floor polisher in front of him. The roar of the machine's motor echoed in the cavernous hall.

An old man with a cane, a woman with an oxygen tank, a man and woman in designer suits with laptops, who were obviously first class passengers, got up and moved en masse toward the gate.

They were the "everyone else".

She shifted her gaze to the magazines still in her lap and the steaming latté in her hand. How am I going to carry these heavy magazines without spilling the hot coffee?

She looked up at the man pushing the floor polisher and a knot formed in her stomach.

I've a bad feeling about this. In her gut she knew the curse was going to strike.

CHAPTER TWENTY-FIVE

HE SHIVERED AS THICK RAIN DROPS POUNDED HIM, soaking through his thin windbreaker as soon as he got out of the back seat of the police cruiser. His arm hurt where the deputy held him in a vise-like grip as she walked under the canopy shielding the front doors of the Sheriff's office. The single story building, not much bigger than a double wide trailer, housed the local sheriff and his deputies. Three police cruisers sat parked in a row to the left of the glass doors.

The two sheriff's deputies were dry in their rain slickers and peaked caps protected by plastic covers.

Look at them. He hated being wet. But he already felt warmer being under the canopy, watching the rain pelt the parking lot. At least, his shivering had eased a little.

The handcuffs though pinched his wrists tighter than ever, making him wince.

The grim-faced female officer, the sheriff called her Izzy, held one of the twin glass and aluminum doors open as the male officers brought him inside. When he passed her he detected the scent of bananas. Banana perfume?

Warm air washed over him as they stepped inside the set of inner doors into the brightly lit lobby. Bryce blinked, trying to adjust his sight to the sudden intrusion of fluorescent lights.

Inside the twin doors was a long black and gray linoleum counter that created an artificial barrier between the reception area and the inner offices.

When the spots before his eyes cleared he saw the office was bigger than he'd initially thought. There were rows of desks five deep that ran to the back of the room. A wall, interrupted at the center by a wood door with a brass placard on that said Sheriff's Office, divided the room in two.

To the right of the counter was another wall with three doors. Each door had a number on it from 101 to 103.

Bryce wondered what happened to room 100.

A thin black woman wearing an identical police uniform to the others sat behind a desk nearest the counter. She wore a wireless headset and her dark eyes were fixed on the computer screen in front of her.

"Hey, Simone," said Izzy. "Got a prisoner to book."

Simone's eyes flitted to Izzy, then Bryce, then back at the computer screen. "The terrorist?"

"Yup." Izzy slapped him on the back. Ouch. Did she have to do that? He was wet so it hurt worse than normal. "This is the guy."

Bryce's eyes narrowed at her and one eyebrow rose up his forehead. They really think I'm a terrorist? Get real. This was ridiculous. "Thanks," he said with a healthy dose of sarcasm in his tone.

"You're welcome," Izzy said without a hint of mirth in her voice.

I swear they're laughing at me, not with me. He'd told Deputy Dobbs all the way to the station he wasn't a terrorist but all he did was grunt and nod. I don't think he was listening to a word I said.

With a smirk Izzy walked him up to the counter. She reached over the counter, her fingers smoothly gliding along under the ledge.

There was a click and a section of the counter opened inward. She looked at him and frowned. "You didn't see that."

Bryce rolled his eyes. Is she kidding? Her frown became a glare. Nope, I guess not.

"Sorry, Officer. If I could cross my heart I would swear never to tell anyone about the hidden button…"

"Nice try, terror-boy," she said. He cringed as she yanked hard on his arm and pulled him past the counter. While her arms were surprisingly strong, her long legs obviously gave her additional leverage.

Waita go, big guy. He had just made things worse.

The counter door closed behind them with a dull thud. Izzy yanked him toward door number 103. Ouch. He winced. The cuffs were cutting off his circulation.

She reached to her belt to a ring of keys that had been jangling since they walked into the office. Izzy sorted through them, mumbling under her breath until she found the one she was looking for.

"Ah, ah!"

Bryce snorted and immediately regretted it. She glared at him. "Sorry. Like I told you in the car, I'm innocent. I am not a terrorist." He offered her a sheepish grin. "Really."

"Yeah. Right. That's what they all say," she said. The key ring had a retractable line on it that she used to pull the selected key away from the others. She slipped the key into the lock as she swiveled to gaze at him, a sardonic smile on her thin lips. "In this job I've heard it all."

"You get a lot of terrorists in Glad Beach?"

Izzy shook her head. "Nope. You're the first." She turned the key in the lock and it broke in half, leaving half in the lock.

Simone looked up from her computer screen at the snapping sound. "Problem, Izzy?"

A puzzled frown wrinkled Izzy's forehead. "No. It's just strange, is all."

Simone rolled her chair on its castors backward with her feet since she was still seated. She accomplished this with the practiced ease of someone who had done this many times before.

She's sorta like the quarterback dropping into the pocket to make the game winning pass.

Her chair came to a sudden stop and tipped back sharply. "Hey!" Simone cried out as the chair fell backward.

Watching this reminded him of one of those old shampoo commercials. The closer she gets the better she looks. Only Simone looked more afraid with each passing second than better.

Cool slo-mo though.

At the sound of Simone's terrified scream Izzy turned her head in time to see her partner land on her hard on back on the thick carpet with her hands gripping the chair arms her eyes fixed on her shiny black leather boots and the ceiling tiles beyond.

"You okay?" said Izzy.

A slow frown spread over Simone's dusky features. "Ya know, I think something strange is going on. This chair has never tipped over. Ever."

Bryce snorted causing Izzy to glare at him. If she only knew.

"I'm fine," deadpanned Simone. She rolled out of the chair to land on all fours just as one of the front doors opened causing the bell over the door to tingle brightly. "But I think there's voodoo at work here." Simone frowned. "I've seen it before."

Izzy stepped back and drew her pistol and aimed it at Bryce.

"Whoa there, dead eye! What's happening?" Bryce tensed and braced himself for a bullet. His guts were knotted with fear. These crazy cops were going to shoot him.

Sheriff Constitution walked in whistling an unidentifiable tune. He stopped like he'd hit the brakes on his police car when he spotted Simone on all fours and Izzy holding her gun in one hand, half of a key in the other. He lowered his sunglasses half way down his long nose and said, "What's goin' on in here?"

Simone scrambled to her feet and smoothed the legs of her uniform pants with both hands. "Sorry, Sheriff. But this man is not a terrorist." Her eyes were wide with fear and she waved her hands like a she would take off any second. "He's possessed!"

Izzy nodded her head vigorously.

They collectively looked to the front doors when the bell over the glass doors tinkled again.

"He is not," said Walter Kelly sarcastically as he came in behind the sheriff. "Ladies, Mr. Kelly has enlightened me," said the sheriff as he walked to the counter and pushed the same button Izzy had earlier. His brow wrinkled when nothing happened.

Walter sighed and walked up to the counter and pressed the button. A section of counter swung aside. "After you," said Walter bowing slightly at the waist his eyes following the sheriff.

"Thank you, Mr. Kelly." Sheriff Constitution walked through the open section of counter. He dropped his hand to the butt of his pistol in the leather holster. With his other hand he whipped off his sunglasses, revealing hazel eyes.

"Mr. Kelly tells me his son, Bryce," the sheriff indicated Bryce with a slight nod, "has a peculiar medical condition."

Bryce glared at his father but he ignored him. He's been telling tales about me. His ears grew warm. Thanks a lot, Dad.

Izzy looked at Simone and frowned. Then she looked at the sheriff, her hands balled into fists on her hips. "Medical conditions can't cause chairs to fall backward. When it has never happened before it is more than mere coincidence." Her lips formed a grim line. "Sir," she added.

Walter nodded. "I agree."

"See?" said the sheriff who went to the coffee maker. He lifted the glass carafe, half full of black coffee, and filled a coffee mug. From a group of six cups sitting on the table next to the coffee maker, the cup he chose had Love Your Peanut Butter, Love Your Life in dark red letters imprinted across it.

He turned and buried one arm of the sunglasses in the left breast pocket of his tan uniform shirt and picked up the mug and brought it to his lips. He took a sip and his features scrunched like he'd drunk something bitter.

"When did you make this mud, Simone?"

"When I came in at seven this morning," she paused. The sheriff's eyes narrowed at her over the lip of the cup. "Sir," she added then averted her gaze.

Bryce twisted his handcuffed wrists from behind him and managed to get a glimpse of his watch. He'd have a kink in his neck later for sure. It was past four in the afternoon.

He smiled. "Well then it's pretty good, for mud."

The sheriff walked to Simone's fallen chair and righted it with his free hand then he sat in it. "Ahhh. It's so good to get off your feet sometimes."

He held the cup cradled in his lap with both hands around it as if it were a cozy fire. "Now, Mr. Kelly, why don't you explain to my deputies about your son?" His eyes twinkled.

Dad's going to tell them about all about my bad luck. It wouldn't be long before the whole world knew about his problem. Then he'd be a leper to everyone including Saxony Edwards. He realized all he really cared about was losing any chance with Sax once she found out about his affliction. Not that he blamed her. No woman would. Even Cinnamon would be living in a different city from him after the wedding. His destiny was to be alone.

CHAPTER TWENTY-SIX

CINNAMON SAT TO SAX'S LEFT HOLDING HER HAND in an iron grip as the 767 lifted off the runway and began to climb away from the airport. Ouch. Did she have to squeeze her hand like a lemon? She wouldn't be able to look out the window next to her if Cin didn't release her. She had hoped to see the city from the air. Sax looked at the little window longingly. Gray clouds filled the sky ahead. Rats! Now she'd never see the Portland skyline from ten thousand feet.

The jet bounced and wobbled as the engine sounds grew in intensity. The clouds shot by faster and faster until the daylight disappeared and was replaced by blackness. Hard to believe it was noon. Double rats!

Cinnamon assured her the coffee stains would come out of her butterscotch Donna Karan jumpsuit. I didn't mean to spill the latte on Cin. How was she supposed to know that floor cleaner would swerve left when she sagged right. The curse strikes again.

Cinnamon said she'd wash out the stains down her right pant leg in the lavatory once they reach cruising altitude. "That's what they call ladies powder rooms on airplanes," Cinnamon explained.

"I said I'd pay for a new one," whispered Sax. She glanced at Cinnamon, her eyes were squeezed tight like the worst dentist in the universe had a drill poised over a bad tooth. Her face was pinched and pale. It wasn't her best look.

"You okay?"

Cinnamon opened one eye. "Yeah. I'll be fine when we reach altitude. I'm not a good flier." She closed the one eye and turned her head to face forward, her eyes squeezed tight.

Sax smiled weakly just as a violent bump shook the plane. She looked at her right hand and saw it trembling. Flying soooo scares me too. The right wing dipped sharply then quickly righted itself. I don't feel so good. My stomach is dancing. Sax covered her mouth to hide a burp.

She looked at Cinnamon, her face pale with her eyes shut tight and beads of perspiration dotting her forehead. Wouldn't it be funny if she was Cin's good luck charm.

Me, bring someone good luck? Now that would be cool.

~~~

Sax looked out the window of the plane at the wet tarmac of JFK Airport and sighed. They made it. Sax had never felt so relieved to be anywhere in her life.

Portland to New York normally takes four hours as the crow flies. Unfortunately, crows with no sense of direction often take longer. Sometimes a lot longer. She thought they'd never make it.

"I'd never been to Omaha, Denver, Detroit, Cleveland, or Miami before," she said as she bent forward to stare out the tiny window, "and certainly not all in the same day." Worst airline ever.

"You have now," said Cinnamon, still seated next to her. "Too bad all airport tarmacs look the same." She sighed wistfully. "Those SWAT guys in Detroit certainly were handsome in their all black uniforms."

She wondered if she should remind Cinnamon some of them were women. Sax turned in her seat to face Cinnamon in her borrowed baggy SWAT jumpsuit. Naw. Let her enjoy the moment. "I think all black is your look," Sax said with a grin.

Cinnamon winked and chuckled.

The plane came up to the gate, halted with a jerk. The engine noise tapered off and finally stopped.

A man and a woman, whose white hair and wrinkles suggested they were at least in their sixties, had been seated in first class ahead of them. They stood and moved into the aisle. The man released the latch of the overhead bin and began to pull out his carry-on luggage and two heavy coats, one grey tweed the other mouse brown.

The woman marched toward Sax and once in front of her said in a low tone, "Dear, please tell me when you're going back to Portland so I can book a different flight."

"In a week. With my friend," Sax indicated Cinnamon with a slight nod of her head. My friend? Where did that come from? Her eyes narrowed. Ya know, she's actually very nice. I think I know now why Bryce likes her.

The woman took a step forward and her wide bottom inadvertently shoved a teenager from across the aisle. The girl was caught off balance due to a large backpack she was lifting down from the overhead bin.

The teenager stumbled forward and the backpack flew out of her hands to land on the head of a man with shoulder length blond hair, broad shoulders, and arms the size of Sax's waist seated a few rows ahead. He hadn't stood yet, apparently waiting for the other passengers to exit ahead of him.

He's a biggie. He needs two seats.

The heavy backpack careened away and landed with a thump in the aisle, scattering the disembarking passengers like bowling pins.

The man stood, bent at the waist to avoid striking his head on the overhead bin, and moved out to the aisle with the litheness of a cat.

Boy, is he fast on his feet for such a big guy.

"Hey! What gives, dude!" cried the teenage girl who whipped round to face the older woman after regaining her balance. The girl had ear buds in her ears so she had no idea who had hit her. She glared at the older woman, her fists balled at her sides.

I wonder if this is what you call a New York standoff?

Sax and Cinnamon managed to get out of their seat into the aisle. The man towered over all of them.

She had never thought of herself as short but next to this guy she was a midget.

The woman froze when a shadow fell over them. Sax watched the older woman's eyes grow gradually wider. Glancing over her shoulder Sax found herself looking directly into a massive shiny brass belt buckle. It read, Hulkster in stylized capital letters.

"Hey," said Sax. "Aren't you Hulk Hogan?"

The man wore a red and yellow bandana around his head and dark sunglasses covered his eyes. A sardonic grin played across his lips. His upper lip and the sides of his mouth were framed by a yellow mustache. Sax realized his head was nearly touching the ceiling of the cabin.

"Yes, I am," he said, his voice a deep rumble.

Sax had the urge to yell out, "Let's get ready to rumble!" but held back. The wrestler would smash this kid into next week if he got mad at her.

"Is there a problem?" said Hogan, his sunglasses scanning each of them in turn.

"Uhhh. No," squeaked the teenager, backing away from Hogan. "Sir," she added, her voice a falsetto.

Hogan whipped off his sunglasses and his gentle blue eyes appeared. "Good. I was worried you all might be fighting back here."

Cinnamon the queen of I-know-nothing-about-American-pop-culture tapped Sax on the shoulder. Sax looked at her. "You know this guy?" she said in a low voice.

Hogan smiled and held out one massive hand across a row of seats with seemingly no effort. "Hulk Hogan. Nice to meet you, pretty lady."

Cinnamon regarded his huge hand with apprehension then reached out and let his hand envelop hers.

"Nice to meet you too, Mr. Hulk." The big man released her hand and she looked at it as if she counting her fingers to make sure they were all still there.

Hogan chuckled. "Well, if everyone's okay I gotta go." He turned and started to walk away.

"Mr. Hogan." The eager tone of the older woman's voice startled Sax. Her features were lit up like a kid on Christmas morning. Oh, brother, does she ever look like Winnie the year he got that new bike, or what?

Hogan stopped and glanced back at her over his right shoulder at them. "Mr. Hogan," she said again, "can I have your autograph?"

"Why certainly, ma'am. Follow me to the passenger lounge." Before he turned away he winked at Sax then quickly covered his eyes with his sunglasses.

"Excuse us," said the woman. With her husband in tow, they grunted and shoved their way past Sax and Cinnamon and shoved past the teenager's backpack before racing up the aisle after the wrestler.

After the couple was gone a man standing in the aisle behind Sax said, "That's not something you see every day."

CHAPTER TWENTY-SEVEN

"DAD!" PROTESTED BRYCE. "I'm going to talk about my problem. Not you."

Walter Kelly held up his hands in surrender. He moved to an empty desk behind Sheriff Constitution and sat in the gray and blue office ergonomic chair. "When you're right, you're right." Walter shook his head and dropped his arms to lay flat on the chair arms. "Sorry, Bryce. I agree it's your curse, you should be the one to explain."

The Sheriff had a sardonic expression on his lips. He swiveled his chair back and forth, causing it to squeak. He took a sip of coffee.

"Sheriff? Are we gonna let them…" Izzy's voice trailed off, her index finger pointing first at Walter, then at Bryce, then back again.

The Sheriff stopped moving the chair to face Izzy, his eyebrows rose on his forehead. "Yes. Hazel Isabel Jean Betsy May. We are. And take off those handcuffs."

She did as instructed but Bryce could see by her expression she was none too happy about it. He added to her anger by smiling at her.

"And Simone, my dear, I want silence please. I think you will both find this interesting." The sheriff used his coffee cup to indicate his deputies should take two plastic chairs set against a wall and sit down.

As they scraped the chairs over the tiled floor Bryce looked at the wall covered with pictures of the sheriff receiving awards and medals from what looked like well known politicians. Bryce's eyes narrowed. One photo depicted a long-haired Sonny Bono shaking hands with the sheriff. Bono was dressed in his traditional sixties hippie garb.

Wow! Is the sheriff that old? Bryce's brow wrinkled. The pose didn't look natural, something was slightly off.

He decided the picture had been photo shopped. Who does such things? Guy must have a giant ego.

The sheriff looked at him expectantly. With one index finger he made a circular motion to indicate Bryce should move on.

Bryce shook his head. "Yeah. Sorry. Ummm. Where were we?"

"You were going to tell us what your affliction is all about?" Constitution took another sip from his mug and rocked back in the chair causing the springs to squeak again.

"May I at least sit down?"

The sheriff nodded toward another empty desk. Bryce moved to the chair behind the desk and sat down. It felt good to get off his feet. He began alternately rubbing his red wrists where the cuffs had irritated his skin.

The desk was empty except for a black telephone. Bryce shifted his weight in the chair.

Bryce sighed. I really don't want to talk about this. But I have no choice or these guys are going to lock me up and throw away the key.

"I have a problem with bad luck," he blurted. Simone and Izzy looked at each other but said nothing. Constitution grunted and shook his head.

"I know it sounds nuts, but it's true." Bryce paused. He eyed his father. "Dad calls it a curse but I think of it as luck gone bad."

It even sounded nuts to him and he lived with bad luck every day of his life.

"What kind of bad luck?" said the Sheriff.

"It's kind of like a black cloud that follows me around. Little stuff," he shrugged, "bad stuff happens around me. Sometimes to me. Sometimes to others."

"Ya see, like I said," said Simone, "he's possessed."

Bryce frowned. "I am not possessed."

"How do you know?" said Izzy.

He didn't. For sure. "All I know is bad stuff happens while doing normal, everyday stuff. But nothing really bad happens. No one dies around me, I don't hear voices, and my head doesn't spin around like that young girl in The Exorcist." At least not yet.

A half smile formed at one corner of the sheriff's mouth. "Glad to hear it."

"And I am not a terrorist," added Bryce.

Izzy shook her head. "He's not making any sense, Sheriff. Bad things happen around him, but it's not really bad? What's that supposed to mean?"

Bryce's attention shifted to the front doors as the bell tingled again. Two men, one white with red hair and freckles, the other black with a scar down his left cheek, in matching dark suits, white shirts, and red power ties came through the door. They looked fit and had identical flat top style haircuts.

You could land a plane on those haircuts.

The black man reached into the inside pocket of his suit jacket to pull out a black leather wallet. He held it up and opened it to reveal a gleaming gold badge and identification card.

Bryce swallowed hard as his mouth dried. Oh, crap. Now I'm in big trouble. These guys are Feds.

"Special Agent Garnier. FBI." He indicated the red-haired man. "This is Special Agent Hanrahan. We're here to see Sheriff Constitution."

The sheriff stood and set his now empty mug on the desk. "I'm the sheriff," he said. He approached the counter and stuck out his hand. Garnier took the sheriff's hand in his and shook it. With his free hand he secreted his ID wallet back inside his suit jacket. His features remained expressionless, his mouth a tight line.

They released each others' hand and dropped them to their sides.

"Nice to meet you, Sheriff. We're with the Portland field office." Garnier reached inside his suit jacket and took out a Blackberry. He pressed a button with his thumb his eyes on the small screen. "A Deputy Isabel May called us saying you'd captured a terrorist."

Constitution glared at Isabel. "Deputy May was a little hasty, Agent Garnier." Izzy's pale cheeks turned bright red and she avoided the sheriff's accusatory frown.

CHAPTER TWENTY-EIGHT

PARK AVENUE, NEW YORK CITY. THE LEGENDARY WALDORF ASTORIA.

Sax took in a deep breath and closed her eyes. The air was tinged with the smell of the finest perfumes and she imagined she could detect the ancient dust of such a magnificent hotel. She imagined the wealthy New Yorkers who had walked through these doors. The Astros and the Rockefellers and the economic elite that once controlled the wealth of this country had stood in this very lobby.

Wow. Awesome. I never could've imagined me in such a place, ever.

Today there was the quiet murmur of the rich and famous as they moved through the lobby, women, men, and a few children, all well-dressed, looking relaxed and casual. And the rustle of fine silks and hand tooled leather high heeled shoes that clicked over the marble floors.

"Owww!" said Cinnamon.

Sax's eyes shot open to see Cinnamon had dropped her makeup bag on her foot. "You okay?"

Cinnamon winced and bent over to pick up the bag. "Yeah. I'm fine," she said between gritted teeth. She grasped the handle on the top of the bag and tried to lift it. The lid suddenly snapped open and the contents scattered with rattles and clicks across the marble.

A number of lipsticks, eyeliners, eye shadow, blushes, bottles of perfume, and tubes of foundation scattered across the marble tiles. A makeup compact skittered loudly across the white and brown tiles finally coming to rest against the antique grandfather clock set against one of the ornate marble pillars that dotted the lobby of the grand hotel.

One perfume bottle broke as it struck the marble. A strong scent of Jasmine filled the air. "Oh, no!" wailed Cinnamon.

Oh dear. How terrible.

"Was that the good stuff?" said Sax, walking up and placed a hand on Cinnamon's shoulder to try to comfort her.

"Yes. Chanel No. 5." Tears rolled down her flushed cheeks. "My last bottle."

This is so my fault. It's my curse. I should never have agreed to help Bryce. All she was doing was wrecking this poor woman's life, sooner or later. She's going to figure out these accidents are my fault, then she'll hate me. And just when I was growing to like her. "I'm so sorry." And perfume sure doesn't travel well. Maybe she should leave the stuff at home next time. Sax's nose wrinkled as the smell of jasmine intensified.

A tall, painfully thin man with grey hair combed neatly to the side of his small head strode up to them, his hands folded behind his back. He offered a closed mouth smile but his eyes were not amused at all.

"Ladies." He bowed his head slightly, his eyes never leaving them. "Is there a problem?" he said condescendingly.

"Yes. Lots," said Sax. But too many to list, pal unless you got all day.

The man's name, according to the shiny gold name tag over the left breast of his dark gray suit was F. Walenburg, CONCIERGE. He looked her up and down as if she were a Dickens street urchin.

I wash my clothes on a regular basis, pal.

Her eyes narrowed. She wondered what Concierge meant. I guess he's never seen a makeup bag break up in the lobby before. Well now you have. Mr. Concierge.

"I am the concierge. It is my job to ensure the comfort of all our guests."

He scanned the collection of makeup scattered across the floor like rings in a still pond when a pebble is dropped in the water. He then looked at Cinnamon with her face buried in her hands crying. His gaze shifted back to Sax. "It seems to me, Miss, you two ladies are in need of assistance."

Sax looked down at her shoes. Collected around her runners were the remains of Cinnamon's makeup. "Yeah. I agree." Boy, do I agree. "Are you gonna clean this up for us?"

Walenburg stiffened, evidently offended by her reference. "No. I will summon a customer service representative for you." He raised one arm above his head.

Sax jumped when he snapped his fingers. What the...?

A lean younger man with dirty blond hair suddenly appeared as if from out of nowhere. He walked briskly across the lobby, his arms swinging.

Sax had to avert her eyes because his shoes were shined to mirror brightness.

Sax realized as he came up to them he was a few inches shorter than Walenburg. "Yes, Mr. Walenburg?" said the bell hop (only they were now apparently called service representatives.) The title on the gold name plate over the breast pocket of his maroon suit jacket confirmed his official title and identified him as Benjamin.

"Benjamin. These lovely ladies are in need of assistance."

The customer service man's dark eyes drifted to Cinnamon standing in the middle of the makeup storm, then to Sax. One eyebrow traveled slowly up his pale forehead as he surveyed the situation. "Yes, sir," he said confidently.

Like the concierge, Benjamin raised one arm and snapped his fingers. A woman dressed in a powder blue one piece dress and matching low heel shoes appeared from the direction of the bank of elevators.

"Yes, Mr. Acorn?"

Sax guessed she was in her mid forties and in very good physical condition. Her green eyes were intense.

She stared at the customer service representative. Benjamin Acorn? I guess he didn't fall far from the tree.

"Ah, good," Benjamin smiled warmly. "Mrs. Lovett!" He called waving one arm over the assorted makeup scattered about the lobby. He made his way across the lobby where he opened a door.

"We have a problem," was the last thing she heard him say before the door closed cutting him off. Whoever Mrs. Lovett was she must behind the door.

Sax watched as knots of hotel guests in groups of two, three, or four strategically avoided them by walking around.

They had to get to the room before this situation got out of hand. Sax dropped to her haunches and started hopping around picking up the scattered makeup as she went.

At least Cinnamon had finally stopped crying. She stood in the middle of the makeup, sniffling. Walenburg pulled a handkerchief from the breast pocket of his perfectly pressed suit then walked gingerly around spoiled makeup as if it were a minefield and handed the cloth to Cinnamon.

She mouthed a thank you then covered her nose and blew three long blasts into it.

After she was finished she tried to hand it back to Walenburg. "Please keep it, compliments of the Waldorf Astoria," he said.

"Thank you." Cinnamon grinned widely at Sax. "My, aren't they nice here."

"Yeah. Nice." She wouldn't want it back either.

Walenburg picked his way back over the sea of spilled makeup like he was walking over hot coals.

Sax stood and dropped what she'd managed to save into the makeup case. She'd ask him to send up the rest to the room later. She looked at Cinnamon's red eyes and tear stained cheeks. I gotta get her to the room. She looked exhausted. It had been a long day for both of them.

"Huh, Mr. Walenburg?"

"Yes?"

"I wonder if Miss Wolthorp and I could be shown to our rooms?"

Walenburg frowned. He gazed at Sax as if he'd swallowed a fly. "Did you say Wolthorp?"

CHAPTER TWENTY-NINE

SIMONE'S GUN LAY ON HER DESK BETWEEN BRYCE AND HER. She scowled at him from across the desk. Dobbs had gone off shift and left the station. A bead of sweat tickled Bryce's back as it rolled down his neck under his shirt.

He looked away. She was making him nervous because she was in big trouble with her boss. It's not my fault she didn't follow orders.

"Simone." Bryce heard the Sheriff's deep voice speaking but it seemed far away. "What are you doing?"

"He's a terrorist," said Simone, "sir," she added, seemingly reluctantly.

"Deputy," said Constitution slowly and deliberately, "holster your weapon."

Bryce locked eyes with Simone. Her dark eyes flitted in the direction of the sheriff's voice then back to him repeating the movement every few seconds. Problem was seconds seemed like years all of a sudden.

Finally the deputy's eyes narrowed and she grabbed her gun and holstered it. The tension in her arms and shoulders relaxed and she exhaled deeply.

The sheriff placed one meaty hand on her left shoulder. "It's okay, Simone. I understand why you called the Feds. I know you had your heart set on capturing our first terrorist. Maybe next time."

Simone emitted a heavy sigh. "Yes, sir."

Oh, brother. Bryce's right foot tingled and he realized his circulation had been compromised. I'm going to be walking like Quasimodo for a while. He groaned. I've been sitting here not moving wayyy too long.

"Sheriff, I'd really like to be out of here."

"Sorry, Mr. Kelly. Simone would really love to capture a terrorist. We've never captured one before you came along."

"But I'm not a terrorist!"

The two FBI agents came out of one of the offices. They scowled at Bryce then threw a folder marked Secret on Simone's desk. "You can file that," said Agent Garnier. "It's not him."

Constitution looked at Bryce and nodded, then sighed. "Yes, I know. Sorry about that."

Bryce stole a glance at Simone. Unbelievable! She's sorry she couldn't shoot me. Bryce gave her a withering stare, which made Izzy avert her eyes and turn to face the computer screen in front of her. Bryce craned his neck and looked at the image on her monitor.

There were pictures of several Gucci handbags.

Bryce eyes narrowed at Constitution. They think I'm a cash cow. "There's a reward, isn't there?" he said, raising his voice. Bryce shook his numb leg to increase circulation.

The sheriff winced and nodded. "Yeah. Sorry. I planned to invest in a banana farm with my share."

Banana farm? What's with these people? Had the whole world gone crazy?

Bryce shook his head and rubbed his leg. I should sue these turkeys. They threatened me and called a terrorist! "Well, I want an apology and then I want to get the heck out of here."

More importantly, I've got to find out if Sax and Cin made it to New York okay. In all the excitement he hadn't called them yet. They might be worried.

"Mr. Kelly," it was Agent Garnier. "Sir, the President is waiting."

"Coming, Agent Garnier." Bryce stood and dragged his numb leg behind him into the sheriff's office. All I need is a hump and a bell tower then Esmeralda would be all over me.

Bryce shuffled in to the sheriff's office followed by the stone faced FBI agent. The glass window in the door rattled when Garnier closed it behind them.

President Tiffany Kimberly Murphy is going to get an earful from me.

Bryce collapsed into faded brown leather that smelled like old runners and let out a breath he'd been holding in. Sweat trickled down the sides of his face and he was breathing hard.

Sure gives you new respect for the hunchbacked. Bryce accepted the receiver from Agent Garnier. He pressed it to his right ear.

"Mr. Kelly?" said a woman's voice he immediately recognized from CNN interviews and White House press conferences.

"Yes, Madam President?" he croaked. *Since when did I swallow a frog?*

"Mr. Kelly, I want to personally apologize on the behalf of the government of the United States."

CHAPTER THIRTY

"HUH. YEAH." SAX WAVED A HAND AT CINNAMON. Walenburg stood in his perfectly pressed suit, his hands folded in front of him, regarding them with indignation.

Other hotel patrons' eyes flitted to the two women as they passed. They walked around them, giving them a wide berth. Oh, brother. They were the center of unwanted attention. Sax decided at the first opportunity she'd take a long bath to wash off the dirty looks they'd been getting.

"This is Cinnamon Wolthorp." She didn't like the disapproving look in his eye.

Walenburg ever so slowly arched an eyebrow and his eyes narrowed even tighter than before. His cheeks paled and Sax took a step backward bumping into Cinnamon. "Sorry."

Oh, oh. I don't like his body language.

His eyes focused on Cinnamon. "Is your father Belmont Wolthorp?"

Cinnamon nodded and she avoided his gaze. Her already pale cheeks turned bone white. "Yes?" she said in a little girl voice and her lower lip trembled.

"The same Belmont Wolthorp who's in jail for grand larceny?" Her dad's in jail? Bryce said she lost her money, but she had no idea it was because her dad was a crook. Poor girl. How embarrassing.

She nodded, her eyes watery and her lean frame had stopped trembling. At least she isn't bawling.

"Good." Walenburg sniffed then turned and walked away, leaving the two women staring at each other.

"What was that all about?" whispered Sax.

Cinnamon wiped one eye then the other with the back of her left hand. "I'll tell you later," she said, her voice hoarse from crying..

Sax glowered at the retreating Walenburg. That was mean. Sax had never liked mean.

~~~

Their suite overlooked Park Avenue. Leafy trees were planted on the grassy divider down the center of the wide street. Sax stood with one hand holding the curtain aside, gazing out the window at the mix of cars, buses, and trucks moving like the ebb and flow of the tides along the rain soaked streets. It reminded her of a nature show on television, where herds of antelope and zebras on the plains of Africa ran free and wild, only the cars, buses, and trucks ran in straight lines.

Cinnamon explained her father had run a Ponzi scheme for twenty five years. He embezzled money from all his friends and relatives.

Sax didn't ask Cinnamon any more questions her about her father being in jail. It must have hurt Cin terribly to open that wound. No way was Sax going to add to her new friend's pain. Cinnamon wasn't involved in her dad's business so why should she suffer?

Cinnamon told her about her favourite department store in the world, Saks Fifth Avenue, that was only a few blocks away. Surrounding the hotel were tall buildings so Sax hoped Cinnamon knew her way around the concrete jungle.

If she was alone she'd get lost for sure.

"My daddy did a bad thing," said Cinnamon said without being asked. She sat on the edge of the king size bed studying her image in her makeup mirror, sighing heavily every few seconds. "I look terrible."

Sax dropped her hand holding back the curtain and turned to face her friend. The curtain made a soft shush sound as it dropped to cover the window.

"I think swindling millions of dollars—" Sax began.

"Wrong," Cinnamon interrupted, her tone edged with anger, "it's billions. Not millions."

Sax walked to the fruit basket on an end table and untied the ornate red bow tied around the top of the cellophane covering. She cringed. The sound of the cellophane crunching reminded her of finger nails on a blackboard.

Man, why did I say that? The cellophane crinkled loudly. She had to make up for opening her big mouth. "Does it matter whether it's millions or billions?"

Cinnamon sat back on the bed her hands splayed behind her to support her. She let her chin drop and her eyes gazed at the thick tan rug. "Yeah, it does. He stole my and my mother's money as well."

A deafening silence closed between them. Sax's heart went out to poor Cinnamon. How sad to have a jailbird father. My family may be odd but at least none of them are in jail.

Sax finally opened a corner of the cellophane and plucked two green grapes off the bunch inside. She popped them into her mouth, bit down and immediately spat them out on the carpet.

"Hey! Those are wax."

"Yeah, I know," said Cinnamon forlornly.

"Why didn't you tell me?" Sax spat out the remains of the faux fruit then ran her tongue around her lips to remove any traces of wax. "Ewww."

Cinnamon shoulders slumped and a tear ran down her cheek.

Seeing her friend's despondency, Sax moved to the edge of the bed and sat down next to her then lay and arm across Cinnamon's shoulders and hugged her. "It's okay. My wax quotient was lacking in my diet anyway."

Suddenly an alarm ripped the silence, ringing loudly from the direction of the hallway.

"Now what?" said Sax. She despaired the curse would ever give her a moment's peace. I guess dinner's going to be late.

The sound of screaming sirens echoed from the street below. Dropping her arm from Cinnamon's shoulder, she stood and walked to the window. After lifting the curtain aside she peered to the street far below.

Fire trucks. It obviously wasn't a false alarm. Curse one, me zero.

Scores of fire trucks with flashing lights reflected off the surrounding glass towers had appeared on the long avenue. The shrill wail of their sirens echoed off the surrounding skyscrapers as they rumbled from both ends of Park Avenue. As if they were a pride of lions surrounding a fresh kill, the white and red diesel monsters were parked in front of the hotel blocking the street in both directions. Sax wondered why there were so many. She didn't see a fire.

Out of the corner of one eye she spotted a puff of grey smoke spurt from the bottom of the door.

"Oh, crap-a-doodle."

CHAPTER THIRTY-ONE

CINNAMON'S GREEN EYES GLANCED FROM SAX to the door and back again. "Is that smoke?" she asked, her voice trembling.

"It'll be okay," said Sax. I hope.

Cinnamon sniffled, wiped her cheeks with the back of her hand to clear away salty tears, then stood up from the bed and walked to the window overlooking Park Avenue. Let me see," she said impatiently grabbing the curtain and pulling it aside.

Her eyes grew ever wider as she stared at the gathering of fire trucks far below. A sharp knock on the door and a woman's voice asking if anyone was in the room caused them to look at each other.

Now Sax knew what fear smelled like. It's smoky. Her mouth dried and a knot formed in her stomach. And it tastes like squid flavored gum. Who knew?

"Yes," Cinnamon called, "we're in here."

There was a bang on the door then another even harder this time, then the door fell inward slapping hard on the carpet. Smoke billowed in from the hallway followed by a firefighter wearing a grey-green jacket with bright yellow stripes circling the torso. Sax could see the firefighter's face, shiny and slick with sweat, through the Plexiglas of her oxygen mask. Her dark eyes were intense and her breathing rapid. In one gloved hand she held an axe.

"We have to go. Now!" The firefighter motioned with her free hand for them to follow her.

Cinnamon ran toward the end table next to the bed. Just before her fingers could wrap around the handle of her Gucci bag the firefighter yelled for her to stop. "Leave that! Take nothing!"

Sax started. Oh, oh. The fire must be close. We're gonna die.

"But my—" Cinnamon started to say before the firefighter again cut her off.

"Never mind, I said. Let's go."

Cinnamon looked at Sax her eyes wide with fear. Sax's voice trembled as she said, "I think we better do as she says."

Cinnamon looked at her hand bag then back at Sax. Her eyes were watery, but Sax knew it wasn't from the smoke. Her heart beat fast. Sweat trickled down her cheeks. I know, Cin, I'm scared too.

Sax and Cinnamon followed the firefighter quickly to the door.

~~~

Sax's knees ached and her hands were sore. She blinked away tears caused by the constant sting of smoke. She coughed. Man, I don't know if we're going to make it.

Though the curse had caused her trouble all her life she'd always thought she was too young to die. Today she feared she might be wrong. Please, please, please don't let me die.

Sax crawled on all fours down the hallway of what she hoped was finally the lobby floor. Behind her Cinnamon alternated between coughing and crying.

The poor girl had never experienced the bad luck curse, so Sax felt sorry for her BFF. Between makeup spills and spontaneous fires she still hadn't found time to check what the initials BFF stood for so whatever it meant she assumed it had to be something good. I hope.

Their leader, New York City Firefighter Ruby Jivers, seemed to be able to sense when to lend them her oxygen mask to get a lungful of fresh air. Sax was thankful the smoke in the stairwell hadn't been as bad as the hallways.

The air exchange system had flooded the hallways with smoke on every floor.

Finally they must have reached the exit door to the lobby because Ruby stood and pushed her body against a metal bar. She held the door as Sax and Cinnamon shuffled through the open door on their hands and knees.

"Ow. Ow. Ow," said Cinnamon.

"You ok?" said Sax.

"My knees hurt. My hands hurt. And jumpsuit is ruined. Other than that I'm fine." Cinnamon began to sob softly.

Ruby let the door slam shut behind them with a bang. A gaggle of firefighters, police, and paramedics stared back at them. They looked as surprised to see the girls as Sax was to see them.

Oh, oh. What had her curse done now? Why are the police here and why are they staring at me?

CHAPTER THIRTY-TWO

THEY WALKED THROUGH THE FRONT DOOR of Bryce's lakeside house exactly five hours after they left. Bryce sighed heavily as he tossed his keys at the side table next to the accordion coat closet doors. They hit the table but slid off to land with a bang on the tiled entry floor.

Bryce groaned. Why does this stuff keep happening to me?

"What's the matter?" asked Walter.

"Nothing, Dad." Bryce slipped his arms out of his jacket and gripped the handle on one side of the bi-fold closet door. The handle came off in his hand.

"Dad!" Bryce covered his eyes with one hand. "It's not fair!"

Walter walked over and slid the other door open and hung up his jacket and then Bryce's. He placed a comforting hand on his son's shoulder. "It's okay. I understand."

Bryce looked up into his father's grey-blue eyes. Walter's eyes crinkled at the corners.

"My father had the same problem." He turned and walked away up the short flight of three stairs to the living room. The house was quiet.

Bryce had noticed Margaret's car missing from the driveway when they drove up. He assumed his step-mother and her sister were shopping at the outlet mall for more knick-knacks to decorate his new home.

163

Not that he wanted or needed Margaret and Elizabeth's help. They bought ostentatious and gauche stuff, not the kind of stuff that suited his taste. Cinnamon didn't like the things they bought either, but she was a good sport, at least in front of her mother.

Bryce found the antiques at Antique Virgin far more charming than what Margaret and her sister bought for the house. And Sax Edwards was certainly intriguing. She's the first woman he'd met who didn't come unglued during his many mishaps. He wondered why.

I'm beginning to really care about her. If Cinnamon and I weren't engaged, I'd really like to get to know her better. There seemed to be some sort of connection between them. It's very confusing.

"Dad, wait," Bryce climbed the three stairs in one leap. His father sat in the padded rocking chair in front of the floor-to-ceiling stone fireplace. The fireplace was the nicest feature in the house. The previous owner had collected the stones off the beaches up and down the coast and had a local craftsman assemble them in beautiful patterns shaped like diamonds and stars and hearts. The stones were a mix of grey, green, tan, and brown. While Bryce loved the look of it, what really sold him was when Margaret said it was the ugliest fireplace she had ever seen.

He didn't hate Margaret, he hated her attitude, and the seemingly inbred tendency to jump into a negative position about anything and everything. His step-mother's attitude grated on him. He'd always made a point of looking on the bright side of life, even in the most adverse situations. As his late mother often said, it takes lemons to make lemonade.

Only now his accident prone nature had gotten worse than ever. He had finally reached the end of his tolerance rope. His grandfather had the curse? I don't remember Gramps having bad luck. In fact he and Gran were the luckiest people he'd ever known. Everything they did seemed charmed.

"Dad, what did you mean about Gramps having the same problem as me? Was he cursed too?" Bryce sat on the couch facing his father who stood with his hands buried in his pants pockets.

He was looking out the picture window overlooking the lake beyond, his back to his son.

Bryce lifted his right butt cheek when the thin, worn cushion sank and the sharp-edged bamboo pinched him. Shifting his weight until he found a spot where the bamboo wasn't poking through the cushion, he settled into the couch. The frame cracking and popping with each movement reminded him of breakfast cereal.

Margaret is right about one thing, this furniture had to go.

Walter turned to face Bryce and donned his reading glasses. They were perched on the end of his nose and he held his new John Grisham novel in his hands. He peered over the top edge of his glasses at Bryce. "My dad had the same problem as you and that Saxony girl," he said.

Bryce gaped at his father, unable to speak. What has Sax got to do with Gramps? His gut sense was his dad was about to tell him about the connection between Sax and him. His excitement grew at the thought he and Sax had something in common. And if she had a bad luck problem it would explain a lot of what had been happening lately.

Walter moved to his chair near the fireplace and sat down. He set his book on the end table next to the chair.

Bryce blinked. "I don't understand. Sax?" Sliding forward on the couch he winced as a shaft of bamboo poked at a particularly sensitive spot. "But what's this about Gramps and her having a problem?"

Walter laid his book on the end table next to him and sighed. "Let me explain." After removing his eyeglasses he placed them on top of the book.

~~~

Bryce glanced at the clock that hung on the wall over the stone fireplace. His father had taken a seat on a rattan chair beside a small pine end table with a glass lamp and his current book. The position of the moose antlers, substituting for clock arms, showed the time was after six thirty. Had it really been two hours since they got home?

But his Dad's riveting story of Shamus O'Rourke, the bad luck leprechaun who was kicked out of Ireland in 1897, held him in a trance.

After arriving in America, Shamus changed his family name to Magee and settled in Hoboken, New Jersey. A big mistake as it turned out, but indicative of how Shamus Magee's future would be filled with bad decisions. This eventually led to Shamus running from New Jersey barely ahead of an angry lynch mob. "Someone figured out the sudden rash of bad luck that befell that community was his fault." His father paused. "Which it was."

He then headed for Florida and instead arrived in Kansas City where he again changed his name.

Shamus' sense of direction was way off. I'm better at finding my way around even though I have been known to get lost a few times.

In Kansas City he changed his name to Buckley, which means cow herd, a name seemingly appropriate since he was now resident in the former cow capital of the west.

After Shamus Buckley arrived in cow town he met and married Kelly Pudmucker of the St Louis Pudmuckers, whose family was very big in gaslight fixture manufacturing. Over the next fifteen years Shamus and Kelly raised fourteen children.

Due to a series of bad investments, the gaslight fixture business went the way of the dodo bird and with it the Pudmucker family fortune. That, combined with Kelly's father running away with his twenty year old secretary to Brazil and the remains of the Pudmucker money, left them destitute. Seeking fame and fortune elsewhere, Shamus packed up his family and once again hit the road.

With his mother-in-law in tow Shamus, Kelly, and their fourteen children they headed for California. Shamus had read about the gold rush of 1849 and hoped some gold was still left.

"Of course, Shamus' sense of direction being as poor as it was they soon arrived in Glad Beach, Oregon."

"Glad Beach! You're kidding," said Bryce. A frown marred his tanned forehead. "But what has any of this got to do with Gramps?"

Walter's mouth formed a wry grin and his eyes sparkled. "There's more."

Walter went on to explain that when they arrived in Glad Beach, Shamus thought it wise to once again change the family name. He decided it would be Kelly.

"So my great-great-great grandmother's name was Kelly Kelly?" Walter nodded. "But that's just stupid."

Walter chuckled. "Yes, I know, but poor old Shamus was clearly no genius."

"So Gramps?"

"Shamus had a son, Todd. Todd married Elsie Moxy. Their son, Harold—"

His father paused to cross his legs then continued, "As I was saying, Harold Kelly married Kathleen Kilpatrick and together they had a son Charles, who was my father."

Bryce couldn't take the awful couch anymore. He stood and rubbed his bottom with one hand as he moved to look out over the expanse of the lake. Rays of sunlight danced off a light breeze-blown chop, making the surface of the water sparkle.

"You never told me all this stuff, Dad. Why now?" He turned away from the window toward his father.

"Because it's time you knew about the family curse."

Bryce laughed nervously.

Bryce'd never spoken to anyone about his troubles. "Oh, c'mon, Dad. You don't believe in such nonsense." Sure, he had a little bad luck now and then, but a curse? "There are no such things as curses. It's just bad luck." Bryce stopped laughing when he realized his father's solemn expression meant he was serious. "Sure, the cops bought that line but I certainly don't. I'm a software engineer, not a sorcerer."

"Sorry, son, but it's true. Shamus brought the curse from Ireland to America." Walter paused and intertwined his fingers in his lap, his gaze dropped to the hardwood floor. "You've heard the expression luck of the Irish?"

He looked up as Bryce nodded. "There's a flip side to that coin." Walter stood, stuffed his hands in his pockets and moved to gaze out the window.

"I think of it as the universe staying in balance." He shifted his gaze to Bryce. "Some people have nothing but good luck. Others, like you and Gramps, have bad luck." He frowned. "As far as I can tell the bad luck cycle skips a generation."

"You mean I have the bad luck of the Irish?" That would sure explain everything that went wrong in my life. But what it meant was the accidents with the sail boat, the bear and the sea lion were his fault.

Oh, poor Sax. I'm not safe to be around. His cheeks grew cold and his gut tightened. He shivered at the thought of Sax being hurt because of him. She could have been killed. I would hate myself if anything happened to her.

Walter smiled and his gaze shifted to glance out the picture window. "Exactly." The smile on his ruddy features slowly dissolved and his eyes grew wide. He jumped to his feet and raced to the picture window looking out at the lake.

"Dad? What's wrong?"

Walter pointed to the lake. "Look."

Bryce looked where his father was pointing and saw a small boat in the distance with two human shaped figures waving their arms above their heads. He squinted and realized the two people in the boat were women. After retrieving binoculars from the book case and raising them to his eyes he focused on them. What he saw made his heart leap to his throat.

Oh, crap. Now Margaret and Elizabeth are in trouble. And it's my fault. Everything bad that happens around here is always my fault, he thought bitterly. His dad was right. He was cursed and dangerous.

CHAPTER THIRTY-THREE

WALTER GRUNTED AS HE STROKED THE PADDLE IN THE LAKE. The sun had dipped behind the stands of tall fir trees that lined the lakeshore. The last of the daylight would be gone soon.

Bryce glanced over his shoulder at his house standing amongst the green trees and the water lapping the sandy beach in front. He looked up at the pale half moon hovering in the purple and orange sky overhead. The canoe rocked gently when a light breeze washed over them.

He lost his grip on his paddle and it splashed into the water. He tried to grab it but missed and it was soon behind the canoe, lost in the dusk.

"Dad, I lost the paddle," said Bryce forlornly.

"I heard," said Walter with a sigh. "I should have listened to the little voice in my head warning me not to leave home without an extra paddle. Sometimes I forget about your disability."

"It's not a disability." Bryce paused. Maybe his father was right. "Never mind. What we need to concentrate on right now is how we get to Margaret and Elizabeth and get home. I don't want to spend the entire night on the lake drifting in the dark. Do you?"

"No, of course not," said Walter, breathing hard.

"Give me your paddle, Dad. I know you're tired."

Walter turned sideways on the seat and handed the paddle to him.

Bryce dipped the paddle in the lake and pulled hard.

A sudden sharp crack startled him and he pulled the paddle out of the water to see the end had broken off.

"Just great!" He tossed the broken handle as far away from the canoe as he could. He heard the splash in distance.

They sat in silence for several moments, the only sound the waves gently lapping against the canoe's fiberglass hull. I must be cursed. He didn't believe in curses but his dad had to be right. My bad luck streaks have to be more than coincidence.

There had to be a way to stop this from happening and he had to find it before it was too late for the people he loved.

Maybe there's a pill I can take? Bryce shook his head. This is nuts. When Cinnamon found out his curse killed her mother she would dump him for sure. And she'd hate him forever. And he was worried Sax would hate him for what his curse did to her. Any way he looked at it he was going to lose everyone he cared about. It was the ultimate no-win scenario.

He paused. Hold on. Cinnamon will dump me? He shook his head. What am I thinking? Just because he didn't like Margaret it didn't justify her dying because of him. I'd never forgive myself if I hurt anyone, even inadvertently.

"Okay," Walter said, startling him out of his blue funk. "We're going to have to use our hands to row to Margaret and Elizabeth. Then we're going to huddle up with them and wait until morning."

"Why can't we just row to shore after we get to them?"

Walter eyed his son. "You're kidding, right?"

"Sure, why not? The sky's clear. The moon is out." He swept the air with one arm. "The stars will be out soon. Once our eyesight adjusts we'll be able to see the shoreline perfectly."

"Normally I'd agree with you, but..." Walter pointed over Bryce's shoulder.

Swiveling on the bench to get a better view of what was behind him, Bryce's eyes widened. Billowing dark clouds were rolling over the tree tops. The clouds were low. Too low. Oh, crap. My curse is turned on full. The inky, billowing clouds rushed at them, reminiscent of a herd of maddened bulls he'd seen in a book about Spain. We're doomed.

"Oh, crap," he whispered.

Bryce and Walter dropped their hands over the sides of the canoe and began to paddle furiously.

~~~

Walter secured the final knot to tie the canoe to the side of the water logged wooden row boat with two lengths of rotting rope. Elizabeth and Margaret's row boat was now secured to their canoe. Bryce was disappointed when they discovered the row boat's oars were gone too. Walter had moved over to the row boat and insisted Elizabeth move to the canoe.

When she protested, Margaret insisted, and she reluctantly changed boats.

Without warning the dark clouds opened up to release a fierce deluge of rain. Bryce let his shoulders sag as rain pounded off his light windbreaker and quickly soaked through the thin nylon fabric. Yuck! I hate being cold and wet.

The sales guy at the store said it was water resistant. He never said it was resistant for less than ten seconds.

At least the sound of rain dancing hard off the lake drowned out Elizabeth's complaining about being soaked.

One eyebrow gradually rose on Walter's forehead and his eyes narrowed to slits. His features darkened. Now she's done it.

It was a sight as rare as the doubled tailed swallow from Capistrano. Dad's finally mad about something.

"Liz," Walter said between gritted teeth, "shut up." Elizabeth stopped in mid sentence and gaped at her brother-in-law.

Margaret rolled her eyes. "Liz, my dear sister, I love you, but Walter's right. Shut up."

Bryce smiled to himself. Margaret siding with his father, who would've thought that would ever happen? Something had changed between them since he last saw them together. His father had one arm draped across her shoulders and she pressed her body into him. Whoa! More than changed. I'd say overheated! Now wasn't the time but Bryce would ask his father about this sudden change when this was over.

Elizabeth scowled, harrumphed, and crossed her arms over her chest. Both Elizabeth and Margaret's normally perfectly coiffed hair lay flat against their heads, rainwater dripping off the limp ends. Bryce knew his step-mother's sister would sulk for hours. A good thing. At least she'll be quiet. But what happened to Margaret all of a sudden? And what about Dad? What had gotten into him?

Bryce repressed the urge to smile. He shifted his weight on the canoe bench and immediately regretted it as cold rain water bled through his chocolate brown Dockers. The clouds shrouded them in fog and the rain pelted them, driving away any body heat. Bryce wrapped his hands around his body, hugging himself to try to stay warm. How were they going to survive the night without catching pneumonia?

He glanced at Margaret and saw the sadness in her eyes. Things had just changed in her world. He realized his beloved Dad had found his inner resolve that had been missing since his mother died. The wind had been knocked out of Walter's sails by the death of Bryce's mother. The fight and determination that made him successful in the business world had suddenly returned. For the first time since Dad and Margaret married they were acting like a couple. He knew his father loved Margaret, but she'd been slow to respond. Now she'd seen the man was ready to protect her.

Today is the turning point between them. He hoped for his father's sake the new them lasted. His dad deserved another shot at love. He knew his late mom would want his father to be happy.

The last of the sunlight that managed to pierce the thick, black clouds finally disappeared. Now Bryce sat in silence and darkness shivering to the sound of a hard rain. Elizabeth's teeth had begun to chatter.

For the first time in his life he wondered if he'd live to see another sunrise. A loud splash off to his left made stiffen. A slight wave caused the canoe to rock up and down.

"Dad," Bryce whispered hoarsely, "what was that?"

"I don't know," said his father.

"If our luck's holding it'll be a great white shark," said Margaret sardonically.

CHAPTER THIRTY-FOUR

WITH CINNAMON BEHIND HER, Sax walked to the front desk of the Waldorf Astoria. She didn't look her best, but then the hotel lobby was still a disordered mess. Her nose wrinkled due to the acrid smell of smoke from burned carpets and lacquered furniture.

I don't care how I look right now.

The elegant rosewood furniture that populated the lobby had been shoved aside by firemen to make way for hoses and to set up a command center to fight the fire. Water had pooled in spots all around the marble tiled floor. Mud, soot, and water covered everything, even the staff.

Mr. Walenburg, Mr. Acorn, and a woman who had to be Mrs. Lovett stood behind the reception desk. Their clothes were wet, dirty, and disheveled, their faces were drawn and haggard. Walenburg was talking on the telephone explaining to someone why they couldn't stay at the hotel. Mrs. Lovett's attention was on a computer terminal in front of her. Her eyes flitted back and forth as she read the screen.

Benjamin Acorn looked up from the desk and spotted Sax and Cinnamon coming toward them. His soot-stained features paled and he patted Walenburg's arm frantically.

Walenburg covered the receiver with one hand. "Benji, cut it out. Can't you see I'm on the phone with an important client?"

Sax approached the desk and stood eyeing the concierge, one eyebrow arched, her lips a thin determined line.

"But, sir," pleaded Acorn.

Walenburg glanced at Sax then back to Acorn. "Tell me lat—
" He paused, his eyes widened and his face paled. He told whoever
was on the line to call back later then hung up.

He cleared his throat and forced a look of calm on his
features then smoothed his unruly hair with one trembling hand and
straightened his tie. "Miss Edwards," he said locking his eyes on
Sax. "How nice to see you again."

"Yeah, I'll bet," said Sax.

Walenburg winced and rolled his neck as if his collar were
too tight. Since the top button of his used-to-be-white shirt was
undone, and his navy blue tie hung loose, his collar was far from too
tight.

"Miss Edwards, on behalf of the Waldorf Astoria please
accept my apology for any inconvenience the fire may have caused
you."

Her eyes narrowed. "Someone said something about me,
didn't they?" He nodded uneasily. Inexplicably his eyes flitted to
Cinnamon who stood quietly behind her, then back at Sax.

Sax frowned and spun round to face Cinnamon. Her BFF
avoided Sax's accusatory stare, her face was flushed, and her eyes
brimmed with tears. "What did you do?" said Sax.

"A guy told me," Cinnamon said, her voice barely above a
whisper.

"Told you what?"

Cinnamon winced and a tear slipped out of her left eye to
travel down her cheek. Her lower lip trembled. "He said you had a
curse. So naturally I thought you started the fire. It's not your fault
you have a curse, after all." She shook her head.

Sax regarded her friend fighting back tears. "Uhhh, Cin how
do you know I have a curse?"

Cinnamon blinked. "Oh, a guy I met at one of the airports
we went through told me."

She was losing her patience for games. Grasping Cinnamon
by her shoulders, Sax smiled tightly. "One more question. Did this
guy have name?"

Cinnamon nodded. "Mr. Hopkins."

CHAPTER THIRTY-FIVE

BRYCE GROANED AS HIS EYES FLUTTERED OPEN and he was forced to cover his eyes with one hand to block out the sunshine. He lay on his back at the bottom of the canoe in a puddle of rain water. Every muscle in his body ached. The musty odor of wet clothes permeated his senses. He shivered.

He lifted his head and saw his father wasn't there. Elizabeth lay curled in a fetal position at the opposite end of the canoe. Her face was pale and her eyes were closed. Like him she was shivering and trembling. Her teeth were chattering and she was moaning softly.

He rolled over and rose to his knee then placed the back of one hand on her forehead. She's burning up.

He looked around in the fog. "Dad?" he said hoarsely.

Ah, there they are…Oops. Dad? Margaret? His father and Margaret were locked in a passionate embrace.

The world had finally gone mad. "I must be dead," he whispered. He moved his head up to peer over the edge of the canoe again and again he saw the two lovers in a private moment. Until now he hadn't realized his father still had it in him.

Suddenly there was an eruption of laughter. That tears it.

Now he knew he had died. Dad and Margaret had never, ever, ever laughed, at least not when they're in the same room.

A groan made him look at Elizabeth who opened one eye and moaned. Bryce was worried. She didn't look good.

Her face was pale and her teeth chattered.

"Dad," Bryce rose to a sitting position and realized the rain had penetrated clear through to his underwear. He shivered, but the warmth of the sun was already making a difference. Rolling his neck he stopped when a sharp pain shot through his neck. "Owww."

"Son?" He tried to look at his father but couldn't turn his head without a sharp pain. Placing his left hand on the side his neck he held it and managed to slowly turn enough one eye on his father.

"Hey, Dad," he smiled weakly and felt his face grow warm.

Walter, his arms around Margaret's waist, grinned. "You okay?"

Bryce wanted to nod, but decided it was best not to. "Yeah. I think so. A few strained muscles, and I'm a little cold."

"Aren't we all?" He looked at Margaret. "But a little body heat can go a long way, right honey?" She grinned, laughed and kissed him on his cheek.

Bryce winced. "Yeah. Right, Dad. Good point. But I don't think Elizabeth fared as well as we did."

The smile on Walter's face disappeared and he shuffled forward on the bench seat of the row boat to look at Elizabeth huddled in the bottom of the canoe. "Oh, oh. Maggie, look."

Margaret leaned over to look and the side of the row boat went lower and lower until the water neared the lip. Bryce winced and closed one eye. If the row boat went under, and the canoe was still tied to it, they'd all end up in the lake. No, no, no, no….

"Liz?" she said, shuffling forward and peering down at her sister's pale face in the bottom of the canoe.

Elizabeth turned her one open eye toward Margaret and mouthed, "Help me".

~~~

It wasn't twenty minutes later when a runabout appeared, planning across the lake at high speed. Behind the speeding boat was a rooster tail that sprayed out the stern as it cut through the water. Bryce stood up and braced his feet as wide apart as he could to maintain his balance then waved his arms above his head.

"Hey!"

Margaret had Elizabeth's head cradled in her lap and was rocking her gently, whispering to her. Elizabeth groaned softly, intermittently.

Walter sat in the row boat waving one arm above his head. He had his baby finger and index finger of his right hand in his mouth to emit a high pitched whistle.

Bryce saw there were two young people in the front seats of the speeding boat. It was about a fifteen foot long fiberglass hull with a black outboard motor attached to the stern. The driver was a teenage girl with blonde hair trailing in the breeze above her bare shoulders. On the passenger side sat a shirtless teenage boy with dark curly hair sporting a chestnut brown tan. They both wore dark sunglasses.

Just when it appeared they wouldn't see them the teenage boy pointed to them and the girl turned the wheel. The speeding boat sliced through the water, the bow now pointed at them.

Bryce sighed and dropped his arms to his sides. My curse hasn't killed anyone. Yet.

CHAPTER THIRTY-SIX

AT THE DOCK THE PARAMEDICS LIFTED ELIZABETH onto a stretcher and quickly rolled her to the ambulance. Bryce sat cross legged on the dock the blanket covering his head and upper body. He held the blanket tight around his neck with one hand. The paramedics wanted to take him to the hospital too, but he assured them once he got some hot coffee in him he'd be fine.

The boy and girl who rescued them were named Ricky and Tania. They were nice kids and had ferried them to shore when Bryce explained how sick Elizabeth was. On the way Tania called 911. The ambulance met them when the arrived at the dock.

After checking his vital signs the two men exchanged a worried glance but left him behind. Wally and Maggie (they were calling each other by their shortened given names now) drove away in Bryce's Mercedes, following the ambulance to the hospital.

"You okay, mister?" said Ricky.

Bryce glanced up at the teenager, offering him a weak smile. "I'll be okay. Thanks, Ricky." He looked around and didn't see Tania anywhere. "Is Tania okay?"

"Yeah. She took the boat back to her mom's so I'll have to walk home." A frown creased his brow. "Stuff like what happened to you is always happening to me."

Bryce eyed the boy. "Really?" He paused to consider how to question the boy about the curse. He may not realize he had a curse. It might frighten him. "Is the stuff that happens what you'd call bad?"

Ricky's eyes were wide as saucers. He nodded his head slowly. "Yeah. I'd call it bad. I guess. How do you know?"

Bryce smiled. "It's okay, Ricky." He sighed letting his shoulders slump. "Bad stuff happens to me too." Looking toward the house he saw a dog had appeared at the head of the ramp leading from the shore to the dock. It was a Golden Retriever if he knew his dogs. The dog wiggled the tip of its black nose and began to wag its tail vigorously. Its long pink tongue hung from the side of its wide mouth.

"That your dog?"

Ricky swiveled his head to look at the dog. He shook his head. "Nope. Not me. Mom and Dad would never allow me to have a dog. Too messy. Too expensive. And too much trouble."

The bitterness in his voice made Bryce smile inside. It was refreshing to be around someone so young. It surprised him a boy Ricky's age could wear his feelings on his sleeve so openly. Nice kid. Too bad for him he had the curse.

"You want to come inside and get a soda?" He flapped his arms as if they were wings. "I gotta get changed anyway. And my dad and step-mother will be gone for a while."

The boy looked doubtful. Bryce chuckled. "I'll drive you home later. Besides, you're the first neighbor I've met." He held out his hand. "We should be formally introduced. I'll go first. Name's Bryce Kelly, nice to meet you."

The boy's expression softened and he took Bryce's hand in his and shook it. "Nice to meet you too, Mr. Kelly. My name's Richard Boone." His chestnut tanned face broke into a wide grin. "Everyone calls me Ricky."

"Okay, Ricky. Call me Bryce and help me up. My legs are Jell-O right now."

~~~

Once they were inside the house he got Ricky an orange soda from the fridge then went to the bathroom to have a hot shower and afterward put on some warm clothes. Before he left the room he started a pot of coffee.

179

Ricky and he agreed to bring the dog inside and try to find the owner.

After the hot shower, and after donning thick sweat pants and a heavy wool, long sleeved sweat shirt, Bryce returned to the living room. He rubbed his hands together. He was finally starting to feel warm again.

The dog, Ricky temporarily named him Max, sat curled at Ricky's feet on the deck over looking the placid, sky blue water. As Bryce stepped out on the deck through the French door, a warm breeze carrying the scent of pine and birch filled his nostrils with earthy smells.

He blinked as his eyesight adjusted to the sunlight and wondered how such a beautiful setting had suddenly become so deadly last night.

Pushing the thought of near disaster away he took a sip of the rich, dark coffee from the red and gold 49'ers mug he'd snagged on his way out.

The deck contained a patio table with an umbrella, surrounded by four padded chairs and four handmade unvarnished pine deck chairs. Ricky sat in one of the deck chairs. Bryce padded barefoot to a vacant deck chair next to Ricky and sat down, setting his coffee mug on the wide chair arm.

He winced and lifted his right butt cheek off the seat. Using his thumb and index finger he yanked out a long sliver of wood from his cheek. Bringing it up to study it he saw the sharp tip was red with his blood.

He looked at Ricky. "Story of our lives, wouldn't you say?"

Ricky showed him a similar sliver and nodded. "Yeah, I guess so, Mr. Kelly."

"Please call me Bryce."

The boy looked hesitant, but nodded. They sat in silence for several moments listening to the gentle lap of the water against the shore. A loon made itself known. The bird's lonely cry echoed across the lake.

Ricky took an urgent sip from his can of soda, swallowed, then set it back on the chair arm. "Huh, Mr...I mean, Bryce, how do you know so much about my problem?"

"Well, Ricky, I've had the same problem, as you call it, since before I was your age." He sighed. "I've always been afraid to tell anyone." He took another sip of warm coffee. "That is until recently when I learned my father knew all about it. Though we've never talked about it."

Ricky looked at him, his brow wrinkled in confusion.

"I'm sorry," he hesitated, avoiding saying Bryce's name again. It obviously made the teenager uncomfortable to use an adult's given name.

This boy was raised right, thought Bryce. "It's okay, Ricky you can call me Mr. Kelly if it makes you more comfortable."

Ricky grinned sheepishly. "Sorry, Mr. Kelly." Bryce smiled warmly. The boy continued, "I wanted to say I'm confused. How did your father know about your problem if you never told anyone?"

"Because it's all about heredity, the problem is not a disease, or because you did anything wrong, or anything you can fix." I wish it was that easy.

Ricky's features relaxed and he eased back in the chair, resting his arms flat on the chair arms. Bryce could almost see the wheels churning in the young intelligent eyes. Finally a look of peace came over the boy's face, as if a great weight had suddenly been lifted from his shoulders.

Suddenly Ricky frowned. "What's heredity mean?"

Before he could stop himself, Bryce chuckled. Seeing the hurt in Ricky's eyes he immediately regretted it. "I'm sorry, Ricky I didn't mean to laugh at you." He'd forgotten teenagers were awash in insecurity. "Heredity means the problem was passed down to you through your genes." The confused look in Ricky's eyes made Bryce wonder if they taught the kids anything about science in school these days.

"What I'm saying is your father, mother, grandfather or grandmother had the same problem and they passed it down to you." He shook his head. "They didn't mean to pass it to you. It just happened."

"Oh," said the boy, "you mean like my Opa. You must know Mr. Hopkins."

"Opa?"

Ricky grinned. "Opa is Dutch for grandfather." Bryce nodded. "Anyway, my grandfather Van Houten, my dad's father, he came here from Holland after World War Two. People always said he's the unluckiest man who ever lived."

"He's dead?"

Ricky shook his head. "Nope. He's in prison."

"Oh." Bryce thought for a second then said, "This Mr. Hopkins, who is he?"

CHAPTER THIRTY-SEVEN

"Mr. Hopkins?" Sax said, surprised Cinnamon had spoken to the strange man on the bus to the Portland Airport. When did she talk to him?

Sax could see the fear in Cinnamon's eyes. She must think I'm mad at her, which I'm not.

"Sax, you're still my BFF, but I just can't be seen with a firebug. It's bad for my image. Someone might think I had something to do with starting the fire. Me? A Wolthorp." She shook her head and chuckled. "Can you believe it?"

Sax smiled then glanced at Benji. "What does BFF mean?"

Benji's eyes were wide as saucers. "Binary File Format?" he croaked.

Cinnamon snorted. "Gamer geek."

Sax eyed her and Cinnamon avoided Sax's glare. Sax shifted her gaze to Walenburg. "What about you, Walenburg, do you know?"

The concierge's soot-stained brow wrinkled in concentration and his eyes narrowed. "Yes, Miss," he said slowly, "it means Boston Film Festival."

Cinnamon snorted again. "Movie fan."

Sax regarded Cinnamon despairingly. "Okay, Cin. Why don't you enlighten all of us, what does BFF mean?" The workmen in their white coveralls working to clean up the fire damage and remove the water-stained furniture froze.

Silence descended like the curtain of a Broadway show with bad reviews. Now all eyes in the smoky lobby were fixed on her.

"It means best-friends-forever," blurted one of the workmen. The other workmen turned and stared at him. "My kid's a Facebook freak, what can I tell ya."

"Huh, thanks," Sax said. Best friends? She says we're best friends and yet she still thinks I'm a firebug? Some best friend she is.

The man smiled at her then went back to sawing a leather sofa in half. The others glanced at each other then went back to work as well. The buzz of activity started around them again.

It was time to set things straight. Sax moved closer to Cinnamon in order to whisper, "I think we have a lot to talk about."

Cinnamon nodded, her eyes wide with fear.

~~~

They sat at a round pink table at a trendy coffee shop on East 49th Street, not far from Saks Fifth Avenue. Cinnamon said Barista's Coffee Boutique was the place to be seen and the place where Manhattan's most influential and powerful elite hung out.

Looking around Sax hardly thought a gray haired lady wearing curlers in her hair, and an old man with Basset hound eyes were the elite of New York City, but since she'd never been in New York City how would she know. Actually it was a good thing the elite were going elsewhere, at least for today anyway, given the state of their clothes and hair.

Cinnamon was right about one thing, the coffee was good. The warm mix of perfectly brewed coffee and cream went down smooth.

"Cinnamon," she began then paused upon detecting the hurt in her friend's eyes. She couldn't help but feel sorry for her friend. Her curse had put them both through the coffee grinder on this trip. I can't blame her for thinking my curse had something to do with the fire. Even I think that.

Sax smiled thinly. "Cin, where did you meet with Mr. Hopkins?" she asked, keeping her tone as neutral as possible.

Cinnamon's hands were wrapped around the pink coffee mug and she blew air across the surface of her latté to cool it off. White foam coated her upper lip. She slowly raised her head, her fingers still wrapped around the cup.

The large picture window to their left was streaked with wind blown rain. After they arrived the skies opened up and a heavy rain had started. Thunder echoed between the steel and glass towers. People rushed by the window with briefcases and folded newspapers covering their heads.

Now I'm the bad weather fairy. But at least she hadn't killed anyone, yet.

Cinnamon cleared her throat. "Uhhh, I met him at the airport."

"Portland?" said Sax.

Cinnamon shook her head. "Miami," she said simply.

Miami? The Albatross Air flight landed there after the attempted sky jacking by a ten year old boy with what turned out to be a toy ray gun. Sax shook her head and chuckled at the memory of the boy holding the crew hostage and the air marshal trying to talk him down. A chubby ten year old on a chocolate and soda high is a terrible thing to witness.

That'll teach the airline to run in flight movies about alien invasions.

Hold on. She thought that man at the Miami airport looked familiar. "He was at the coffee stand, wasn't he?"

Cinnamon's lower lip stuck out, reminding her of a pouty child. "Yes," she whispered. Her eyes flitted to the people rushing by on the street. A rain-drowned dog walker went by, her black hair pasted to her narrow head like a glove, the dogs yelping and whimpering.

How did Mr. Hopkins know they were going to be at the Miami airport, and how did he get there from Oregon?

Cinnamon certainly wouldn't have the answers to these questions. Sax leaned forward, resting her elbows on the table. "What did he tell you about me, exactly?"

Cinnamon, her eyes fixed on her cup, said Mr. Hopkins told her Sax was cursed.

185

She didn't believe him, until Hopkins showed her pictures of Sax as a child being chased by giant crabs on a rocky beach, and another of her being carried aloft by a handful of multi-colored balloons. In both pictures Sax was crying, her face squished and tears running down her cheeks. Cinnamon looked at Sax in awe.

"Are those pictures for real?" Cinnamon said. "Did those things really happen?" she added.

How did Mr. Hopkins get those pictures? Sax nodded. "Yes, I remember. There was a freak wind funnel that dropped giant crabs onto the beach at Mississinewa Lake when I was five. They chased me for an hour before they gave up. They were some mad crustaceans." She looked wistful and shook her head at the memory. "That was the best family picnic ever.

"The great balloon ride happened at the Indiana State Fair when I was eight. A clown had an itch that needed scratched, without thinking he handed me his big bunch of helium filled balloons. I floated away and ended up hovering over the Pepsi Coliseum until a nearby giant hot air balloon racer floated over and rescued me." Sax snorted again. "I really had to hold the balloon strings tight let me tell you."

"You're kidding," said Cinnamon, her jaw hung open and her eyes were wide.

Sax smiled. "Nope, 'fraid not. Bad luck follows me where ever I go."

Cinnamon's cheeks flushed. "Then you did start the fire?"

Sax frowned. "Of course not. That's ridiculous." A soft smile played over Sax's lips. Sax wrapped her fingers around the cup then lifted it to her lips. She took a loud slurp then set it back on the table. "But I was only a few floors away from where it started."

"Do you have a range?" asked Cinnamon, her eyes now wide as saucers.

Sax chuckled. "Not that I know of." She paused as a frown creased her brow. "I wonder if the government could use me as a weapon. People like me would be perfect as weapons of mass destruction. The possibilities are endless. Imagine North Korea brought to its knees because of bad luck." She smiled. "We would change the world order."

"There are others like you?"

Sax nodded. "Mr. Hopkins said Glad Beach is crawling with my kind."

"Wow." Cinnamon looked at her in awe then her expression shifted to a frown. "But then who is Mr. Hopkins? And how does he know this stuff?"

Sax crossed her arms in her lap and eased her back against the padded chair back. It surprised her she hadn't thought of this earlier.

Cinnamon Wolthorp was an amazing woman capable of identifying the central question that had been niggling at the back of her brain since she met him.

Yeah, who was Hopkins, really? It bothered her she had more questions than answers.

"I have no idea," Sax said finally.

CHAPTER THIRTY-EIGHT

SAX'S FATHER, JACK, EAGERLY AGREED TO COME TO BRYCE'S HOUSE to pick up him and Ricky, and drive Ricky home. Right now Bryce didn't trust himself to drive anyone anywhere. He knew he was growing increasingly paranoid with Ricky in the car with him. *I'd never forgive myself if anything happened to the kid.*

And it would give me a chance to talk to Jack alone and find out more about him. He was Sax's father, after all, and since he had grown to care about her he knew he had to get to know her family a little better.

Jack stopped the '50's era Land Rover on the driveway to the sound of squeaking brakes and the crunch of gravel. The passenger door flew open as the jeep-like vehicle came to a stop. The door hinges squealed in protest. The ancient diesel engine made the steel frame rattle and shake until Jack turned the engine off. It ran on for several seconds until, with a loud pop, it stopped but not before there was a final violent tremble through the vehicle's frame.

Whoa! That's something.

Jack was seated on the left side behind the oversized steering wheel. He smiled at them through the dirty windshield. *Funny, I thought English cars were all right hand drive.*

"Hey, lads." Jack's ruddy complexion was split by a wide toothy grin.

"Hi, Jack," said Bryce. Placing one hand on Ricky's shoulder he introduced the teenager, "This is Ricky O'Malley. He lives on Squidrider Street. Do you know it?"

Jack's grey eyes narrowed as he stared at the boy one grey eyebrow raised on his sun-wrinkled forehead. "He old enough?" he said with an easy smile.

Oh, oh. Here he goes again into eccentricville. "Old enough for what, Jack?"

"To be your love child, of course," he said as if it were obvious.

Bryce laughed, but stopped when he saw Ricky's tanned features had a bright crimson tinge to them. He stared at Bryce. "It's okay, Ricky. Jack's only kidding."

He helped the boy clamber into the middle seat next to Jack. There were three well-worn army-green seats all next to each other. Behind the row of seats was a flat bed, Jack no doubt used it to transport the treasures for sale at his shop. A weathered canvas top acted as the roof. If the rays of sunlight coming through the top were any indication then the roof would do little to protect the occupants from inclement weather.

"Kidding?" said Jack with quizzical expression on his haggard face. "About what?"

"It's a joke. Like a Monty Python skit, Jack." One thing Bryce had learned about Jack was when he was in eccentricville you had to play by the eccentric's rules. Even if it sounded a little loopy. Bryce grinned and slapped Jack on the shoulder. He was beginning to appreciate how Bertie handled him.

Jack laughed. "Yeah. I love those guys." He turned the key in the ignition and the diesel rattled to life. I think I'm beginning to understand Jack a little. I like him.

Once the door was closed Jack shifted the Land Rover into first with a nerve shattering grinding noise, then the engine roared and they jerked forward snapping everyone's heads back. Bryce gripped the window frame beside him to hold the door shut.

"Whoa," said Bryce as the wide tires kicked up a cloud of dust that quickly enveloped the truck's interior. Ricky began to cough.

Jack roared with glee as the old truck roared and groaned into a sharp turn in the driveway and they headed for the paved highway back to Glad Beach.

"This is a '50 original," he said shouting over the unmuffled engine, the gravel crunching under the tires as they bounced up and down on the barely padded seat.

"Hey, Jack, take it easy. I need my butt," said Bryce. He smiled because he couldn't help but love the ride. Sure beats roller coasters.

It's no wonder the Brits loved these things. People paid good money for a bone-crunching amusement park rides and they were getting one for free.

Jack steered the swaying truck around a couple of deep potholes. The back end slewed back and forth, but the Land Rover managed to stay on the road.

"So, Bruce, how's the brothel biz working out for ya?" asked Jack, his eyes fixed on the driveway ahead.

Ricky glanced at Bryce, his eyes wide with wonder. Bryce offered the boy a half smile. "He thinks I'm a pimp for some reason," he said to Ricky in a low voice so Jack wouldn't hear. "I'm not."

Jack glanced over at Ricky then his eyes flitted back to the road as he steered around another bend in the road. The truck tipped onto its side to balance on two wheels. "Hey!" Ricky emitted a terrified yell.

The truck dangled in space for what seemed an eternity, then crashed down on all four wheels and surged ahead again as if it were a wild animal. Gravel pinged off the truck's under carriage then shot out into the trees on both sides of the road.

"You like ice cream?" he said to Ricky.

"Oh, c'mon, Jack, he's sixteen not six," said Bryce. Not that he knew Ricky's age but he was a teenager.

Ricky leaned closer to Bryce and whispered in his ear. "I'm fifteen." Bryce looked at the boy and smiled. Ricky grinned.

"Huh, yeah I like ice cream," said Ricky responding to Jack's question.

Bryce rolled his eyes. This oughtta be good.

~~~

The three of them walked into Peter's Ice Cream with Jack in the lead. During the twenty minute drive from Bryce's house to the ice cream shop Jack regaled Ricky non-stop with the illustrious history of the Land Rover.

"And that's why Gerry was defeated during the North African campaign in '43," Jack was saying as they arrived at the counter.

Peter's Ice Cream was an institution in Glad Beach. The owner, Mark Owen was the great grandson of the founder, Moses Owen. Moses arrived on the Oregon coast in 1891 and starting making ice cream in 1919. When he opened the shop, under the name Moses' Ice Cream, he sold four flavors; vanilla, chocolate, strawberry, and caramel swirl.

Caramel swirl made his shop famous all the way from Portland to San Francisco. When tourism flourished in the 1920's and city dwellers began to escape the summer heated cities, they flocked to the sandy beaches and ocean breezes along the Oregon Coast. Moses' ice cream shop became more and more renowned with each passing year. And each year he began to experiment with new flavors. He asked his summer customers to judge the new flavors. This culminated in the Labor Day fair when one new flavor would win an ice cream eating contest sponsored by Moses Owen. He didn't actually add every flavor his customers said were good, but the contest was fun and everyone enjoyed it.

By the outbreak of World War II he was selling fifteen flavors, in addition to the four originals. By this time the flavors ranged from licorice to crème de menthe. During the war, for reasons lost to the mists of time, he changed the name of his shop to his son Peter's name. Peter assumed control of the shop in 1946 and the rest is, as they say, history.

Today the freezer cases contained twenty seven different ice cream flavors that were alternated with new flavors every three months.

Jack walked to the counter and nodded to the cases.

"Hey, Mitch," Jack smiled at the pasty faced man. The worker's dirty blond hair stuck out like wings from beneath the brim of his paper hat. The white and black name tag over his left shirt pocket read, MARK.

The man's eyes gazed at Jack and a slow frown creased his brow. "Jack?"

"Yeah. I'm back. Isn't it great?" He waved one hand at Ricky and Bryce. "These are my friends, Robby and Buck."

Mark scowled at Bryce then he shifted his gaze to Ricky then back to Bryce. "Sorry," Bryce whispered, "Jack is a little eccentric."

"A little?"

Bryce chuckled then put on his best nice–to-meet-you smile and said in his normal voice, "Hi, Mark. I'm Bryce and this lad is Ricky."

The scowl eased on the ice cream man's features, but he raised one eyebrow and eyed them skeptically. "How come he calls me something different every time he comes into the shop?" He tipped his head at Jack who had his face near the glass of the ice cream display case. The look on Jack's face was the same expression that could be found on a child who had never seen so many ice cream flavors before. Jack pointed at a round container of green ice cream, "Hey Mick, what's that flavor?"

"Pistachio," said Mark raising his voice. He lowered his voice and looked at Bryce. "That woman isn't with him is she?" There was a hint of fear in his tone.

Bryce's mouth formed a lopsided grin. "Nope. Just us." I think he means Sax. Something must have happened in here with her that scared him. I hope she's okay wherever she is right now. He winced. And Cinnamon too, of course.

He couldn't help it but he couldn't get her out of his mind and it made him feel guilty. I should be concerned about my fiancée.

"And that?" Jack asked eager as a child.

"Licorice," grunted Mark. He looked at Ricky. "What do ya want, kid?"

Ricky glanced uneasily at Bruce who nodded then shifted his eyes to the ice cream man. "Thank you, sir. I'll have strawberry, please."

Bryce was impressed with Ricky. His parents had evidently done a wonderful job raising him. The boy was so well mannered. He reminded Bryce of himself at his age. Fifteen was a tough age and more so when you were cursed.

192

Jack spun to his left to face Bryce. "You gonna have sumthin'?"

Bryce shook his head. "No, thanks. I've got to watch my waistline." He patted his stomach. He glanced at his watch. "Jack, can we go soon? I should get to the hospital to see if Elizabeth's okay."

Jack dismissed him with a wave of his hand. "Don't be silly, Bart. Marty. Give him two scoops." He eyed the case. "One scoop of Monkey Blood, the other of Cotton Mouth." He stroked the tip of his chin with long fingers. "I'll have a scoop of the licorice and," he paused, "chocolate hazelnut."

Jack smiled as Mark worked his magic with an ice cream scoop.

Mark handed a cone stacked with two scoops of ice cream to each of them after Bryce paid. He hoped Monkey's Blood didn't contain real blood, and cotton mouth didn't taste like the inside of his mouth after a bad nights sleep.

They walked out the front door to the chime of the twinkly bell over the door. The sun had risen high in the sky now and Bryce estimated it was somewhere near eleven o'clock. There were a few cars and pickup trucks moving up and down the street and the shops were busy with locals running their errands.

They stood on the sidewalk licking their cones. "Say, Jack, tell me about Sax."

"What ya wanta know?"

"Why doesn't she have a boyfriend?"

Jack chuckled then took a bite of the licorice ice cream. "She has bad luck."

Bryce raised one eyebrow. Bad luck? What did he mean? "With men you mean?"

Jack shook his head. "Nope. With everything."

Bryce looked at Ricky and they exchanged puzzled looks. Bryce's gut twisted and his heart rate increased. It couldn't be. Or could it? Was it possible Sax had the same curse?

Jack was unreliable so he decided to question Bertie about Sax's bad luck. He had to know more about her. If they had this in common it would explain a lot.

He had a weird hope she was cursed and it made him feel guilty.

His shirt pocket vibrated signaling he had an incoming call on his cell phone.

"Hold this, please," he said to Ricky as he handed his ice cream cone to the boy. He retrieved his cell from the shirt pocket and flipped it open. He noticed the number was his father's cell phone. Oh, oh I hope this isn't bad news. It was his father's phone number.

Raising it to his ear he said, "Hello, Dad?"

As if in a dream he listened to his father words. Finally he said, "Okay, Dad. I'll be right there." He closed the phone.

"Something wrong?" said Ricky. Melting ice cream trailed down his fists then dripped off to land in splotches on the sidewalk.

With trembling fingers Bryce stuffed his cell into his shirt pocket and frowned. It was as if his stomach had fallen into his shoes. "Yeah," he whispered. "I think I may have finally killed someone."

His life had suddenly spun out of control and there was nothing he could do about it.

CHAPTER THIRTY-NINE

THEY HAD TO GET OUT OF NEW YORK before any more damage occurred. Correction: before I do any more damage, thought Sax.

It had only been a day and a half since they left Glad Beach but that was long enough to know she had to get home.

Sax looked out the window of the bus at the sea of white clouds hovering over the magnificent Pacific Ocean.

The bus pulled into the parking lot of the hotel where their trip started just as the sun sunk below the horizon. It seemed to disappear into the ocean swells that streamed toward the sandy shore. Sax look up and spotted two gulls, their wings spread wide, floating on updrafts caused by the change in temperature, as the last of the daylight gave way to the night. The edges of the horizon were gold and purple, tinged with orange and traces of fiery red.

Sax sighed. Whatever. But still it was good to be home. She had traveled enough. What started as an adventure had ended in disaster. And she never completed her mission for Bryce. Could it be any worse?

How could I think this trip would end well? What an idiot I am.

Still, she wondered how Hopkins could be in so many places so far apart. Who was he? And why did he know so much about her? There were too many questions and not enough answers.

Her heart skipped a beat when she spotted a figure leaning back against the grill of his Hummer with his hands in the pockets of his blue jeans. She recognized Bryce's grin when he spotted the airport bus. Sax nudged Cinnamon who snored softly in the seat next to her.

"Bryce," she said simply, her voice gentle. Her heart pounded in her chest at the sight of Bryce.

He looks happy to see us.

"Ummm," said Cinnamon, raising her head, her eyes unfocussed. "Who?"

"Bryce. It's Bryce," said Sax. "He's here to pick us up. He must've gotten the message we left for him when we called from JFK."

"That's nice," said Cinnamon dreamily. She curled her knees to her chest in a tight ball and closed her eyes again.

Sax gazed at her BFF. Poor woman was worn out. She sighed heavily. Just like everyone who traveled with her.

The bus lurched to a stop under the canopy that protected the twin glass doors of the hotel lobby from rain. The driver, a tall, rail-thin man with grey hair and lifeless brown eyes, stood up. He was forced to stoop slightly to save his head from striking the ceiling.

"Glad Beach Hotel," he said, his voice flat, dull, and difficult to describe. He stepped out the open door.

There was no point in waking her yet. Sax crawled around the still sleeping Cinnamon and shuffled down the aisle to the door. The distinct smell of salt carried on the breeze from the ocean filled her senses and comforted her. She stepped off the last step to the cement pad and took in a deep breath.

"Hey, Sax," said Bryce, his hands still in the pockets of his blue jeans, his head slumped, his wide shoulders stooped as her walked toward her. Her stomach muscles tightened. She realized she missed him more than she realized. He looked positively yummy.

"Hi, Bryce," she licked her dry lips. He stood beside her now, his dark eyes dull. She didn't know what else to say to him.

The sound of the driver busy at the back unloading bags filled the silence between them.

A middle aged woman with mouse brown hair and a pinched face disembarked from the bus with her young daughter in tow. Glaring at Sax, who smiled thinly, the woman disappeared to the rear of the bus, one hand wrapped tightly around her daughter's smaller hand. The little blond girl's eyes shone brightly at Sax and Bryce as she passed them.

Was it my fault she got stuck in the gas station washroom and the driver drove away without her? Sax would have thought the girl's mother would have stayed awake to keep an eye on her own daughter. I can't control my curse, but I wish I could.

Her eyes filled with tears. She wanted to tell Cinnamon she loved him but couldn't do it. She'd failed him but Cinnamon was her friend now and Sax couldn't hurt her.

Bryce watched the woman disappear round the back of the bus. "Problem?" he said, shifting his gaze to Sax.

"No, of course not." Sax turned away to hide the fact she was about to start crying. "Sorry. Things have been a little stressful lately."

"You can say that again."

Sax wiped her eyes with the back of her hand. "Things have been a little stressful lately for you too?"

Bryce laughed and Sax chucked.

"Yeah. I'm as welcome around here as the plague." Sax pointed to the woman and her daughter as they came round the end of the bus. The mother glared at her. The woman frowned, harrumphed then disappeared once again. The bus driver, a thin smile playing over his bloodless lips, disappeared after them. The girl smiled at them until an adult-size hand grabbed her arm and dragged her out of sight. Before she disappeared she waved.

Isn't she cute. Sax and Bryce looked at each other until, like a release valve, their tension broke. They laughed together until tears rolled down their cheeks. Sax's sides ached.

Finally the laughter subsided and they both gasped for breath. She'd needed a good laugh. Bryce Kelly was sure a good guy. She hoped he still liked her after he discovered she failed him, but she doubted he would. Their growing friendship was about to end.

"Hey," said a sleepy voice. Cinnamon exited the bus.

She wobbled and looked about to collapse when Bryce rushed to her side and wrapped a strong arm around her slender waist. She seemed to melt into him.

"Thank you, honey," she said in a soft voice. She smiled sweetly at him and sighed. Sax's heart beat faster. *Cin really cares for the man I love.*

As if a dream had ended where she and Bryce would suddenly fall into each others arms and declare their undying love for each other, she came crashing to back to reality. They were still going to be married and there was nothing she could do about it.

Bryce looked at Sax. "Luggage?"

Sax shook her head. "Long story." Surprisingly Bryce nodded then half carried, half dragged Cinnamon toward his Hummer.

Sax followed them. *Odd.* He didn't seem at all surprised they were such a mess—she ran a hand through her tangled hair—and that they had no luggage.

Bryce settled Cinnamon into the passenger seat and closed the door, then he turned toward her. "You can ride in the back," he said then added, "if that's okay."

"Sure," she said.

"Say, did you tell her about us?" He winked. He leaned closer and she detected the scent of his aftershave. He smelled of mint and orange, her favorites. It reminded her of summer. His voice lowered to a whisper, "About our love?"

"No, sorry. The opportunity never presented itself."

His brow wrinkled slightly. "Uhhh, too bad." His features brightened and he grinned. "Oh, well you can tell her later today."

"Yeah, sure." She wondered if she would ever get out of this mess. Trapped with no escape. She hoped he was telling her the truth when he said she didn't really want to marry him, or she'd sound like a complete moron.

Bryce opened the rear passenger door and held it open for her until she was seated in the truck's back seat.

"I really love this truck," Sax said, changing the subject as Bryce climbed in behind the steering wheel.

"Thanks. Cin says I have to sell it after we're married. Want to buy it?"

"No, sorry. My budget would die of shock."

His eyes smiled at her in the rearview mirror and he chuckled, sending a shiver of passion through her. The curse was breaking her heart. She was desperately in love with a man already spoken for.

"If we were together I'd let you keep it," she whispered softly.

"You say something?" he said.

"No. Sorry."

Bryce started the truck. The engine came to life with a soft purr and a slight vibration.

This truck sure beat the piece-o'-crap her father drove.

Sax's eyes flitted to the sleeping Cinnamon in the passenger seat then back to the rearview mirror. "Yeah, that makes sense." Not. She crossed her arms and eased back letting the soft leather envelop her.

~~~

They were almost to Sax's house when both tires on the right side blew at the same time. What the...? Does my curse ever take a day off? She gripped the door handle beside her as the heavy truck swayed side to side.

Bryce managed to wrestle the Hummer to the side of the highway. A pickup truck behind him honked its horn and the driver waved his fist as he swept past them. Sax scowled at the truck as it shot by and disappeared round a bend in the highway.

"What's the matter with him?" she said. "Hasn't he ever seen a flat tire before?"

Bryce sighed and stepped out the driver's side door without looking first. Sax swiveled her head to see what was coming from behind in time to see a large motor home bearing down on them. "Hey, Bryce! Watch out!"

Bryce looked up and broke into a run leaving the door open behind him.

He dove around the front bumper of the Hummer where Sax lost sight of him. There was a sharp scream of air brakes being hit too hard as the motor home swerved and swayed back and forth on the two lane highway out of control. It struck the truck's driver's side door with a loud bang.

The Hummer's door broke away with the rending sound of steel hinges breaking loose. The door crashed and banged as it struck the pavement in front of the massive motor home's bumper. It then skittered across the pavement leaving behind a cascade of sparks and disappeared beneath the massive vehicle accompanied by the sounds of breaking glass and tortured metal. A shower of yellow sparks flew out from under the motor home until, with a loud bang, the mangled door shot out the back. The odor of burnt rubber filled the air.

Sax winced as cars and trucks skidded off the road, or changed to the other side of the highway to avoid hitting the car in front of them. Horns blared and angry voices mingled in a roar of surprised indignation.

Sax got out and peered up and down the highway. Vehicles of all sizes and descriptions were scattered like seeds in both directions, but no one appeared to have been hit except Bryce's car. Wow, that was scary. Her heart had been beating fast but now began to slow as she realized no one appeared to be injured.

"Good thing no one was hurt," she said to herself.

"Yeah," said a voice behind her.

She turned around to face a grinning Bryce. She resisted the urge to leap on him and hold him forever. He wasn't dead, thank God.

The sleeve of his leather jacket was torn from elbow to shoulder and his chin had an angry gash across it, blood dripping from the tip of his chin. His right cheek was scraped and bloody from impact with the gravel shoulder.

"Bryce! You're hurt," Sax took a step toward him but stopped before she could wrap her arms around him. Her eyes filled with tears.

He opened his mouth to say something but Cinnamon interrupted him.

"Bryce? Hurt?" came sleepy voice from the passenger side of the Hummer. The door swung open and Cinnamon stepped out. She yawned, scratched her head absently. Her eyes were slits. She looked around at the mayhem of vehicles scattered up and down the highway in both directions, parked at odd angles, then swiveled her head and fixed her sleepy gaze on the motor home sitting lopsided straddling the center line in the middle of the road. The two tires on the right side had burst in all the excitement so the Hummer sagged to the right.

"Did I miss something?"

CHAPTER FORTY

SHERIFF CONSTITUTION TIPPED BACK HIS COWBOY HAT with one finger and whistled softly. A wooden toothpick rolled in one side of his mouth. He stood by the sagging motor home after examining the blown tires.

Bryce sat on the tail gate of the ambulance while the paramedics cleaned his wounds and applied bandages to his cheek and chin. Fortunately the tear in his leather jacket hadn't reached through his shirt underneath. Other than a few scrapes and bruised ribs he was fine.

A wave of nausea washed over her. The paramedic told her this might happen. Sax's stomach tightened and she thought she'd throw up any second. "Shock has after effects," he explained, "nausea, vomiting, headaches are common."

What concerned her more than anything was the accident might be her fault. She coughed and the sour taste of bile filled her mouth but she managed not to vomit. She might have killed them all.

Still in the driver's seat of the Hummer, her elbows resting on her knees, she watched Deputy Dobbs and Izzy work the accident scene. Dobbs grunted as he pounded wooden stakes into the ground then ran yellow police tape around everything. Izzy was directing traffic around the motor home. The Hummer's crumpled, scarred door lay at the side of the road surrounded by yellow tape.

"What do you think?" It was Cinnamon from the passenger side of car. "I'm glad Bryce is okay, but then he usually is."

"I think this is one big mess." Bryce was usually okay? What does she mean by that?

"Yeah, I know. Stuff like this happens all the time to my Bryce."

"What do you mean?"

"What?" said Cinnamon grumpily.

"About Bryce. Stuff happening to him all the time. What stuff?"

Cinnamon waved a dismissive hand at Sax. "I don't know. Nothing." She closed her eyes and pulled her legs up into her chest. "He doesn't like to talk about it," she said.

Cin wasn't gonna be any help, but Sax knew better than anyone what she was talking about. It wasn't like Bryce had the same problem with bad luck as her, but the accident was clearly her fault not Bryce's. Unless he did? Sax smiled to herself. What a ridiculous idea.

The paramedic had just finished bandaging Bryce's wound and was handing him a package of pills she presumed were pain killers.

Sax got out of the truck and walked toward him.

Upon seeing her coming toward him Bryce's mouth formed a sly smile. A strange warmth tingled below her waist. Just because he was engaged it didn't mean she couldn't dream. But why was she torturing herself like this?

"Hey, Bryce. Can I talk to you for a minute?" Sax said, walking to stand next to the ambulance.

She cringed inside when he winced and his right hand went to his rib cage. His ribs must have taken a beating when he dove for cover.

"Sure," he said with a grimace. "What's up?"

Sax sat down on the tailgate of ambulance next to him. He reeked of antiseptic cleaner. She gazed into his now puzzled blue eyes.

"Cinnamon said you have a problem," she said letting the sentence hang without further explanation.

His eyes shifted to one side then back at her. "Problem? What problem?"

Touché pal, but it's not gonna work. "I think you know what I'm talking about."

His chin dropped to his chest. "Owww." He raised his head and gazed at her. His eyes brimmed with resignation.

"You've outed me," he said simply.

Sax blinked and chuckled. "You're gay?"

He laughed. "No. No. I'm not gay. The truth is I have the bad luck of the Irish."

Sax snorted. "Now you're just making fun of me because I have bad luck sometimes." She placed her hands flat on the ambulance's tail gate on either side of his thighs boxing him in.

"No, I'm not, Sax." He paused. "Listen, you're my friend right?"

Sax nodded because he was her friend and because her feelings for him had grown deeper than she thought possible. I can't help it I've fallen in love with him. She wanted to lean in and kiss him but held back for fear he'd reject her.

Long ago she had concluded a true relationship with any man was impossible. Her curse made it impossible. Every time she got close to a man something happened that scared them away.

Her first boyfriend in high school, Kelly Winterbourne, had been the star basketball player until he fell and broke his ankle in three places during the State Championship game. The Big Soda— grape, sixty-seven ounces—she spilled on the court wasn't her fault. Amy Snog had bumped her elbow when she jumped up to cheer on the team.

Of course, Kelly blamed her for losing the game, and ending his budding basketball career. Last she heard of him he was an insurance executive in Cincinnati with a wife and four kids. He'd done okay.

If she revealed her true feelings for Bryce now something bad would happen to him for sure. Her eyes flitted to the motor home now on the hook of a tow truck about to be towed away.

That motor home could easily have squished him into pulp. She had to bury her feelings for him and make sure he married Cinnamon. She had to keep him safe because she had feelings for him.

But Cinnamon was a woman of the world, far more knowledgeable about the finer things in life than Sax would ever be.

Saxony Edwards, a small town single girl, a spinster who'd never been kissed. The curse would ensure she stayed alone for the rest of her life. But she could be friends with a man, in particular this man. Friends, but nothing more. Ever.

An arm came across her shoulders followed by a hug. "You okay?" Bryce said, his voice thick with concern.

"No. I'm fine." Sax pressed her hand into his side. He groaned and grabbed his side. She yanked her hand away as if it were on fire. Oh no! She didn't mean to hurt him.

Sax drew in a breath and her eyes filled with tears. "Bryce! I'm so sorry. I hurt you."

"No," he gasped between gritted teeth. He held up one hand when she leaned toward him and was about to hug him again. "Please don't. I can't take anymore." He grinned weakly. She leaned back and her cheeks grew warm.

He drew in a breath and winced. "Sax, I have a problem and I think I know how to fix it."

CHAPTER FORTY-ONE

WALLY KELLY ARRIVED AT THE ACCIDENT SCENE driving a flint-grey Mercedes sedan after Bryce called him on his cell phone. Maggie sat on the passenger side, her arm resting on the open window frame. Her dyed auburn hair was wind-tossed.

She looked so different. She was smiling, joking, and laughing. For a moment it occurred to Bryce that his father may have had the real Margaret murdered and replaced her with a robot duplicate like in the movie The Stepford Wives.

"Where'd you get the car, dad?" Bryce asked when the truck rumbled to a stop beside his damaged Hummer.

His father's grey-blue eyes traveled over the car. "Never mind about me. What happened to your truck?" Bryce snorted and gazed knowingly at his father.

Wally chuckled. "Yeah, I know. Stupid question. Hop in." There was a click and the car's rear doors popped open.

Bryce helped Sax climb in behind Maggie then ran around and got in behind his father. Cinnamon squeezed in beside Bryce. He winced when she pressed against him and let a out a ragged breath.

"How're you doing, son? You look a little banged up."

"No worries, Dad. I'll be okay."

"Okay. Great. Where we going?" asked his father in his too-cheery voice.

"Do you know a guy named Hopkins?" asked Bryce.

In the rearview mirror Bryce watched his father's expression change from carefree giddiness to something he'd never seen in his father.

Raw fear is a terrible thing.

Wally swiveled in his seat and glared at his son. "You don't want to meet him."

The corners of Bryce's mouth curled and he glanced at Sax then his eyes shifted back to his father. "Dad, I talked to a local boy. He told me all about Mr. Hopkins." Bryce had a sinking feeling this was not going to be good news. His father might be right. But the Hopkins character begged further exploration.

Sax's eyebrows rose on her forehead and her eyes reflected her recognition at the name. He wondered if she knew Mr. Hopkins too.

Bryce said, "Do you know Mr. Hopkins, Dad?"

His father grinned sheepishly. "I don't know him exactly. Well, not really. He's a coffee pal. Good guy actually."

Maggie frowned and her eyes reflected her puzzlement. "You're being evasive, my darling." She crossed her arms over her chest and harrumphed.

Bryce looked at her then at his father. Darling? Her strange behavior on the boat was still going on. Bryce wondered if Maggie had a new angle.

She shifted in her seat to face his father. "Wally, if you know this man you tell these kids right now." Maggie turned to smile at Bryce. Has she had a personality transplant? "These two good kids deserve your help. Tell Sax and Bryce where they can find Bob."

Oh, brother. Why was Maggie helping? She'd always hated him. He decided he must be dreaming.

"Who's Bob?" he said.

Maggie smiled slyly. "You'll see."

~~~

They found Bob Hopkins on the sundeck of the Coffee Hut reading a book, a steaming cup of herbal tea on the table in front of him.

A seagull riding the breeze cried over the sound of the surf pounding the wide expanse of sandy beach far below the sundeck. Dark sunglasses covered Hopkins eyes.

"Hi, Bob," said Wally, leading the way through the French doors from the interior of coffee shop. Cinnamon, Sax, and Bryce came out after Wally.

Hopkins looked up from his book. A frown crossed his otherwise placid features. His smooth, tanned complexion belied his age. The deep smile lines at the corners of his eyes and his steel grey hair were evidence he was older than he looked.

Hopkins took off his sunglasses revealing eyes as green as fine emeralds. His warm smile was inviting. She'd liked this man since she met him on the airport bus. Closing his book he set it on the table beside his tea cup.

"Please," he waved to the four chairs surrounding the table, "sit down."

Sax sat at Hopkins' right and Cinnamon took a seat in an empty chair beside her. Wally and Bryce took seats across from him. The waitress came out the door and took their orders.

After she was gone, Hopkins had a bemused expression on his face, folded his hands in his lap and scanned the four new arrivals. His eyes settled on Bryce, Cinnamon, and Sax each in turn. Sax suspected they looked awful after all they'd been through. The bags under her eyes were leaden.

"You three look a little worse for wear, except of course you, Wally." A silver eyebrow rose on his forehead. "But where's the lovely Margaret?"

"She dropped us off and went to the hospital to visit her sister."

A look of surprise registered on his face. "Oh? Is Liz okay?"

Does he know everyone? She'd never met him before that day on the bus yet he seemed to know all about them.

"Yes, she's going to be fine," said Wally with an easy grin. "A touch of pneumonia. Nothing a good antibiotic can't cure."

Sax stole a glance at Bryce and saw the relief reflected in his chiseled face and his dark eyes. What was with him? He'd told her he didn't like Liz.

A gentle smile tugged at the corners of Hopkins mouth. "Saxony Edwards," he said with a twinkle in his voice. "How are you're parents? Bertie and Jack certainly have an eye for wonderful paraphernalia."

Sax chuckled uneasily. How did he know her mom and dad? Her father must have made quite the impression. She hoped her father hadn't insulted him too badly. "Yeah, right. Junk. The stuff they buy for the shop is all junk." Hopkins grinned then lifted his cup to his lips and took a sip. "And in case you were wondering I know your brothers as well."

Now he's a mind reader.

Sax gaze shifted to Bryce. She was nervous. "What gives here? Who is this man?"

"Let's hear what he has to say, okay?" said Bryce

This is too weird. How did Hopkins know so much? She looked around the sun drenched deck. The five of them were alone. It creeped her out to think he had been watching them.

"Bob Hopkins knows our secrets." Wally wiggled his eyebrows up and down. "All our secrets."

CHAPTER FORTY-TWO

"OUR SECRETS?" SAX BEGAN TO TREMBLE. She'd been outed too. Everyone was going to know about her curse now. Her black cloud of bad luck had done its work again. This time though it had ruined her chance with the one man who overlooked her problem and had accepted her as his friend.

Hopkins would reveal her secret to Bryce then he'd never love her. He'd think she was a freak.

Her heart sank.

I'm doomed to be an antique virgin until the end of time.

Bryce's expression changed to one of concern. "You okay?"

Swallowing hard she said, "Yes. I'm fine."

Before Bryce said anything more the waitress appeared carrying a round plastic tray filled with steaming coffee cups. The tip of her tongue stuck out the side of her mouth, her attention focused on the cups brimming with tea and coffee.

Just as the young woman stepped gingerly over the door sill onto the sundeck a grey and white seagull landed at her feet. Sax realized the waitress didn't see the bird since it was obscured by the drinks on the tray. She was going to trip and they were about to be covered in hot drinks.

The waitress will crash. She'd be blamed and Mr. Hopkins would tell everyone she was the cause. The curse comes full circle.

"Freeze, Shelly," said Hopkins sternly.

The waitress froze in place and waited. A single oil-black beady eye of the bird seemed to glare at Hopkins. Then suddenly the seagull made a shrill, angry cry, extended its wings and lifted off. It floated over the wooden railing overlooking the beach beyond, flapped the air hard with its wings, and was gone.

"How did you do that?" said Sax, turning in her chair to face Hopkins.

"Happens all the time," explained the waitress with a grin, her tone bubbly and infectious.

The waitress set the tray on the table and began to distribute the drinks. "When the regulars, like Bob here, tell me to freeze, I freeze. Otherwise the results could be," she paused and raised both eyebrows, "messy."

A round of chuckles and knowing nods followed the waitress as she disappeared through the French door sliding it closed behind her with a thump.

Am I the only one who doesn't know what's going on?

Sax, her cheeks warm, looked at Bryce, Cinnamon, and Hopkins as if they had gone mad. "Mr. Hopkins, is this magic?" she said sarcastically.

Hopkins sighed and shook his head. "No, Saxony my dear. Not magic." He paused and seemed to gather his thoughts then said, "Bryce's family is cursed with the bad luck of the Irish."

Hopkins continued. "Wally knew it because his father also suffered from the curse."

"But what about me?" She still didn't believe him. "On the bus to the Portland airport you said something about Glad Beach being filled with people like me," her eyes drifted to Bryce, "and there are others like me."

Hopkins gazed at her, his eyes puzzled then he became serious. "Yes, you and many others in Glad Beach have the same problem." His brow wrinkled. "For some reason Glad Beach acts like a magnet, attracting people with the bad luck gene."

"Genes?" Sax's said. "You mean the problem is genetic?"

Hopkins nodded.

Sax stole a glance at Cinnamon who watched expectantly, listening and sipping her cinnamon (what else?) latté.

Sax leaned closer to her BFF and said in a low voice, "You buying any of this?"

Cinnamon nodded. "Sure, why not? It's as good an explanation as anything else for what happened to us."

Sax winced. "Huh, sorry about that." Her friend shrugged.

Turning her attention once again to Hopkins she said, "Do I have this gene?"

"Yes, I'm afraid so. It was handed down to you on your mothers side," Hopkins paused, "and before you ask, no, your brothers do not have the defective gene."

"In my family Dad said the bad luck skips a generation," piped up Bryce. "What about Sax's family?"

"That's true for your family, Bryce but not, unfortunately, for Sax's."

Sax looked wide-eyed at Hopkins. "My mom?" she said in a squeaky voice. Her eye brimmed with tears and her breathing came in gasps. Did her mom know about her curse? "Why didn't she tell me?"

"You'd have to ask her about that," said Hopkins, "but I can tell you she managed to find a cure."

A cure? Her heart rate increased. There was a way to rid her of the curse? It sounded too good to be true. "But you said it was genetic?"

Hopkins nodded. "It is."

Bryce jumped into the conversation before Sax could say anything more. "This doesn't make sense. How could Bertie Edwards cure a genetic problem? Gene therapy is still in its infancy. I know. Before I sold my software company we were developing software for some of the premier genetic laboratories in the world."

She shifted her attention to Hopkins once again. "So Mr. Hopkins, tell us how my mother cured her back luck gene."

A wry smile formed, his eyes sparkled then he said, "She found true love."

~~~

Bob Hopkins explained the history of the bad luck gene.

It stretched back as far as there were written records. Some noted archeologists even claimed the cave drawings found in Lascaux, France, in 1940 depicted sufferers of the same genetic disorder. Of course, like all scientific claims subject to interpretation, this claim was immediately hammered into the disputed or acknowledged camps. There's no room for gray areas in the scientific community.

History, explained Hopkins, records tragedy after tragedy as a result of the effects of the gene. Hannibal's right hand man's elephant slipped on the ice. This triggered an avalanche that buried half his army.

"I don't remember reading that in history class," said Sax.

Hopkins ignored her and continued, "The great London fire of 1666? Bad luck. And the fall of Rome to the Vandals and the Goths? Bad luck." He shook his head sadly. "The destruction of Spanish Armada and the destruction of the Yuan fleet, both due to bad luck. The Armada because of a bad luck weather forecaster named Hector Alonso. The destruction of the Yuan fleet was due to a bad luck boat builder whose name was wiped from the ancient Chinese records. In fact you can still see on the scroll where his name was blacked out."

Oh, c'mon really? She rolled her eyes. She had no idea what he was talking about, but if he was right then it explained her whole life. And if true love is the cure then she had to find the HIM. The man who was her one true love would finally remove the curse. Then she could live a normal life. Her heart ached to be normal.

"What about the Chicago fire?" said Wally with an amused glanced at Sax.

"Accident," said Hopkins definitively.

"Okay, Mr. Hopkins, we get it, but what does this have to do with my mother?" Sax said finally interrupting the history lesson.

Hopkins leaned forward in his chair and scanned Cinnamon, Sax, Bryce, and Wally each in turn his face a grim mask. "Unless you and Bryce find your one true love, your bad luck gene will cause untold destruction, and in fact could lead to the end of the world as we know it."

CHAPTER FORTY-THREE

SAX'S BROW WRINKLED. What a load of crap. She eyed Hopkins suspiciously. There was a twinkle behind his eyes.

"End of the world?" she said.

He chuckled. "Sorry, I was just making a little joke."

Wally snorted. "He's such a kidder."

She shivered. She'd forgotten how thin her jacket was and how filthy and grubby she felt. What she needed right now was a long soak in a too-hot bath. She had never been this tired in her whole life.

It was time to confront the elephant on the sundeck. "Mr. Hopkins, who are you and how do you know about the curse?" said Sax.

Hopkins shoulders drooped a little as the tension in his shoulders released. Been there, done that.

"Sax," Hopkins began then paused as a frown marred his forehead, "I know you think we met on the bus to the airport but that wasn't me. It was my brother, Max."

Sax stared at him and saw this time he wasn't kidding. He has a twin brother? Cinnamon giggled as if she were a school girl. Sax shot her a look of 'Really, do you have to?' and she fell silent. Cinnamon's cheeks flushed crimson. She raised her cup to her mouth and her eyes disappeared behind the cup's rim.

Bryce snorted. "Then he must be your twin."

One side of Hopkins mouth curled. "Triplets actually," he replied matter-of-factly.

214

Wally laughed. "Now that's what I call a twist."

~~~

Bob Hopkins explained that his two identical brothers, Max, lived in Detroit, and Harry, lived in Miami, and he and his brothers once jointly owned Albatross Airlines. They made a lot of money until they eventually sold the airline to a cookie company, but not for peanuts. (Wally laughed at that bad pun too). The proceeds of the sale were used to fund a scientific research foundation whose mandate was to find the source of bad luck.

Bryce groaned. "Oh, now c'mon, Bob. Are you kidding us? You can't be serious."

Hopkins scowled at Bryce. "Yes, I'm serious. Deadly serious." Bryce rolled his eyes, but remained silent. Sax looked at Cinnamon again.

Oh, brother. Whoever said melodrama was dead hadn't met Bob Hopkins. Guy has a loose screw or something. He wasn't making any sense.

Sax stood and walked to the railing. Just as she was about to lean on the rail Bob shouted, "Freeze!"

She did and held her breath. What did I do now?

Bob rushed over and with one hand pushed gently against the rail. The sound of wood cracking sent a shiver of fear through Sax. A large section of railing broke off and fell away to crash repeatedly into the cliff side until it impacted the gray sand on the beach far below. Bob placed one hand on Sax's shoulder and gentle drew her back from the edge.

She let out her breath in ragged gasps, her heart pounded hard in her chest. "I nearly..." her next words caught in her throat.

"You certainly nearly," said Bryce. Coming up to her he wrapped his strong arms around her and pulled her to him. She wrapped her arms around his torso, closed her eyes, and buried her head in the warmth of his muscular chest, then began to sob softly, her body trembling as her fear subsided.

For the first time in her life she felt safe and deeply loved by someone.

She held back tears and pressed her face into Bryce's chest to hide her feelings from him. But she hurt deep in her soul because she knew she could never be with him.

"Boy, that was close," said Cinnamon slurping the last of her latté. "If Bob hadn't known the railing was rotted through..." She let her words trail off into obvious land.

"I didn't know the wood was rotten," Bob said with a shrug.

Sax pulled back from Bryce to stare at Bob. "Oh crap-a-doodle," she said.

"My bad luck curse," she and Bryce said in unison.

Bryce looked down at her. Looking up her eyes locked on his. "It looks like you and I have a lot more in common than either of us realized," Sax said.

Reluctantly she stepped out of Bryce's comforting arms and swiveled to face Bob Hopkins. "Mr. Hopkins, please tell me about this foundation."

His silver eyebrows rose on his forehead. "Then you believe me now?"

Sax shifted her gaze to the missing section of railing then back at him. "Can you say, duh?"

CHAPTER FORTY-FOUR

MAGGIE KELLY STOOD BY HER SISTER'S HOSPITAL BED holding her
sister's hand. The antiseptic smells of hospitals had always made her
queasy. Liz Wolthorp's watery, gray-green eyes gazed back at her.

"How're you feeling, dear?" said Maggie patting Liz's hand
affectionately.

"I'm feeling much better. Thank you, Maggie," said Liz,
her voice dry as a dusty room. She coughed. Maggie released Liz's
hand to retrieve the plastic cup off the bedside table. There was a
bendable plastic drinking straw above the rim of the cup.

Liz sighed as she accepted the offered cup then positioned the
cup so she could easily slip the straw between her lips. She slurped a
deep draw of water.

"Ah," she sighed releasing the straw and handing the cup
back to Maggie. "That really hit the spot."

Liz's eyes shifted to her sister's. "So what's happened since I
went to la-la land?"

Maggie smiled at her, turned and retrieved a hard plastic
chair from where it sat against the plain whitewashed wall.
Dragging the chair closer to the bed she sat and crossed her legs.
"Oh, not much," she said brightly.

A sly smile crossed Liz's pale features. "C'mon, sis, you can
tell me."

Maggie giggled, causing Liz to frown. "I'm in love!" She
waved her hand in front of her as if it were a fan.

"Oh, my. I'm as giddy as a school girl."

Liz, being the older of the two, scowled at her younger sibling. "What's wrong with you? I'm the one who's sick, ya know. It's like you don't care about me at all."

Maggie looked cowed. "Sorry. It's just that I've never felt this way about anyone and I'm enjoying it."

Liz's scowl released. "I understand, sis. Being in love is a wonderful illusion. Men are so easily fooled by such romantic nonsense. Dreamers, the lot of them. All men really care about is sex and sports."

Maggie shook her head. "No. I mean it. I'm really in love. Really." She sniffed the air. "Besides, Wally isn't like other men." Her cheeks flushed crimson when she realized she'd just let the proverbial cat out the proverbial bag.

Liz stared at Maggie, her cheeks paled, and when she didn't say anything, Maggie began to worry she'd suffered a stroke. Maggie considered taking out her makeup mirror and using it to check for breathing, but quickly dismissed the idea when Liz finally spoke. "What? You..." she sputtered "...and Wally...you're in love?"

Liz's eyes brimmed with tears and her lower lip trembled until she buried her face in her hands and began to cry.

Just then a smiling male attendant walked in carrying a food tray. The man hesitated upon seeing Liz crying, the smile disappeared. He froze in place and looked to Maggie for direction.

"Put it on the bedside table and leave us, would you please." The man edged into the room, placed the tray on the table then quickly retreated. The door thumped closed behind him.

Maggie took Liz's hand in hers again and patted it gently. "There, there, dear sister. Don't fret. It's not the end of the world."

Liz removed her head from her hands, hiccupped and gulped in air. "What if Bryce doesn't want to marry Cinnamon?" She gasped and sucked in a lungful of air. "How are you going to manipulate Walter?" Fat tears streamed from both red-rimmed eyes and ran down her cheeks. Her nose began to run.

Maggie task, tsked. "What a mess you are." Moving to the four drawer dresser under a mirror across from the bed she grabbed a box of tissues sitting atop the dresser.

She pulled out a wad of tissues and handed them to her sister. Liz accepted the bundle of tissues and used them to blow her nose noisily. Once, then twice more.

Maggie frowned. "Liz, why are you making such a fuss?"

Liz's red eyes gazed at her. There was a world-gone-awry look behind them. "Is Cinnamon still going to marry Bryce?"

"Of course. What made you think they weren't going to marry?"

The corners of Liz's eyes drooped. "Because I thought the sun had gone nova."

Maggie snorted then laughed. "So you think if I'm in love with Wally the world is going to end, is that it?"

Liz sniffled and grinned sheepishly. "Yes," she said meekly.

"Oh, is that silly or what?" She patted her sister's knee through the bed covers. "I'm in love. And it's real. I've fallen in love with my husband, not his money. Is that so strange?"

Liz nodded then dabbed at her nostrils with the wad of tissues.

Maggie grinned then said, "Actually I was thinking of a double ceremony. Bryce and Cinnamon getting married, and me and Wally renewing our vows. Wouldn't that be fun?"

Liz's face broke into a wide grin and her eyes brightened. "Yes, you're right." She patted her sister's arm. "When we girls put our heads together we can really tie these knots tight can't we?"

"Yes, dear sister, yes we can."

Liz's brow wrinkled slightly. "One thing though." Maggie looked at her expectantly. Liz added, "Don't snort, dear, it's not ladylike."

Liz tossed the gooey tissues into the trash bag hanging off the bedside table then flopped her arms to her sides on the bedcovers. "We have to make plans. The sooner the kids get married the better."

CHAPTER FORTY-FIVE

Now that the railing was gone and it had started to rain, Bob suggested they move indoors. "Safety and staying dry go together," he explained.

Sax stood in the middle of the coffee shop with her hands in the pockets of her jeans. Through the windows facing the ocean the inky boiling clouds continued rolling in from the horizon. The size of the waves streaming toward the shore had doubled in size in the ten minutes since she'd been watching.

Fat raindrops began to dot the deck and the French door rattled in its frame as the wind strengthened. A storm was on its way and it looked to be a doozy.

Shelly the waitress lived in a one bedroom house next door to Coffee Hut. She invited Sax and Cinnamon to use the shower to clean up and lent them bulky sweaters and jeans afterward until they could get home and get into fresh clothes. She finally began to feel human again. Cinnamon was over there now showering.

Sax turned away from the window and gazed at Bob's friendly face. His eyes were so gentle and he was such a sweet old man, but he was mad as a hatter. Her mother would have called him a nutter in her English vernacular, and probably to his face too. Sax hardly had such nerve to be so direct.

"So what you're saying is this research foundation is called the BLT Foundation and they discovered a love gene?"

When she said it out loud it sounded completely crazy. Oh, brother. Sax glanced at Bryce.

As nuts as it sounded she really hoped it was true. If it was true then she may have a shot with Bryce, if she managed to break off his engagement to Cin.

She shook her head. What am I saying? I must be sick.

Bob nodded. Bryce wore a bemused expression on his chiseled features. In contrast his father sat rapt, his attention hanging on Bob's every word.

Wally's a nutter too.

"Yes," said Bob after taking a sip from his fresh cup of tea. "The Bad Luck Technology Foundation has the largest collection of evidence that supported the Bad Luck theory until we found the evidence it truly exists."

Bryce snorted. Sax looked at him and shook her head. We really do have a lot in common. They were perfect for each other.

She turned away and wiped at her eyes with the back of her hand. It wasn't fair. Why now? Why did she find the perfect man she loved only to lose him to someone else?

She turned back to face them and Bryce looked at her quizzically. She nodded and offered him a weak smile of reassurance. He nodded.

"So the researchers found evidence of bad luck in the human genome?" said Bryce, his tone heavy with sarcasm.

Sax tapped him on the arm and he looked at her. "It's the only thing that makes sense." Bryce frowned. "C'mon, Bryce, think about it. You and I have accident after accident all the time." She raised both eyebrows, "The sailing adventure, the bear and the snake, the crazy seal, the car door and the motor home?" She eyed him. "Don't you see a pattern in all this?"

"Maybe," he said then looked at Bob. "Okay, let's assume for a moment you're not off your nut," he paused and winked at Sax. She frowned. Now he's being pig headed. "You're saying the only cure is to find your one true love." Bryce eased back in the chair and crossed his arms. "I'm getting married to Cinnamon so maybe that'll cure my problem. But somehow I doubt it."

He told her he didn't love Cin so marrying her won't work. If what Mr. Hopkins told them is true Bryce needed to find his one true love.

Her gut sense was Bryce was her one true love, but she wondered if she was his. Could it be? She snorted. That would be too good to be true but she wanted it to be true more than anything.

Bob's mouth curled at the corners and his eyes sparkled with amusement. "Is Cinnamon your one true love?" he asked Bryce.

Before he could respond Cinnamon strolled into the room humming to herself. "Hi, everyone," Cinnamon said brightly. She had a pink towel round her neck and smelled of Lifeboy soap and peach shampoo. "I'm back."

Sax shook her head. Oh brother, is her timing off or what?

Cinnamon stopped humming and stared at Sax when she realized they had stopped talking. "Hey. What's wrong with everyone?" She sniffed the air. "Do I still stink or something?"

~~~

After they watched the sundeck break away from the front of the Coffee Hut they decided it best to head for home. Shelly explained the deck broke loose every few months, no matter how big the supports underneath were, and no matter how far they were drilled into the cliff side. A railing breaking away usually meant the deck would break off within a couple of days. She explained this time it broke away sooner than normal.

Shelly thought it odd it broke away so soon after the railing went down the cliff, but sloughed it off as bad luck.

Yeah. No kidding. It's like the perfect storm of bad luck with me around.

Bob left before them.

"We should go to my house," said Bryce, riding in the passenger seat of the loaner car the mechanic who was fixing his Hummer had dropped off for him. "I need to change." He sighed tiredly.

"You know, son, you never did answer Bob's question," said Wally, his eyes narrow, concentrating on the road ahead as he drove. The rain was heavy now and the car's wipers were beating hard to keep the windshield clear. The oily clouds created an illusion of night except it was only two in the afternoon.

He's boxed in as if he were the cheese in the mouse trap, thought Sax. Maybe he's finally getting it that even if he and Cin marry it won't defeat his curse. Her heat skipped a beat. She still had hope, slim as it was.

"I don't need to answer. Isn't it obvious?" Bryce pivoted in his seat and peered into the rear compartment at Cinnamon. "Right, honey?"

Sax thought he was speaking to her since they suffered from the same affliction. When he addressed his question to Cinnamon she had to stop herself before she answered him. Nope. She had no hope. Her shoulders slumped and she looked out the window of the car. He was marrying her anyway and there's nothing she could do about it.

"Yeah, right," acknowledged Cinnamon sullenly. Before they left the Coffee Hut, Bryce assured her she smelled fine and told her everything was fine. He told her about the conversation with Bob Hopkins and the foundation and the bad luck cure. He said it was a ridiculous theory and more magic than science.

Cinnamon wasn't so sure. While they were alone in the shower room earlier she confided to Sax her concerns with the impending nuptials and her reluctance to marry a man who she liked but didn't love.

Since they were BFF's she also shared her part in Maggie and her mother's scheme. She told Sax the marriage was destined to save the family from financial ruin.

Sax's eyes narrowed at her friend, "But I thought your father ruined the family finances?" Her eyebrows rose on her forehead. "Being convicted in a Ponzi scheme tends to do that ya know."

Cinnamon grunted. "Yes, you're right of course, but my mother wants me to marry a rich man, like Maggie did. Mother seems to think love isn't what men really want." She wiggled her eyebrows suggestively. "If you get my meaning?"

Sax got her meaning all right. Amazing how some people used sex to get what they wanted and missed the experience of true love. For her part Sax had always believed in true love. Too bad her curse had created a seemingly insurmountable barrier.

Bob Hopkins' theory may finally provide the answer she'd been seeking all her life. If only Bryce agreed.

The rest of the way to Emerald Lake, Sax ran through all she'd been told. By the time the truck turned onto the gravel road leading to the house Sax had made up her mind. The car bounced on the gravel as they neared the Alpine style house. A black and green taxi was parked in front.

If Bryce married Cinnamon they would both be unhappy, but it might cure his bad luck. While she still wasn't a hundred percent convinced what Mr. Hopkins said about love curing the curse was true, she wanted to believe it.

If the marriage was Bryce's shot at the cure then how could she stand in his way? She had to find a way to do the right thing. But what was the right way to the right thing?

Sax would help Bryce in any way he asked even if it meant losing the one man in the world she had feelings for, and the one man who understood her.

Sax raised her eyes skyward. Why me?

CHAPTER FORTY-SIX

WALLY WENT IN THE FRONT DOOR FIRST. The sky around the lake was dotted with wispy white clouds. The storm nearer the ocean hadn't come this far yet. But the black clouds on the horizon were headed this way. A woman's voice echoed cheerily from the top of the stairs as soon as the door swung open on squeaky hinges. "Wally, is that you?" Maggie said.

"Yes, dear, it's me." He ushered Cinnamon and Sax inside and Bryce entered last. "I brought the kids home with me." He shut the door cutting off the pine-perfumed breeze.

After they doffed their shoes and hung up their coats in the closet they walked up the short flight of carpeted stairs to the living room.

A man wearing tan slacks and a jean shirt stood in front Maggie. His deep set, hazel eyes studied them as they came to the top the stairs. Maggie had her open purse in one hand, with the other she searched for something.

Her face was scowled like a prune. "That's funny," she said, "I thought I had a couple of twenties, but I can't find them."

Wally smiled and pulled his wallet from his back pocket. "Don't worry, honey. I'll take care of it."

After he paid the driver the man left. "So where's Elizabeth?" asked Bryce, swiveling his head. He stopped when he saw a figure on the sundeck sitting in one of the deck chairs.

225

Whoever it was was hidden beneath a red, gray and black tartan blanket. "Oh, she's out on the deck. Is she okay?"

One side of Maggie's mouth curled. "Yes, dear boy, she's fine. She wanted to sit and feel the sun on her face for a while." Maggie glanced out the window and saw the dark clouds were headed their way. "I was about to go get her and bring her inside."

She smiled coyly at Cinnamon. "Why don't you go get her, Cinnamon? I think she wants to talk to you anyway."

Cinnamon eyes betrayed her uncertainty. She glanced at Sax who offered a weak smile of encouragement. "Ok. You guys wait here," Cinnamon said. Cinnamon sighed then walked to the French door and, with one last look at Sax, stepped onto the deck.

Bryce got up and asked to be excused saying he needed a nap. Sax thought he looked tired, so before Cinnamon, Wally or Margaret could respond she said it was okay. He smiled weakly at her then disappeared to the bedroom he shared with Cinnamon. She wanted to join him.

Before he left he asked his father to drive her home.

After they were alone Wally exchanged a look with Margaret then went to sit in his favorite chair in front of the floor-to-ceiling stone fireplace. Sax joined him in the living room sitting on the creaking rattan couch.

Maggie left the room saying she would put on a pot of coffee. She disappeared in the direction of the kitchen.

~~~

Closing the door behind her she walked to stand beside the chair where her mother sat. Her mother had the blanket pulled over her head like an Arab woman's Hejaz. Her mother looked up as Cinnamon came round to face her. Her green eyes were weary and her face was lined by fatigue.

"Darling," said her mother with a gentle grin. "I'm so happy to see you."

"Hi, Mom," said Cinnamon, avoiding her mother's eyes.

A frown creased her mother's forehead. "Is something wrong?"

Cinnamon shook her head. "No, of course not."

Her mother grinned then looked away at the expanse of the blue-green water of the lake. A soft breeze carried with it the fragrant smells of wildflowers beginning to bloom along the shore line. Brilliant slashes of red, yellow, purple, and blue flowers were beginning to appear now that the days were getting longer. The winter storm season had finally begun to wane, giving way to a new spring.

Elizabeth sighed softly. Cinnamon sat in a matching wooden deck chair next to her mother's. She rested her arms flat on the wide arms of the chair and let out a breath. She didn't want to marry Bryce. Sax wasn't about admit she loved Bryce but she did. And it wasn't because he was rich and handsome, which he was, it was because he was her one true love. And she'd bet her life Bob Hopkins knew it, too. It seemed the only one who didn't know was Bryce.

She'd rolled up the sleeves of the bulky sweater and the sun felt warm on the skin of her arms and face. Nature was so not her thing. But the truth was she would miss this place.

The party girl stuff was getting old but her image was who she was. Birds chattered in the gently swaying pines and firs that lined the lake. I wish I loved Bryce, but I don't.

At least love was in the air for someone, Cinnamon thought glumly looking at the birds flitting from branch to branch in the trees.

"Mother," began Cinnamon, "I don't know if marrying Bryce is such a good idea."

Out of the corner of one eye Cinnamon saw her mother's head snap round to face her. Her eyes were watery and her cheeks were flushed. "What's the problem?" Her mother's voice trembled with barely restrained fury.

The marriage to Bryce had always been more important to her mother than her. Cinnamon really liked Bryce and he was handsome, but he was a bit too much of a nerd for her taste and the socialite life wasn't his cup of tea. He bought this house in the middle of nowhere USA, and he liked the outdoors with all its bugs and snakes and bears.

227

She rubbed her hands together as if washing them. Besides, nature was dirty.

Art shows, museums, Broadway plays, and the opera bored him to distraction. She knew he attended those things for her sake, but he preferred old movies, hiking, sailing, and his taste in art leaned toward pop culture not fine culture.

But still Bryce was a very nice man and had boatloads of compassion for everyone and everything. And he loved animals. She could learn to love him, but then there was his problem. His bad luck. The trip with Sax showed her what could happen and it scared her.

Cinnamon had to find a way out of this marriage, not just for her sake but for his. She had to tell her mother the truth about him. "Mom, I really like Bryce."

"But?" Her mother said, the bitterness thick in her voice.

"But he has a problem." She finally managed to look at her mother. Her mother's forehead was furrowed and her eyes blazed with anger. "Bryce has the bad luck of the Irish." Cinnamon knew how ridiculous the words sounded as soon they passed her lips.

Elizabeth's frown eased and she emitted a harsh, bitter laugh. "What are you talking about? Bad luck?" She shook her head, grunted and waved one dismissive hand at her daughter. "There's no such thing."

"But, Mom, he does have bad luck. Really. Mr. Hopkins said—"

"That old fool?" her mother snapped off her words. "Don't listen to him. He's a lunatic. A quack."

Cinnamon sat in silence, her shoulders slumped, her heart heavy. She felt trapped. Bryce had a curse and the only cure was to find his one true love.

Cinnamon's eyes shifted to her mother who had pulled the blanket tighter round her neck. Her mother grumbled about how ungrateful she was and how a good daughter would care about her.

"Yes, Mother I do care about you but I don't love him." She was proud of herself she finally admitted it to herself out loud.

Now how would she convince her mother.

CHAPTER FORTY-SEVEN

Sax looked up from the well-read 1992 issue of Cosmo as Bryce shuffled into the living room, his slippers scuffing over the hardwood floor. The article on hairstyles of the rich and famous fascinated her.

Bryce sat down heavily in his father's chair. Wally had left a while ago to join Elizabeth and Cinnamon on the sundeck. Maggie was out on the deck already, setting a coffee pot and mug laden tray on the round wood table.

Bryce's eyes were sunken and dull, his strong jaw dark with stubble, giving him the rough and ready appearance of an Indiana Jones-type adventurer.

They were alone. She swallowed hard. It was the first time they'd been alone in a while and for some reason she was nervous.

Sax closed the magazine and set it on the rattan side table next to the couch. "You okay?" she said.

His mouth formed a wry smile and he gazed at her with weary eyes. His red and black plaid housecoat, tied around his waist, was open just below his neck. The nest of brown curls on his chest was showing.

Bryce sure is one sexy piece of manhood.

He smiled weakly and shook his head. "No. Not really." He paused and her heart went out to him, but she knew she couldn't share her feelings for him no matter how much she wanted to. She fought the urge to race to him and wrap her arms around him.

229

All she wanted to do right now was to protect him, comfort him.

He continued, "I'm having trouble taking it all in. The last twenty four hours have been…," he paused. Conflicting emotions swept across his features as he searched for the right word, "difficult," he finished.

Sax snorted. "Boy, you can say that again."

The familiar spark flashed in Bryce's eyes. "Why don't you tell me about the trip to New York?" he said, changing the subject.

The grin on Sax's features faded. "I don't think you want to hear about the trip." This worried her. They'd nearly died so many times Bryce might not want to be friends with her anymore. The death of a fiancée on a person's watch tended to dampen friendships. Or so she'd read somewhere.

Bryce produced a half smile and shrugged his broad shoulders. "Why not?" he chuckled. "Sure, bad stuff happened, but that's our lot in life isn't it?" He looked at her and his eyebrows raised knowingly. "But I wasn't there was I?"

Sax chuckled uneasily and her face grew warm. "No. Just little 'ol me." Bryce dropped his hand to his lap. The other arm remained on the arm of the wing chair. "We are cursed," he said bleakly. "And what are we going to do about it?"

Sax heart rate increased and she opened her mouth to respond when Wally stuck his head in the French doors. "Hey, guys come outside," he said brightly. "We've got some big news." His face split with a wide grin.

Sax's stomach tightened. She had a bad feeling this was not good news. She hoped it wasn't bad news about the wedding. Or did she?

Bryce cast his eyes down at his housecoat. "Not in this I'm not." He winked at Sax. Her mouth dried and she shivered with pent up yearning.

If he took that robe off in front of her she wouldn't be responsible for her actions. She'd jump his bones for sure. He got up and hurried away, headed for the bedrooms. "I'll be right there, Dad," he called as he disappeared down the hallway.

"Okay, Bryce, I'll meet you outside," Sax called after him. She winced. Yeah, right he wasn't talking to me. Stupid. She lowered her voice to a whisper and added, "Then I'll tell you everything."

"What did you say?"

She swung around to face Wally. His blue-gray eyes reflected his puzzled expression. "Nothing, Mr. Kelly. Nothing at all."

~~~

Bryce was back within ten minutes dressed in a tight white t-shirt that emphasized his six pack abs, and blue jeans, his bare feet stuffed into flip flops. His dark hair lay flattened against his head still dripping with water. He ran a hand through his tangled locks.

He looked one hundred percent male. Why had she ever thought he could love a plain girl like her? Cinnamon was glamorous and worldly. She was just a small town girl afflicted by a curse. She had no chance with Bryce even if he broke it off with Cinnamon.

But Cinnamon sat in the deck chair staring at the deck, her blond hair hung loosely over her pale cheeks, and her hands gripped her knees, pulling them to her chest. Sax sensed her friend was avoiding eye contact with her mother and her aunt.

Liz and Maggie were smiling like Cheshire cats who'd each swallowed a canary. Wally stood with his back to the railing, his hands flat on the rail on either side of him. His eyes sparkled and he wore a wry smile.

Bryce stepped onto the deck, closing the door behind him. A bird's cry made Sax look in the direction of the stand of fir trees on the left side of the lake. She didn't see anything. A movement at the corner of her left eye made her swivel her gaze to the left in time to see a white headed eagle lift off a high branch. The bird spread its wings as it flew toward the surface of the lake.

"Well, Dad," said Bryce. "What's so important?"

Wally's eyes flitted to Maggie. "Why don't you tell him, dear?"

Maggie stood and walked to stand beside her husband. He enveloped her waist with one hand and pulled her into his side. A slightly embarrassed frown crossed Bryce's face and the tips of his ears took on a reddish tinge.

"Your father and I are going to renew our vows," she said. Liz snorted. Maggie added, "We've finally fallen in love. It took time, but it finally happened." Liz snorted harder. Maggie frowned at her. "Regardless of what some people think."

Bryce smiled. "That's wonderful."

Didn't he know Liz and Maggie were scheming to see Cinnamon and he get married so they'd get closer to his dad's money? Family politics were so confusing. She smiled to herself. Like I should talk.

If anyone looked up the definition of eccentric they'd see her dad's picture. And her mom coddled his strange ways. Her brothers were in denial and their daughter had a bad luck curse. We really are a crazy bunch.

Shifting her gaze to Cinnamon she saw a single tear escape her left eye and roll down her cheek. Someone was sure unhappy. She wondered if there was anything she could do to help.

"And there's more," said Maggie.

Here it came, the catch. Sax had a sinking feeling she knew what was coming.

"Liz and I've arranged for an engagement party tomorrow for you and Cinnamon and to formally announce the double wedding ceremony this Saturday." Maggie giggled like a school girl until Wally pulled her round to face him and pressed his lips hard into hers.

Sax averted her gaze. Yup, as she suspected, more bad news.

"Saturday? That's two days from now," said Bryce.

"Why wait?" Liz growled from beneath the blanket.

Sax looked at Bryce as his eyes flitted to Cinnamon then back to the Liz-lump under the blanket. "Uuuh, I guess?"

Sax's cloud of bad luck descended on her like a curtain. It was over. She had lost Bryce forever.

CHAPTER FORTY-EIGHT

THE NEXT DAY THE SMALL DIRT-STRIP AIRPORT AT NEWPORT had never seen so many chartered aircraft. Wally had rented a nearby restaurant called Boys Town where he asked the arriving guests to wait for the bus he hired to take them to the Rembrandt Hotel in Glad Beach.

Glad Beach-ites referred to the Rembrandt as the hotel with one ear to the ground.

Given these people were mostly society friends of Liz and Maggie none of them looked too pleased when they were served by the fat owner Markus Dubinsky and his equally fat daughters, Bertie, Brunta, and Daphne.

No fancy coffee drinks in here, Markus explained when some guests ordered lattés and other fancy coffee drinks. "And no champagne, I see." complained one indignant man.

Sax sat on the stool behind the cash register near the front door. She should have stayed home. It was killing her to help with Bryce's engagement party and wedding preparations. But she'd agreed to help Wally fetch the wedding guests. It was ten thirty now and the last of the planes from Portland was due to arrive by eleven thirty. The party was scheduled to start at six o'clock.

So far every plane landed safely. My curse hasn't struck yet.

The uncomfortable looking lot of well dressed arrivals was a mix of Wall Street types and women who looked Botoxed, face-lifted, implanted, and liposuctioned to within an inch of their lives.

The age of an individual woman didn't seem to make a difference to the level of enhancement.

There's more plastic in here than at a mannequin convention.

Sax covered her nose and mouth with her hand, so as not to attract attention, and snorted softly at the thought.

She glanced at the rooster shaped clock that hung over the framed autographed picture of Spencer Tracy dressed as a priest. Beyond the bad luck gene, she and Bryce snorted and loved the outdoors. Even with its snakes and bears. Maybe after his marriage we can go hiking again. They'd be just friends, of course.

She'd try to keep her bad luck gene under control. On the way to Newport, Wally told her the BLT Foundation was working on some new and radical gene therapies they hoped would lead to a cure.

After Bryce married Cinnamon maybe he'd be cured. But how was she going to find her one true love so she'd be cured? She had no idea where to even start looking.

"Hey, Sax," Wally's voice cut through the din, snapping her back from her introspection.

She glanced at Wally seated at a table across from a man with a round, ruddy face. The man's brown eyes sparkled as he spoke excitedly. The hum of conversation made discernment of individual speakers virtually impossible.

Sax grinned easily as she caught Wally's eye and he waved her over. She slipped off the stool and said, "Yeah, Wally, I'm coming." Walking toward to the table she studied the brown-eyed man.

After sitting beside Wally across from the strange man, Sax noticed the slight odor of machine oil in the air and it made her feel slightly queasy. Her nose wrinkled. The man looked from her to Wally. "Is something wrong?" he said.

Wally chuckled. "No, Harold." He grinned. "As I was telling you there are some very unique people around here. Saxony here is one of them."

Wally had been so kind to her that she had grown very fond of him. He'd be the perfect father-in-law to whoever married his son.

Harold eased back on the bench seat his forehead furrowed, his eyes clearly perplexed.

Wally introduced them. "Saxony Edwards, this is Dr. Harold P. Wilson. Dr. Wilson heads the research lab at the BLT Foundation."

Dr. Wilson nodded. "Bob Hopkins suggested I come to the wedding to observe and record the moment the curse is removed from Bryce. It will enhance our understanding of the effect of love on this genetic disorder."

Wally grinned and cocked an eyebrow at Sax. "Should be interesting, don't you think?"

Sax grinned. "I'm sure it will be." Yeah, but too bad it wouldn't be her who married Bryce. She was smiling on the outside but dying on the inside.

~~~

Sax smiled to herself as the bus bumped underneath her and swayed around a corner. Wally had taken Dr. Wilson with him in his car.

The A-listers from New York, Paris and London seated in the rows behind her gasped and sweated as the bus rolled around the switchbacks along the coast highway making its way back to Glad Beach. She glanced at her British made Dolphin watch. The glowing red digital numbers read 3:14 a.m.

Good. If it's three fourteen in England it's eleven fourteen right now. They'd pull into the hotel parking lot at about noon. Plenty of time.

Good 'ol Brit tech, she thought. Reliable in its unreliability. Some things just work as they are meant to and if your eccentric parents give you a watch made in England it's going to be set on English time.

She smiled to herself eyes. Oh, brother, my life is so not boring.

A man gagged from somewhere behind her.

A sudden bang at the rear of the bus made several passengers gasp.

She snatched the microphone off the bus' dashboard. The driver glanced at her and smirked but didn't say anything. His eyes shifted back to the winding highway.

Sax pressed the open mike button on the side with her thumb. A burst of static forced everyone to cover their ears.

"Sorry. It's okay, everyone. This bus has double tires on the rear wheels. One blow out does not mean we have to stop," she said.

Sax glanced at her watch. "We should be at the hotel in about forty minutes, after which you'll have sufficient time to check-in and freshen up before the welcoming cocktail party on the deck off the main dining room. Don't forget the party starts at six sharp."

After replacing the microphone on its hook on the dashboard Sax sighed and crossed her arms over her chest.

Yup, it's gonna be a good time for everyone but me. I'll be alone and still cursed.

CHAPTER FORTY-NINE

SAX GLANCED AT HER WATCH AS THE BUS STOPPED in front of the Rembrandt Hotel lobby doors. 3:59 a.m. in London. Right on time.

The air brakes sighed and the door swung open. After a grin and a thanks to the driver Sax bounded down the three steps and stood at the bottom watching as the nervous passengers began to disembark.

One man, wearing a heavy wool coat, dark glasses, an ivory-white scarf around his neck, and reeking of stale scotch, stopped to ask if the presidential suite was available.

Sax smiled tightly and directed him to the lobby where he could enquire at the front desk. Great. A drunk. Just what every wedding needs. He looked her up and down, grunted, and headed for the doors. "Have the porter bring my bags to my suite," he said, walking away with a dismissive wave of one hand.

Yeah, pal, good luck with that.

An elderly woman, a Miss Marple-looking type, stepped off carrying a small puffy dog in her arms as if it were a child. "Hello, dear," she said gently. "Where do we go?" Her gray-blue eyes swept the area like radar.

Sax swept one arm toward the lobby doors. "Right through there, ma'am. What about your luggage?"

The older woman stopped scanning and stared at her with a tight smile on her lips. "Yes, dear. Have the help bring my bag to my room," she said.

Sax shook her head as she turned to watch the old woman enter the lobby.

From behind her a male voice with a thick Italian accent said, "Allow, signorina."

She turned around and frowned when there was no one there.

The man coughed then he said, "Scusi, signorina, downa here."

Looking down she realized a small man was standing in front of her. Startled she jumped back. Whoa! How did he sneak up on her?

The man had to be no more than five feet tall. At five seven she was a giant compared to him.

His olive complexion had a reddish tinge and his magnificent handle bar mustache was shiny as if it were soaked in olive oil. Next to the rest of the passengers streaming by her in their designer clothes, this little man in rayon slacks, a plain white Wal-Mart shirt and faux leather jacket was the epitome of the phrase out-of-place.

He bowed slight at the waist his oil-black eyes never leaving hers. "I am the Great Oliveira," he said sticking his chest out in an exaggerated fashion. "Prego, direct me to my dressing room."

Before she could respond Wally burst through the lobby doors. "Signore Oliveira! Wonderful! You made it."

"No worries, Sax, I'll take it from here," said Wally after placing one hand on the Great Oliveira's back and guiding him inside. Wally glanced over his shoulder at Sax and winked.

Now what was that all about?

~~~

The party on the deck of the hotel overlooked an expansive ocean vista that stretched north to south as far as she could see. The gray beach seemed to go on forever into the distant horizon.

The party was already underway when Sax arrived at six fifteen. She suspected this crowd would never miss a chance at an open bar. The man with the white scarf had donned a white tuxedo. He looked like a waiter as far as she was concerned.

She was thankful now she'd brought a new dress and shoes with her on the bus. She didn't want to be the underdressed one people talked about later.

Looking around she spotted the elderly lady with a knitted shawl covering her narrow shoulders. Sax wondered if the dog was off peeing in a corner somewhere. She covered a snort with one hand over her mouth.

"Don't snort, dear. It's not ladylike," said a voice behind her. Mother? Sax whirled to face her mother and her jaw dropped.

Her mother wore a full length Union Jack dress and British flag earrings dangled from her ear lobes. Her mother smiled warmly, her blue eyes dancing with humor and warmth.

Sax stepped forward and wrapped her arms around her mother.

"Mom! You're here?" She closed her eyes and let out a small breath. Great. Just great. Everyone here was going to think she was as eccentric as they were. She sensed disaster in the making.

Sax released her mother and stepped back. She held her white sequined evening bag in front of her as a shield.

"My, don't you look nice," said her mom. She had to agree. The strapless white gown and matching high heels had broken the bank but the new dress and shoes made her feel pretty for the first time in a long time.

Her mother wiggled her eyebrows suggestively. "Special guy?"

Sax chuckled uneasily and her cheeks grew warm. She wasn't ready to talk about her feelings for Bryce with her mother. "No, Mother. I thought I'd treat myself is all."

"Oh," said her mother in the disappointed voice she knew so well. "Well, never mind, dear. One day," she said, her eyes wistful.

At least, she hoped so.

"Huh, Mom where's Dad?" Her eyes widened as the crowd of A-listers parted like the red sea to let a grinning, ruddy-faced Jack Edwards stride across the room toward them. He had his thumbs hooked over the too-wide, gleaming white belt holding up his bell bottom pants.

The pants matched the Union Jack pattern of her mother's dress and he wore a bowler hat, also stenciled with the British flag, cocked at an angle over one eye.

Sax recognized her father's ruddy complexion. It meant he'd drunk a glass of scotch. Her father didn't normally drink, but when he did the embarrassment needle was buried in the red zone. This was so not good. The good ship disaster had just docked. Sax slapped her forehead with the flat of one hand.

"Hey, you two," said Jack with a giggle as he came up to them. He was swaying where he stood. "How're my two favorite ladies doin'?"

She turned to face her mother. "Mom, don't tell me you guys are gonna lead a pub sing-a-long, again?"

Five years were not enough to bury that memory.

Her mother's brow wrinkled in puzzlement. "Why not, dear? It's a party, isn't it?"

Sax shook her head and walked away leaving her mother and father laughing and snorting.

Oh, no. They'd both had a drink. This was a date that would go down in infamy. Can this day get any worse? The man she loved was about to marry someone else and now her parents were on the booze.

The sound of swooshing over head made her look up. Shielding her eyes from the brightness of the setting sun she spotted what she first thought was a very large lime green bird. Squinting she saw the bird had a waxed handle bar mustache.

The Great Oliveira? Did he have a kite attached to him?

Something falling off the flying man suddenly blotted out the sun. She realized there were many something's falling. Before she could react an object struck her left eye.

"Hey! Ouch!" Looking away she covered her injured eye with one hand. Roses. There were pink, red, and white roses falling from the sky like rain. The Great Oliveira swooped overhead, dropping roses as he went.

She spun round intending to find Wally and warn him how dangerous it was to drop anything from the sky when she froze. Bryce was walking toward her. Bryce!

Oh, no I must look ridiculous. Bryce was so handsome and she was such a train wreck.

She quickly dropped her hand from her wounded eye but kept it shut. She could feel the eye swelling already. Darn allergies.

Great. The Cyclops strikes.

"Hey, Sax," said Bryce as he approached. In his hands he held two glasses of champagne. "I've been looking for you."

Looking for her? Her heart rate increased. Maybe he was going to tell her of his undying love for her and how he and Cin had broken up. I hope. I hope. I hope.

She smiled weakly as he handed her one glass of champagne. "Huh, how's it goin', Bryce." She must sound like a doofus. 'How's it goin'?' What a hick.

Bryce grinned and took a sip from his glass. A girl can dream can't she? She'd read wayyy too many fairytales when she was a kid.

He looked incredibly handsome in his black tuxedo. He'd even shaved, his strong tanned features accented by his dark curly hair and always mirthful blue eyes.

"Ever had champagne before?" he said.

"No." Not on her beer budget. She took a tentative sip and smiled. The bubbles tickled her nose. "Hmmm. This is good."

"Cinnamon's mother had it flown in special. I like a good glass of beer myself." He appeared to be uneasy, the way he shuffled his feet and ran a finger around the rim of the glass over and over. What was wrong with him?

"I've been meaning to tell you something," he began before she interrupted him. There was no use talking anymore. He was marrying Cin and she was going to be single for the rest of her life and that was that.

She hoped the champagne would deaden the pain in her heart. "Well, bottoms up," said Sax with a snort. She upended the glass and drained it.

Bryce gazed at her, his eyes reflecting concern. "Do you think that's a good idea? This stuff can go to your head pretty quickly."

"Sure. Why not? This day is the worst day of my life." She hiccupped.

Bryce eyebrows rose in surprise. "Really?"

She dismissed him with a wave of one hand. "I've said too much." She looked around for an empty chair. The staff of the hotel had lined the perimeter of the cement deck with chairs from the restaurant.

The only empty one was next to where a glum faced Cinnamon and her smiling mother sat beside each other.

At the other end of the deck the Great Oliveira landed, attached to a hang glider. Sax slapped Bryce on his arm. "Hey, B man, let's go see what's happenin'," she slurred her words. Well what do you know, she felt better already. Champagne was cool.

She grabbed another glass off the tray of a passing waiter and downed it in one gulp. Hmmm…better.

"Yeah. Okay," said Bryce tentatively.

Sax wrapped one arm around Bryce and practically dragged him toward the glider. As they came up to watch, Oliveira was undoing the straps of the safety harness attached to the hang glider.

The Great Oliveira wore a skin tight lime green spandex suit and matching goggles covered his eyes. After removing the harness he pulled the goggles up onto his forehead. He grinned and held his arms theatrically from his sides.

She giggled and clapped her hands. "Ta-da!" she said brightly.

People around her sniffed their distain. Oliveira scowled at her and walked away leaving the glider on the deck.

Sax let go of Bryce's arm and walked up to the glider to study it more closely. It looked relatively simple to operate.

A nylon harness held you suspended under the single large wing and you held onto a triangle shaped cross bar while in flight.

"I'm going to get you something to eat," said Bryce.

"Whatever," said Sax, waving him away. She didn't need him or anyone else. All she needed was more champagne.

Sax glanced over her shoulder as he walked away. Her eyes flitted to her parents urging a sweating waiter to roll an upright piano onto the deck. This just gets better and better.

They were going play British pub music at a society wedding.

Her eyes drifted to Cinnamon, slumped in her chair. What was the matter with her? She was marrying the greatest man in the world yet she looked like she was at a funeral.

She took in a deep breath then puffed her cheeks out and slowly released the air from her lungs. That's it. It was time to leave. She couldn't take it anymore. Bryce was marrying the wrong woman. She loved him. This should be her engagement party.

Her eyes shifted back to the hang glider and she made up her mind. And there's my ticket outa here.

Before anyone could stop her she had the glider harness on and locked in place, lifted the glider off the cement, and wobbled as she carried it stumbling toward the edge of the sundeck.

"Hey!" she glanced to her right and saw Wally running toward her, his face frantic, his arms waving wildly. The A-list party guests around her stared at her.

"Good-bye all!" she shouted as she gripped the cross bar in white-knuckled hands, closed her eyes, and leapt off the deck. The wind picked that moment to strengthen and lift the hang glider into the air. With the salty breeze whipping her hair she opened her eyes and her stomach twisted at the sight of the beach flying by below her.

Oops. She realized this kite idea wasn't such a good idea after all. Her curse made her do it. Or maybe it was the champagne. She couldn't be sure. Next time she'd take a car to get away from an engagement party.

She struggled against the harness and the hang glider's left wing dipped violently. She froze and the large wing-shaped craft stabilized and leveled off then began to climb into the sky. She knew one thing for sure, she didn't know how to fly!

The gray beach whipped by faster now beneath her. She glanced back and saw Bryce standing at his father's side looking up at her.

"Bryce!" she cried. "What did you want to tell me?"

Can she pick the moment to ask or what?

The glider's speed increased with each passing second as the strength of the wind increased.

She was quickly leaving Bryce behind but his mouth moved and he shouted something. She could barely make out his shouted words, but she thought she heard him say he loved her.

Her features broke into a wide smile and her heart soared. Tears welled in her eyes. Bryce loved her?

Her heart soared just as an updraft caught the kite and it shot upward. Sax's stomach heaved and her breath was knocked from her lungs. She swallowed the sour taste of vomit in her mouth as the kite settled at its new altitude.

Breathing again, she looked around and realized the hang glider had just left the beach behind. The glider was heading out to sea going west and carrying her farther away from her one true love. It wasn't fair.

She had finally found the man she loved and who loved her and what did she do? She flew away on a giant kite headed for Japan. She felt so stupid not to have seen the signs. She had to find a way to get back to him.

She struggled desperately against the harness but she flew on and on, farther away from shore with each passing second.

Finally she stopped struggling, resigned to her fate. Two things were obvious, she had no idea how to work a giant kite, and she was doomed.

CHAPTER FIFTY

Bryce looked at his father, whose mouth hung open. They stood side by side leaning forward against the cement railing, shrouded in the glow of the last light of day, staring at the hang glider retreating into the distance. An ever darkening sky crowded with thick black clouds split by streams of gold, yellow, and red as the sun settled below the horizon. The sky looked foreboding and filled with danger.

His heart tightened in his chest. He was not going to lose his one true love forever. He wouldn't accept losing her. He had to save her, or die trying.

He glanced at his father. His father was in shock. "Dad? Are you okay?"

"Uhhh, yeah...I mean yes...at least I think so." His father's eyes flitted back and forth which signaled he was processing the words Bryce just shouted to Saxony before she was just about out of hearing range.

A cool breeze coming from the north made Bryce shiver. Bryce placed one hand on his father's shoulder. "Listen, Dad, I know this is confusing." He paused. "It's confusing to me too." His gaze drifted to the hang glider with its struggling rider dangling beneath. "But I think right now we have something more urgent to attend to."

His father nodded. "Yes. I agree." Abruptly his eyes hardened and his expression became serious. "I know someone who can help."

"Mama mia! Mya glider!" cried an Italian accent behind them.

The corner of Bryce's mouth curled as he locked eyes with his father. "We know someone who will rescue her."

He grabbed his father's arm and practically dragged him through the doors to the reception room. "Dad, come with me."

~~~

The thumping blades of the red and white Dolphin helicopter made hearing with the headphones off impossible. His father had arranged with the commander of the U.S. Coast Guard station at Newport to dispatch a helicopter to rescue Sax before she flew too far out to sea.

It was night now and oily clouds had rolled over them like a shroud in the last few minutes. The first spits of rain struck the windshield in front of the pilot and the aircraft was buffeted repeatedly as if it were a boat on a choppy sea.

Before they lifted off the pilot told his father and Bryce the winds had shifted from east-west to north-south. Sax would be headed south now. He also told them the hang glider would be difficult to spot on radar since it was constructed using light, porous materials like nylon and aluminum.

The interior of the helicopter glowed green and white from the lights behind the pilot's control board and the soft light in the rear compartment where they sat. Bryce watched the rescue technician check her equipment. She assured them if Sax was out there they'd find her. The name on her uniform patch read Reed. She'd introduced herself as Cristina before they lifted off from the Coast Guard Station at Newport.

The helicopter bucked beneath them. Bryce wasn't so confident in Cristina's assessment of the situation. Thankfully, Cinnamon had understood why he had to rescue Sax. She said she too had doubts about their impending marriage.

She said she really liked Sax and hoped she really was his love match. In his heart he knew Sax was the woman he'd been looking for all his life. If only he hadn't been afraid to admit he loved her. He couldn't believe he'd been so blind about Sax. He knew now Sax was the one. She was his one true love.

Now he was scared she may be lost forever.

Sax was out here alone and probably afraid. All he wanted to do was protect her. For the past several minutes he'd been mentally kicking himself for leaving her side when she gulped that champagne. It was obvious she couldn't handle it. This mess was his fault.

Given the shift in the winds the pilot radioed to the Coast Guard station for a rescue cutter to be dispatched to aid in establishing a search grid.

They flew on for an anxious half hour when a man's deep voice came through Bryce's headset saying the cutter had spotted the hang glider south of Newport near Cape Disappointment.

Bryce caught the brief look of fear flash through Cristina's eyes. He swallowed hard. Sax? "Something wrong?" he said into the microphone in front of his mouth, attached to the headphones.

She shook her head, avoiding his gaze. "Cape Disappointment. Not a nice place to be."

"Why?" asked his father. His father's voice sounded tight with tension through the headphones.

Her dark eyes became hard. "We usually find the bodies there."

Bryce knew immediately what she meant. He'd heard the stories about Cape Disappointment on the coast. No one was ever found alive there.

His father's eyes narrowed. "I don't recall that name on any map."

"That's because its real name is Cape Humor." She paused and turned her attention to looking out the window set in the sliding door. "Some joke, eh?"

Yeah, thought Bryce. Some joke.

Suddenly Cristina visibly tensed. "There she is."

Bryce scrambled to the window. Sax? Where? Oh, please be okay my love. There, caught in the white glow of the spotlight affixed to the belly of the helicopter was the hang glider with a figure hanging limp underneath. His heart skipped a beat when he saw her.

Sax hung limply, her arms at her sides, her head lolled to one side. Her eyes were closed but he thought he could see the rise and fall of her chest as she breathed. "She's hurt," he said grimly and his heart beat faster. But she's alive. "We have to get to her fast! She's unconscious!"

Cristina nodded. "But that could make things easier."

"How?" said his father.

Cristina stood up halfway bent at the waist to avoid hitting the ceiling and moved across the cabin to a locker affixed to the opposite wall. "Have you ever heard of someone drowning while trying to save another?" She turned the handle on the locker and it popped open. "A drowning person is panic-stricken and has unbelievable strength." After lifting a rope off a hook inside the cabinet she shut the door again with a click of the lock. "I know of several cases where a trained lifeguard drowned while trying to save children half their weight."

Bryce glanced at his father. Unable to stay still, Bryce bounced in his seat. He had to get to her.

His father raised one hand and signaled he should stay calm. Bryce nodded and stopped bouncing. His father was right. He had to calm down. "So if Sax is out cold she'll be easier to retrieve," said Bryce, "correct?"

"Exactly." She moved back to the door with the rope in one hand and crouched down on her haunches. "Ken, bring us closer will ya?"

"Roger," said the pilot.

The helicopter swayed side to side then gradually turned toward the hang glider. Bryce bent forward to peer out the window. Sax was bathed in white light but hadn't stirred. Hurry! He couldn't bear to lose her now they were so close. He wanted to leap across the air between them and take her in his arms.

Cristina pulled on the door handle and the door slid nosily along the track.

A blast of sea air filled the cabin and the sound of the rotor increased to mingle with the rush of air.

"Not too close, Ken," said Cristina.

"Roger," said the pilot again.

"I'll need to be twenty five feet or so," she added.

"Twenty five feet, acknowledged," said the pilot. "Proximity alarm set."

"Proximity alarm?" said Bryce.

"The Dolphin has a built in radar operated proximity alarm. When we have to make rescues from cliffs or mountain sides we don't want to run into the mountain. The alarm alerts us when we get too close to the target. In this case we'll set the alarm to indicate when we are within twenty five feet of Sax so the helicopter blades don't get too close."

"But I thought you said the radar doesn't see hang gliders?" said his father.

"Normally it doesn't," she shrugged. "We got lucky."

Good luck? Was she kidding or had something changed? He looked at Cristina and she looked as staid and professional as ever. Okay. Something had definitely changed. He'd never felt such confidence in anything in his life. This will work. Sax will be saved.

"How're you going to bring her in if we can't get too close?" said Bryce.

"Catapult," she said as she worked to attach one of end the rope to a device that looked like a harpoon.

"You're going to shoot this at her?" Bryce said shifting his gaze between the catapult and the hang glider that was quickly getting closer.

She might hit Sax. What then?

"Is this thing safe?"

Cristina's only response was a nod. She finished tying the knot then lifted the handheld launcher to her shoulder. She locked gazes with Bryce who had shifted toward the front edge of his seat.

"Stay where you are," she said.

He stopped and nodded. He looked out the window anxiously at Sax.

Bryce closed his eyes and held his breath. He really loved Sax. She was his one true love. Please be okay. Please.

He flinched at the sound of the catapult being fired.

"Perfect," cried his father within seconds. "She's got her!"

Bryce opened one eye and didn't see the hang glider. His dad and Cristina were crouched by the open door looking down. They had their safety straps affixed to the belts around their waists. Bryce opened both eyes, got up from his seat and attached his strap to the stainless steel loop next to the door. He then leaned forward to gaze out the open door.

His father chuckled and moved out of the way to the other side of the cramped cabin. Cristina pointed below with one gloved hand, a wide grin split her pale features.

There, dangling upside-down, was Sax. The glider flipped over twisting in the wind, the wing torn, now useless as a flying device.

After firing, Cristina stuffed the launcher into a holder that secured and held it in place and supported the combined weight of Sax and the hang glider.

She slapped a button next to the holder and the rope began to retract.

Bryce sat back and sighed. He couldn't take too more much of this.

Within ten minutes Sax and the hang glider were secured inside the helicopter and they were on their way back to the Coast Guard station.

Bryce cradled Sax's head in his lap and brushed her cheek gently with the backs of the fingers of his right hand. My poor girl. My love. "You're safe now," he whispered.

Her eyes fluttered open. He smiled down at her. He'd never been so happy in his life.

"Hey, sailor," she said, "going my way?"

Bryce looked up at his father, then at Cristina. The tension of the last few hours suddenly burst like a dam and all three began to laugh.

CHAPTER FIFTY-ONE

BRYCE SMILED AT SAX AS HE ENTERED THE LIVING ROOM carrying a tray with a teapot, mugs, and plate with four shortbread cookies on it. It had been four weeks since the hang glider incident, and two weeks since they were married in a quick ceremony. Neither of them wanted to wait.

The best news of all was their curses had disappeared. Dr. Wilson had run tests and declared them both cured.

Sax had never been so happy in all her life. She was truly in love.

She reclined on the leather couch, her gaze focused on the red, blue, and yellow of the crackling flames in the stone fireplace.

His father, Wally, looked up from the book he was reading. "It's funny how things work out," he said with a chuckle in his voice.

"How's that, sweetie?" said Maggie, who came in behind Bryce. She rushed over and plopped down in Wally's lap. He let the book go and it thumped to the floor. She wrapped her arms around Wally's neck and they shared a passionate kiss.

"Why don't you two get a room?" said Sax her eyes shifted to Bryce as he set the tray on the recently purchased oak coffee table.

"Hi, sweetie," she said with a giggle. She felt silly acting like a teenager but she couldn't help herself. If this was what true love was like then she was happily addicted.

"And hi yourself, sexy," said Bryce with a grin. Her cheeks grew warm.

Maggie eased back and said, "Oh, we have one of those," her eyes narrowed at Wally, "don't we, my little pumpkin."

Wally laughed and wiggled his eyebrows. "Yes, dear, we certainly do."

"Have you heard from Cinnamon?" said Wally, changing the subject. "I'm very fond of that girl."

Sax grinned. "Me too. I received the wedding invitation just the other day. Who would have thought she'd marry a Mr. Hopkins' son?"

"And my dear sister would be one of the true loves of another Mr. Hopkins," added Maggie.

Bryce filled two cups with the fragrant jasmine green tea then carried them to the couch. She accepted the cup from him with a flirtatious grin. Her heart beat faster as their fingers briefly brushed each others. She loved this man. He made her truly happy. The couch sighed as he sat next to her.

She felt his warmth beside her and sighed inwardly. Who knew there could be such contentment possible in the world?

"I guess Dr. Wilson's theory about the curse is correct," Bryce said with a grin.

Sax nodded. "I guess so. He was right about my mom and dad," her eyes flitted to Bryce, "and us." She lifted the cup to her lips and took a sip and winced. "Ouch, that's hot."

Bryce chuckled. "But at least it's not bad luck."

The room echoed with laughter.

True love had saved them all from the bad luck gene and for the first time Sax's luck had changed. She glanced at Bryce and smiled at the memory of their wedding night.

She was no longer the antique virgin. That ship had sailed. Life was good and about to get better.

About the Author

International selling author, Russ Crossley writes science fiction and fantasy, and mystery/suspense as well as their various subgenres.

His latest science fiction satire set in the far future, *Revenge of the Lushites*, is a sequel to *Attack of the Lushites* released in 2011. The latest title in the series was released in the fall of 2013. Both titles are available in e-book and trade paperback.

He has sold several short stories that have appeared in anthologies from various publishers including; WMG Publishing, Pocket Books, and St. Martins Press.

He is a member of SF Canada and is past president of the Greater Vancouver Chapter of Romance Writers of America. He is also an alumni of the Oregon Coast Professional Fiction Writers Master Class taught by award winning author/editors, Kristine Katherine Rusch and Dean Wesley Smith.

Feel free to contact him on Facebook, Twitter, or his website http:www. russcrossley.com. He loves to hear from readers.

Also by the Author

Other titles from 53rd Street Publishing you may enjoy
http://www.53rdstreetpublising.com

Other books by the Author

Razor and Edge Mysteries
The Kidnapping of Billy Buttons
String of Pearls
Death by Clown
Beggin' For Murder
Ragged Ice
The Grand Central Mystery
A Strange Case of Undead Murder

Jazz Stiletto Mysteries
A Day Without Sunshine
Skullduggery
Instrument of justice (first published in Over My Dead Body online mystery magazine)

The Amanda Dark paranormal mysteries
Hook Island
Grind Manor
Moonrise Diner

The Trudy Wilson Mysteries
Bad Loyalty
Shear Murder
Buzzcut coming in 2015

Novels
Attack of the Lushites
Revenge of the Lushites
My Zombie Prince
Antique Virgin
The Fire In Their Hearts
with R.S. Meger (from Champagne Books)
Zomopolis
The Last Serial Killer

Short Stories
Countdown
Shoeless Moe
Round Up At The Burger Bar:
The Story of Trixie Pug, Parts 1, 2, 3, 4, 5, 6, 7, 8, 9
Five Minutes
Blossom Queen, Barbarian
The Secret
The Family Line
End of the Flies
Death by Magic
The Penguin Sleeps With The Fishes
Only The Worthy
Hero For A Day
End of Empire
Strange Bedfellows
Big Business
A Perfect Crime
The Wise Guy and The Pirates
In Search of the Perfect Cup
T.I.N. Men
The Legend of G and the Dragonettes
The Incredible Mr. Fix-It
Lock Stock and Barrel
Divided Loyalties
Cave of Wonders

A Family Empire
Until We Meet Again
Dragon Rising
Solitary Man
The Keel Mountain Conspiracy
Angel on My Shoulder
Heroes of Old
The Great Bicycle Race
Tikka's Big Day
"My Partner the Zombie" —
Hungry For Your Love Anthology
(St. Martin's Press)
Big Hairy Deal
One Red Shoe
A Bad Day in Lunden Texas
Bloody Betty, Queen of the Pirates
Mirror Image
Dangerous Waters
Cape Disappointment
Boomerang
The Watcher of Wayburn Street
The Apprentice
Drip!
A Beautiful Friendship and The Parrot of Doom
Robine's Diary
The Christmas Club
Loose Ends
Splatter Pattern
It Takes Two
Lexicon
Replacement Parts
Sidekicks
Lost Stories
Time and Space

Anthologies
Tales of Urban Fantasy

Five Tales of Bizarre Detectives
Tales of Mystery and Suspense
Tales of Weird Fantasy
Spies, Detectives, & Heroes
Tales of Twisted Crime
Tales of The Unexpected
Tales From Space
10 by Russ Crossley
Round Up At The Burger Bar: The Story of Trixie Pug,
Parts 1- 5 The Beginning
Worlds of Science Fiction and Fantasy
More Tales of Mystery and Suspense
Ladies of the Jolly Roger
Justice Served
Love Stories
Ladies of the Jolly Roger with R.S. Meger
The Adventures of Razor and Edge:
Five Tales From The Quirky Detective Team
An Unexpected Journey

Non-Fiction
The Writers Tools - The Synopsis

Also available from 53rd Street Publishing

Aloha Armstrong, The Woman from L.I.P.S returns in an exciting new adventure. Her mission: to go undercover as sheriff of Zomopolis, a domed town where incurable zombies are kept until a cure can be found, to discover the fate of the previous sheriff who went missing under mysterious circumstances.

She soon discovers a town filled with secrets, people who might not be who they claim to be, and a deadly conspiracy than threatens to destroy humanity. Handsome diner owner Hanson Braddock, a man with his own secrets, offers his help but can she trust him?

Surrounded by possible enemies Aloha must face a decision that will change her life forever.

Will Aloha save the world from certain doom or is this her final mission?

The book may be purchased from your favorite online bookseller or ordered from your local book store.

www.ingramcontent.com/pod-product-compliance
Lightning Source LLC
Chambersburg PA
CBHW020553180626
46810CB00007B/2493